D0209573

Strength IN Numbers

STORIES *from* HOPE HAVEN

Strength IN *Numbers*

CHARLOTTE CARTER

Guideposts
New York, New York

www.guideposts.com
(800) 932-2145
Guideposts Books & Inspirational Media

Cover design and illustration by Lookout Design, Inc.
Interior design by Lorie Pagnozzi
Typeset by Aptara

Printed and bound in the United States of America
10 9 8 7 6 5 4 3 2 1

This book is dedicated to my writer friends who face the challenges of multiple sclerosis every day of their lives—Bonnie, Liz and Deb—and to my readers who share the same courageous battle.

Special thanks to Lori Wilde for her insights into the world of nursing, to my amazing fellow authors of the Stories from Hope Haven series, and to all the ladies of the loop for their humor and unfailing support.

The Best Medicine by Anne Marie Rodgers

Chasing the Wind by Patricia H. Rushford

Hope for Tomorrow by Patti Berg

Strength in Numbers by Charlotte Carter

Strength IN Numbers

Chapter One

JAMES BELL WALKED ACROSS THE PARKING LOT TO the entrance of Hope Haven Hospital, the chill morning air clouding his breath.

The Lord had blessed this mid-December morning, the sun just beginning to rise into a clear sky, a cold front moving in from Canada. If the weather stayed cold, the fire department would flood the basketball courts at the Deerford town park. Neighborhood kids would search their homes for ice skates they hadn't seen since last spring.

James grinned as memories of his youth played like an old video through his imagination. Pom-pom-pullaway on the makeshift rink. Pickup games of hockey. Friday date nights with music playing from an old boom box.

Deerford, a small community in north-central Illinois, was a great place to grow up and raise a family.

He picked up his pace, his unzipped parka flapping open with each step. As a registered nurse, he was eager to do his bit to help bring healing to others, body and spirit.

The automatic door swished open. As he entered the three-story building, the warm interior air struck James.

He took the stairs to the third floor to the staff lounge and locker room. A few steps inside the door, the bulletin board was draped with silver garland for the holidays. Various notices were posted, most of them old and faded. Information about filing a workers' compensation claim. A request for volunteers to serve as counselors at a children's winter camp.

He spotted an envelope in his employee mailbox. Shrugging out of his jacket, he opened the envelope and read a memo addressed to all employees:

Due to a continuing financial shortfall, salaries of all Hope Haven Hospital employees will be reduced by 10 percent, effective January 1. This change will be reflected in the first paycheck following January 15.

The administration regrets the necessity . . .

James's knees went weak. His mouth dropped open and his heart sank to his stomach.

He'd known for some time that the hospital was struggling financially, but he'd thought the problem had been solved. He hadn't imagined Albert Varner, the hospital CEO, would take such a drastic step.

A 10 percent cut in salary meant James would earn several thousand dollars less per year to support his two teenage sons and his wife. Fern suffered from multiple sclerosis. Their insurance didn't cover all the necessary medications to control her MS, and the excess came out of their pockets.

In time, that expense would only grow larger.

Same thing with his boys, Gideon and Nelson. Each year their expenses for clothes, cell phones, school activities and just plain being teenagers increased. Sometimes exponentially.

A 10 percent cut would be disastrous.

What could he do?

His mind in a fog and a sick feeling in his stomach, he went into the staff locker room and changed into green hospital scrubs. He left and slowly descended the stairs to the second floor where the General Medicine and Surgery units were located. Still a half hour until his shift officially started, he was in no rush to get to work.

The quiet of early morning on the nursing floor would soon be replaced by the hurried footsteps of doctors and technicians coming and going, meds being administered and patients leaning on their call buttons.

A pair of poinsettias sat on the counter of the nurses' station, supplied by the families of grateful patients.

Anabelle Scott and Candace Crenshaw, his nursing colleagues, were behind the counter, their expressions as grim as he felt.

"You look like you heard the bad news too," James said. His throat felt tight, as though he'd have as much trouble swallowing a simple aspirin as he did accepting such a huge pay cut.

Anabelle, the nurse supervisor for Cardiac Care, gave him a sympathetic smile. "Not exactly good news just before Christmas, is it? Particularly for those of you with young families." An experienced nurse and wise woman, Anabelle's short, salt-and-pepper hair was neatly combed, her expression calm. As was usually the case, she wore a white lab coat over her street clothes.

Candace, who worked in the Birthing Unit, shook her head. "I've already bought most of the presents for Brooke and Howie. I always start my shopping early so I can spread out the expense." Her forehead furrowed and she bit her lip. "Now I'm wondering if I should take some of the presents back to the store."

As a young widow and the single mother of an eleven-year-old girl and a five-year-old boy, Candace was understandably worried about the impact of a salary cut on her family's finances.

So was James.

"Varner sure picked a bad time of year to do this." James stepped into the supply room.

"I can't think of a *good* time of year," Candace countered.

From force of habit, James checked the automated computer system to see how many patients he had—one prostate, a pneumonia on oxygen, a hand surgery. He skimmed the rest. He really needed to pull himself together. His patients deserved his best efforts and all of his concentration.

He shifted his attention back to his friends. "You know what they say, adversity makes us stronger." Somehow he'd cope with reduced income in a way that wouldn't hurt his family. Just how he'd do that eluded him for the moment.

Candace eyed him skeptically. "Who says that?" She removed her stethoscope from the pocket of her pale yellow scrubs and looped it around her neck.

"I don't know, but it sounds good."

Anabelle laughed. "For months the hospital has been teetering on the brink of disaster, and somehow Albert Varner has pulled us out. Maybe he'll find a way to pull us back from the edge again."

James wasn't all that optimistic. The news had really shaken him. Maybe that was because Fern was going through a rough patch with her MS and he was worried about her.

The stairwell door burst open. Elena Rodriguez, a nurse from the Intensive Care Unit, hurried across the floor to the nurses' station, planting herself right in front of James.

Lifting an eyebrow, he looked into her brown eyes, so dark they were almost black. They sparkled with an intensity that would not be easily subdued.

"Okay, Mr. Hotshot Spelling Bee Guy," she said. "I've got a new word for you."

Her energy forced a smile from him. All of his friends knew he was addicted to watching the annual spelling bee championships on TV. Once upon a time, he'd almost made it through the state championships to a regional event. "Okay, Ms. Moderator. What's today's word?"

"Exacerbate."

"Ah, a good one. Can you use it in a sentence?"

"You betcha. The ten percent pay cut we're all going to be hit with is going to *exacerbate* our families' financial problems."

"Amen to that," Anabelle said.

"She's right on," Candace agreed.

Thinking, James rocked back on his heels, looked up at the acoustic tile ceiling and carefully spelled the word.

Elena snapped her fingers in a gesture of dismay. "Shoot, I thought I'd catch you on that one."

"Not even close. That's a first-round word for sixth graders." He grinned at her. "How 'bout this? Albert Varner seems determined to *pauperize* all the hospital employees."

"If you think I'm gonna spell pauper-whatever, think again. I had enough trouble with *exacerbate*. What I want to know is what we're supposed to do. Cesar and I won't starve, but the cut is sure going to put a crimp in my savings for our trip to Spain. Just yesterday I got a brochure about festivals in the Andalucia region. They have something going on every month, and I was trying to figure out the best time of year to go." She pulled her lips back to a discouraged angle. "Now I have to worry about if I'll be able to go at all."

James rubbed his hand across the back of his neck. He knew Elena had been planning and saving to go on the trip for years, dreaming of the day when she could visit the ancestral land of her paternal great-grandfather.

Anabelle spoke up. "I'm afraid the cut in pay will cause some employees to look for work elsewhere. That could impact all of us."

Candace said to Elena, "James claims adversity is good for us."

"That's not exactly what I said but close." He exhaled, bent his head and studied the toes of his white work shoes. "Maybe we ought to do what we always do when things get tough. We ought to leave it in God's hands and have faith everything will work out for the best."

Anabelle touched his arm. "Prayer helps too."

He shouldn't have needed that reminder. But he did and was glad Anabelle had shared a bit of her strength with him.

"Will you all join me?" he asked.

Elena nodded and Candace smiled, then bowed her head.

"Dear Lord, we come to You in search of Your comfort and Your strength," James began. "We need Your help as we face this new adversity. Guide us on Your path to find positive ways to deal with the proposed salary cut and to maintain our faith that all things are possible in You. Bless our work here at Hope Haven and our patients. Amen."

His co-workers echoed soft amens, and some of the despair James had felt earlier lifted from his shoulders.

As though a starting bell had been rung, the activity on the second floor picked up. Graveyard-shift nurses updated the day-shift nurses on patients, reviewing medications and adding insights about the patients' health and morale as needed.

The hospital loudspeaker paged doctors. Meal service carts rumbled through the hallway bringing breakfast to waiting patients.

It was a long-established routine, and James mentally settled into the changeover as he met patients held over from the previous day. This was what he did. He was good at his job. He'd learned as a medic in the first Gulf War that this was what he wanted to do with his life.

About nine o'clock, he received word that a transfer patient from a hospital in Springfield was being moved into his unit later in the morning—an amputee who had lost his leg in a motorcycle accident. The kid was only seventeen.

James's heart broke for the young man. Losing a limb was a tough adversity to handle for someone so young. During the war he'd seen soldiers far older than seventeen come apart emotionally when they realized they had lost a part of themselves.

Recovery from that kind of trauma required more than a few stitches and a handy bedpan.

As the morning progressed, James prepared the discharge paperwork for the prostate and hand surgery patients and made sure a room was ready for the new amputee patient. According to the computer system, the young man's name was Theodore Townsend.

He's hardly more than a boy, thought James.

A soft *ping* announced the arrival of the service elevator on the floor.

The boy lay on a gurney, his gaze riveted on the elevator ceiling as though it were a Rembrandt on loan from the Louvre. The boy's mother held his hand while Dad stood stoically looking straight ahead. Both parents were simply dressed, the dad a muscular guy who looked like he might be a plumber or in the construction business.

"All ashore that's goin' ashore," the orderly everyone called Becker announced, pushing the gurney out of the elevator. An IV dripped medication into the boy's arm and the transfer paperwork rested on top of the kid's stomach.

"Room 207," James told Becker.

"Got it, boss." The stocky orderly, not much older than the patient, expertly rolled the gurney down the hallway and made the turn into room 207.

James picked up the paperwork to make sure everything was in order.

"Hi, Theodore," he said, flipping quickly through the printed pages. "You like to be called Theodore or Ted?"

"Ted," the boy replied in a monosyllabic grunt.

"Okay, Ted, how're you doing?"

"Great. I'm having a blast." The youngster's sarcasm fell flat against the pain etched in the boy's face and the fear visible in his hazel eyes. An all-American kid with a blond buzz cut, he had a couple of stitches on his forehead and road burns on his cheek and right arm. He'd apparently taken quite a tumble off his motorcycle.

If James had his way, his two sons would never ride anything that didn't cocoon them safely inside a couple of thousand pounds of steel.

He rested his hand on the boy's shoulder for a moment, speaking in a low voice meant to both soothe and reassure. "I'm James, your nurse. We'll get you settled in a minute, then you can get some rest."

Ted's eyes cut toward James, but the boy didn't speak. His mother still had a death grip on her son's hand, her complexion almost as white as her knuckles. Worry lines etched her face.

"Mr. and Mrs. Townsend, if you'd like to step outside, it'll take me just a few minutes to make your son comfortable. Then you can come back in and visit for a few minutes."

Having a child injured or seriously ill was probably harder on the parents than it was on the kid. Sometimes they didn't understand that James needed room to do his job, and their son probably didn't want them to witness his pain. Mothers, in particular, often didn't want to leave their child's bedside for even a few minutes.

Fern had been the same way when their son Gideon had been hospitalized with a respiratory virus at the age of two. As James thought about it, he realized he had felt the same.

"Come on, Cynthia." Mr. Townsend hooked his hand through his wife's arm. "I saw a waiting room down the hall. We can wait there."

Bending down, Cynthia kissed her son's cheek. "We'll be right back, Teddy, I promise."

"It's okay, Mom. I'm not going anywhere."

As the mother turned to leave, James saw tears welling in her eyes. *Tough business, being a mom.*

When the parents left, James and Becker positioned themselves to shift the young man onto the bed. Physically fit with good muscular development, the youngster probably weighed in the area of 170 pounds.

"We're going to lift you up and place you on the bed, Ted," James said. "Let us do all the work. Think of it as a free ride."

"Yeah, right," he mumbled.

James slid his hands under the boy's shoulders, Becker had the patient's hips and legs. "This may hurt, son, but we'll make it quick."

Ted visibly gritted his teeth.

Checking with Becker, James gave him a one, two, three count. Together they hefted the boy. Ted sucked in a quick breath and then he was safely on the bed.

Becker adjusted the IV pole and pulled the gurney away. "He's all yours, James. I promised you'd take real good care of him."

"Will do," James said.

Becker left, and James went to work adjusting the boy's position in the bed and checking the dressing on his wound. James noted that the kid had lost his right leg just above the knee, leaving him with nothing but a stump.

"How's your pain level?" The doctor's orders included pain medication as needed.

"I can handle it." Ted squared his jaw tough-guy style.

"How'd you mess up your leg?" James asked.

"I hit a patch of gravel. The bike slid and took me with it." Ted turned his head away. "It would've been better if it had killed me instead of turning me into a stupid cripple."

James's breath caught in his lungs and he felt a stab of concern. Depression and grief for a physical loss wasn't unusual, and this boy was experiencing both. Ted's comment that he'd be better off dead was more than a little troubling.

"They're doing a lot of good things with prosthetics these days, Ted. You'll be surprised how quickly you'll be up and walking under your own steam again."

The boy's head whipped back, and he glared up at James with a combination of anger and regret. "I'm a soccer player, man. I'm the striker on my team. I've scored more goals than anybody ever has at Lincoln High. Soccer players don't walk. *They run!*"

James had vaguely recognized the Townsend name, and now he realized he'd read about Ted in the local paper—a star high school athlete with a great future ahead of him.

A future that a single moment of carelessness had suddenly reshaped.

"Maybe you'll be the first high school soccer player with a prosthesis," James said in an effort to provide encouragement.

The boy hissed out an expletive. "Get outta here, man. You don't know anything about me or soccer or anything else." Awkwardly, he rolled onto his side, presenting James with his back.

Knowing further conversation was useless, James left and went to the lounge where the Townsends were waiting. Sitting together on a love seat holding hands, they looked as forlorn as their son, but less angry.

Mrs. Townsend hopped to her feet. "Can we go back to his room now?"

"In just a minute," James said. "I imagine his surgeon in Springfield talked to you about the psychological effects some amputees experience."

"Dr. Lang told us Teddy should make a full recovery," Mr. Townsend said. "And with modern prosthetics, in time he'll be almost as good as new."

James indicated his agreement with the doctor's prognosis. "Ted isn't quite buying that yet, which is understandable. He's grieving for his lost leg and he'll go through all the stages of grief just as he would if he'd lost a loved one. He'll be angry at everyone—probably including you, himself and even God—if he's like most amputees."

"Oh dear." Cynthia covered her mouth with her hand and more tears welled in her eyes. "We've both prayed so hard since we got the call that Teddy had been injured. We wanted him at Hope Haven to be closer to home."

Mr. Townsend looped his arm around his wife's shoulders. "I wish I'd never given him permission to ride that bike. It's all my fault."

"Blaming yourselves won't be productive," James said gently.

"Hard not to," Mr. Townsend said.

James nodded that he understood the problem. "As time goes by, Ted may slip into denial. He may attempt things he can no longer do and then hurt himself in the process."

"Rest assured, I'm not going to let my boy out of my sight ever again," Cynthia announced.

A smile tugged at James's lips. *Typical mom reaction.* "You don't have to go that far and probably shouldn't. But it will take time for Ted to adjust to his new situation. You'll have to be encouraging without promising the impossible and keep him focused on the long road to rehabilitation and recovery."

"We'll do our best," Mr. Townsend promised.

James was sure they would. But it was still going to be a rocky road for the entire family over the next several months, long after Ted was discharged from Hope Haven.

He didn't envy them the ride.

Before James could take a break for lunch, his cell phone vibrated in his pocket. Because of his wife's illness and the fear that she might need him, he always carried the phone with him.

Flipping the phone open, he checked the number. *Fern.* His chest tightened with anxiety. He brought the phone to his ear. "Hi, sweetheart. Are you all right?"

"I'm fine, just a little more tired than usual." Fern's voice sounded weak, as though she was speaking to him from a great distance. "I'm just leaving Dr. Chopra's office. The doctor's calling in a new prescription for me." Fern's breath was audible. Simply talking had become an effort for her. He was glad her mother went with her to appointments. "Could you pick up the prescription on your way home?"

Fern, no doubt trying to protect him, hadn't even mentioned this morning that she planned to see her neurologist. A skilled doctor originally from India, Amala Chopra specialized in

MS cases. Today's appointment meant Fern's disease was cycling down again. James felt the sudden press of tears.

He cleared his throat. "Of course I can pick up the new meds. Sure you don't need it sooner? I can run out on my lunch break."

"No, she gave me a couple of samples. I'll be fine 'til evening."

"Okay, but get some rest this afternoon. Don't overdo it."

After telling Fern good-bye, James slipped the cell back into his pocket and closed his eyes.

Please, God, help my wife.

Chapter Two

ON THE FIRST FLOOR OF THE HOSPITAL, CANDACE stood staring at the vending machine outside the cafeteria entrance. She tucked her hand in her pocket and fiddled with her lunch money.

She wanted something to munch on but didn't know what. Ever since she'd read the memo about the cut in salary, her stomach had been on the verge of rebellion.

A full meal would be more than she could handle.

"Doesn't matter how long you stare at the machine. The choices aren't going to get any better."

She turned at the sound of Heath Carlson's voice and smiled at the down-to-earth radiology technician. Candace had begun to think of him as a good friend.

"After this morning's bad news, I didn't think I could handle a full lunch," she said.

His blond eyebrows lowered into a concerned frown. "Bad news?"

"Didn't you see the memo?"

"Oh yeah, that." The easy smile that creased his cheeks suggested he wasn't worried about a little detail like money. "I was afraid you'd had some personal bad news."

"Oh no, just the continuing assault on my bank account."

"Sorry about that." He slid his hand into his trouser pocket, bunching up the hem of his white medical jacket in the process. "How 'bout I treat you to an extravagant vending machine lunch?"

"No, you don't have to do that. I'm not that broke. Not yet, anyway." She had to admit Heath's friendship felt increasingly important, but she wasn't in a position to dwell on any possibility beyond the existing situation. She still thought about her late husband a great deal and was in counseling for her grief. With two young children to care for, her life was too full to add any other relationship.

"The truth is," she said, "I hate that they've gone to healthy food in the vending machine. I know we should encourage it in a hospital, but I mean, really, how can they think a granola bar is a decent substitute for a giant, calorie-laden, dark chocolate bar when a girl is feeling down?"

Heath laughed out loud, a hearty masculine sound that Candace couldn't help but enjoy.

"My mother claims chocolate is medicinal," he said with a grin. "Says the Aztec priests were the first to figure that out."

"Ancient truths are worth remembering." Feeling lighter in spirit than she had since reading the morning memo in her hospital mailbox, she dropped the necessary coins into the slot and pulled the lever for a granola bar. It dropped down into the tray, where she retrieved it.

"Tell you what," Heath said. "I'll start a petition to require Varner to disburse chocolate bars with every bad news memo he sends out. That way employee morale won't need a crash cart."

"Good idea." She smiled and saluted Heath with her granola bar.

Chocolate would be nice, but she knew it wouldn't solve her precarious financial situation. Not with the substantial pay cut on the horizon.

In ICU, Elena scanned the three active monitors at the nurses' station for heart rate, oxygen absorption, breathing. Though all the patients' vital signs were steady, her car-crash victim worried her. She would be happier if he had come out of his coma by now.

From her desk, she could see her patients through the glass partitions. All seemed comfortable.

She would have been happier, too, if the hospital CEO hadn't issued the memo about pay cuts. How could anyone deal with that news nine days before Christmas?

This was supposed to be a joyous time of year.

Now there was a dark cloud hanging over every employee, herself included.

Over the past few years, her special travel savings account for her trip to Spain had grown steadily month by month. But this pay cut would flatline her savings.

She'd been so hopeful and excited about the prospect of seeing—

Elena was startled from her thoughts when the monitor on her coma case beeped a warning. Before the shrill sound ceased, Elena was on her feet.

Immediately Elena saw one of the leads had been pulled off when the patient rolled over. "Easy, Mrs. Cole. You're all right." Elena reattached the lead and reset the monitor. The beeping stopped. The lines tracking across the monitor resumed their steady rhythm.

Crisis over, Elena exhaled and returned to the nurses' station.

By the time James's shift ended at three o'clock, he felt as though he'd been at a dead run all day while carrying a five-hundred-pound weight on his back.

There'd been three more admissions to his unit: a mastectomy, a perforated ulcer and a compound leg fracture in traction. All of that was in addition to young Ted Townsend, whose mood vacillated between stoic acceptance and anger at the entire world.

Poor kid. James ached for what he and his parents were going through.

Worry about Fern had contributed to the long day, he realized as he walked across the street to the Deerford Medical Services Building, which claimed HHH Pharmacy as one of its tenants. The lobby of the building was decked out with a giant Christmas tree. Swags of plastic garland draped gracefully above the entrance to the pharmacy.

James usually looked forward to the holiday season. With Fern's MS in a bad spell and a pay cut in the offing, he felt as though a wet blanket had dampened his enthusiasm.

Instead of Harold Hopkins in his usual place behind the pharmacy counter, there was a young Asian woman. Her shiny

name tag read Dee Yang, Pharmacist. She had three people waiting in line.

"Picking up a prescription for Fern Bell," James said when it
was his turn. He watched as Dee searched through a pile of filled
prescriptions that apparently hadn't been sorted alphabetically.
Finally she found what she'd been looking for.

"Here you go." She placed the pill bottle on the counter,
swiped the bar code and told him the cost.

Mentally wincing at the price, he handed her a credit card.
"Where's Harold?"

She swiped the card. "He had a death in the family and had
to go to Chicago for a few days." She glanced behind James to
those who had joined him in line. "Sorry for the wait."

"No problem." He signed the receipt she handed him.
The young lady appeared inexperienced, and James gave her a
smile of encouragement.

Before leaving the counter, he glanced at the label on the
bottle. Fern's name was in bold letters, and he recognized the
name of the medication as one his wife hadn't previously been
taking. MS had been dragging Fern down lately, and he hoped
the new medication was potent enough to reduce and control
her debilitating symptoms.

He walked back to the hospital parking lot. A few minutes
later, he wheeled his minivan into the driveway of his two-story
brick home. The neighbor's fifty-foot fir tree cast a long shadow
across his yard, much like Fern's multiple sclerosis touched every
part of his family's life.

James's job was to make sure plenty of sunshine broke through
whatever clouds showed up.

He parked and switched off the ignition, a sense of dread filling his chest.

He couldn't tell Fern about the upcoming cut in pay. She'd worry and fret. He didn't want to add to the burdens she already carried because of MS.

There were so many days when he wished he could reach inside her and physically battle her MS into permanent remission.

But that's not how life—or medicine—worked.

James remained confident God knew what He was doing when He gave Fern the burden of a progressive disease. James just didn't know why the Lord had picked his sweet wife.

Scrubbing his hands over his face, James drew a deep breath and got out of the van. The day had warmed to well above freezing. No ice skating today for the neighborhood kids.

He let himself into the house. In the living room, he found Fern napping on the beige microfiber couch they'd bought a few years ago. Colorful throw pillows were propped behind her back. Sapphire, their fifteen-pound Maine coon cat, lay curled up beside her in a variegated pile of silver, gray and black fur. The tufts on the tips of the cat's ears twitched in silent recognition of James's presence.

Fern's walker stood next to her. That meant she'd been having a bad day, as James had feared. On good days she could get around with a cane.

She stirred in her sleep, and James was struck once again by how lucky he'd been to find her twenty years ago. Ten years younger than he, and as sweet and kind and funny as an angel, she could have married any guy in the county. But she'd picked him. He'd forever be grateful for that.

Her eyes blinked open. She squinted, trying to bring her vision into focus. "Hi, honey. Is it after three already?" Her words were slightly slurred.

A band of anguish tightened around James's chest and it hurt to draw a breath. Slurred speech was a sure sign her MS was worsening.

The disease worked in cycles. But each time she hit a low spot, she didn't bounce back up as far as she had been in the prior cycle.

"Almost three thirty," he said. "We had four new patients admitted to my unit today, which means lots of paperwork. I picked up your prescription for you." Crossing the room, he moved her walker out of his way and knelt beside Fern to kiss her. Without makeup, she looked pale; but her lips were warm and welcoming.

"Bad day, Sleeping Beauty?" He placed her pills on the end table next to her unopened laptop. She had an online MS support group, which had been invaluable to her. The fact that she hadn't opened her computer all day spoke of fatigue and depression.

Her lips shifted into a crooked smile. "The usual, I suppose. I get so tired when I go to the doctor."

Sapphire stretched and yawned, then hopped down from the couch and made her way toward the kitchen, no doubt in search of an afternoon snack.

"You know Dr. Chopra says you have to listen to your body. If you're tired, it's okay to take a rest."

"I know. But I feel so useless." She cupped his cheek with her hand. "You work so hard."

"They, too, serve who sit around looking beautiful all day waiting for the joyous return of the master of the household."

She sputtered a laugh, and James's heart lifted at the happy sound.

He brushed another quick kiss to her lips. "The boys aren't home yet?" He stood and set the walker back in place where she could easily reach it.

"Gideon's at ROTC drill practice, and Nelson's helping to build the stage sets for the eighth-grade play."

"Oh yes, our young thespian." Nelson's English teacher, Mrs. Murphy, was a recent college graduate and enthusiastic teacher new to Deerford Middle School. Apparently she decided eighth graders weren't too young to learn a bit of Shakespeare. The first week of January, the class was going to perform a simplified version of *A Midsummer Night's Dream*. Nelson had landed the part of Puck.

"Nelson's so excited about the play." Her quick smile of enthusiasm momentarily overcame her fatigue. "Every day he tells me how cool Shakespeare is. I can hardly wait to see him perform."

James couldn't wait to see the show as well.

Glancing up the stairs to the second floor, he said, "I'm going to get cleaned up, and then you can help me start dinner."

"I doubt if I'll be much help today." The spark of energy faded, and Fern sounded as weary and melancholy as when James had awoken her.

"You help me by simply being here, Fern. I wouldn't have it any other way."

She looked away, and another small piece of James's heart broke. He was trained to help heal others, yet he couldn't do a thing to heal his own wife.

"Dad, you're officially the greatest mac-and-cheese maker in the world." Gideon helped himself to another heaping serving.

"Everything I know about cooking I learned from your mother." James smiled at his family sitting around the table in the kitchen. His two boys were a study in contrasting personalities.

Gideon, having recently turned fifteen, a freshman at Lincoln High and a natural athlete, was still growing and would soon top James's five foot eleven inches. No wonder the kid ate about as much as his entire ROTC unit.

Nelson, at thirteen, was somewhat more academic in nature and had a witty sense of humor, which is why Shakespeare appealed to him. He had recently dropped swim team to focus more on Scouting which gave him an outlet for both physical exercise and challenging problem solving.

Both boys had inherited Fern's wavy brown hair and James's blue eyes, a handsome combination which girls had already noticed, based on the amount of text messaging that went on. Although never at dinnertime. That was a family rule.

Reaching across the table, Nelson dragged the bowl of macaroni and cheese toward him. "Mrs. Murphy says I'm a great Puck. I've got a really good feel for the part. 'My fairy lord, this must be done with haste, for night's swift dragons cut the clouds full fast,'" he quoted.

Gideon snorted a laugh. "That's because you've been a clown all your life."

"Yeah, and you've been a silly jock all your—"

"Boys!" Fern waggled a shaky finger at them.

It took only that small rebuke to silence the boys' bickering. It seemed that their mother having MS had made them more sensitive and sympathetic than the average kid.

James couldn't have been more proud of his sons.

"Have you got your lines memorized yet?" Fern asked Nelson.

It took the boy a moment to understand her slurred speech. "Not really, but it's still three weeks until we do the show. Besides, the third act is a killer. Puck has lots of lines."

"I hope your play won't conflict with the camping trip the Scout troop has planned." James had taken over as troop scoutmaster when the previous leader had to drop out. He knew he'd enjoy the young teenage boys; he thought the discipline and character building that the Boy Scouts provided helped boys to grow into fine young men. But he'd been reluctant to leave Fern for evening meetings and occasional overnight trips. She'd been the one to insist he needed time away from her to recharge his own batteries.

"Remember, we have a special troop meeting Monday evening to check everyone's camping gear," James said.

"I know. The guys will all be there. And the play is right before the camping trip. So no problem."

Dismissing the Scouting activities as settled, Nelson waxed on about the play and regaled them with stories of his fellow actors and set painters. James only half listened. He wanted both boys to be able to go to college. Even if they landed scholarships, the expense would still be daunting. Saving for their future had never been easy.

He'd also been hoping to remodel the downstairs by adding a bedroom so Fern wouldn't have to struggle upstairs every night.

Now, with a cut in pay added to the increasing cost of medication for Fern, climbing that financial mountain appeared even more formidable.

Please, Lord, show me the way.

Tension pulled his neck muscles taut. He sat back and rubbed his hand across the nape of his neck. There had to be options. Ways to increase his income, not decrease it—or at least maintain his current salary level. He just needed to find a way.

After dinner, the boys helped James clean up the kitchen, then went upstairs to do their homework before bedtime. Fern sat in her usual after-dinner spot, a rocking chair by the double-sided fireplace, a colorful lap robe crocheted by her mother draped over her legs.

Giving the counter a final wipe, James hung the dishcloth over the faucet. Deep in thought, he stood staring out the window into the dark night.

"Are you going to tell me what's bothering you?" Fern asked.

He didn't immediately turn around but continued to look into the distance. A streetlight glowed on the block behind them. "It was a long day. I'm just tired, that's all."

"James, we've been married twenty years. I know when you're troubled." A hint of annoyance crept into her tone.

He turned his head slightly. "You know me that well, huh?"

"And you know I'll keep bugging you until you tell me what's wrong." Her brows lowered with concern and her eyes pleaded with him. "Is it about me? Did you talk with my doctor?"

"No, nothing like that." Defeated, knowing he'd have to tell her now, he dragged a kitchen chair next to her rocker. He took her hand, warming it between his palms, her skin as soft as a baby's. "It's nothing for you to worry about, I promise. The hospital board is up to its old tricks. We all got notice today of a pay cut. Not a huge one. Really. We'll be fine."

A shake of her head told him she'd seen right through his story. "How much of a cut?"

A sigh escaped James's lips. "Ten percent."

He saw her mentally calculate what the cut would mean to them. MS had slowed her physically, but she was still as mentally sharp as she'd always been. As sharp as she'd been when she'd managed the office of a medical clinic that served transient farm workers and folks who were down on their luck.

He knew she hated that MS had forced her to give up her job.

"That's a lot of money," she finally said.

"We'll be okay. I was thinking I might check around for some part-time work. Maybe at St. Francis in Peoria. A couple of shifts a week."

"James, that would mean more than an hour commute each way. You'll wear yourself out and be exhausted all the time. Not to mention you wouldn't be here for the boys."

Or for Fern, he realized as the knot pressed down harder in his stomach.

She squeezed James's hand, a weak grasp but one filled with determination. "I still get my monthly disability check. We'll find a way together to make it work."

Leaning forward, James kissed his wife. His chest filled with so much admiration for Fern, he thought it might burst. Her courage, her determination in the face of adversity, her strength of character had the power to bring him to his knees. She was the force that kept this family together. Kept him striving to be worthy of her.

"I love you, Fern. I always will."

Chapter Three

ELENA RODRIGUEZ STOOD IN HER BEDROOM AFTER dinner, sifting through the thick manila folder filled with information she'd collected about travel to the Andalucia region of Spain. A new brochure about festivals had come yesterday. The photos of Easter events made it look like an oh-so-lovely time of year to travel there. She'd found a company that offered cooking classes in traditional dishes of southern Spain. Another outfit helped people track their family's ancestors. She'd even discovered a school where she could take flamenco dancing lessons. She could hear the click of castanets already.

Heartsick that the pay cut would delay her longed-for trip, she swiped the back of her hand at the tears that threatened. She was being such a silly goose about this whole thing.

Her husband, Cesar, walked by the bedroom, reversed course and poked his head in the door. He'd changed out of his police uniform earlier and now wore his favorite flannel shirt and jeans.

"I thought you were putting Izzy to bed," he said.

She cleared the lump in her throat. Her dream would still come true. Someday. "Rafael is reading her a story first."

Their son and his five-year-old daughter, Isabel, had moved in with Elena and Cesar when Rafael's girlfriend deserted both him and their new baby girl. An indefensible act for a mother, as far as Elena was concerned, but one that showed the young woman's true colors. Sarah had decided keeping herself supplied with drugs was more important than her own child.

Elena gritted her teeth. She did not want that woman anywhere near her son or her beloved Izzy ever again. She'd agreed once to meet Sarah for coffee. The girl hadn't shown up. She wouldn't fall for that ploy again.

Cesar stepped into the room. "You ought to have every word of those brochures memorized by now. Are you looking for something?"

"No." Sighing, she closed the folder and placed it back on her dresser. Her sewing machine was tucked into a corner of the room, the pieces of a red velvet dress for Izzy ready to be sewn together. "I didn't want to tell you in front of Rafael and Isabel. The hospital's cutting my pay."

"What? Why?" He straightened to his full five foot ten inches, immediately jumping to her defense. "You're the best Intensive Care nurse they've got. How can they—"

"Easy does it, Officer Rodriguez." She loved that he was so protective of her, but sometimes his reactions were over the top. An occupational hazard for a cop, she supposed. "It's not just me. The hospital is still in financial trouble, so they're cutting everyone's salary by ten percent."

"Oh well..." Knowing everyone was affected, not only Elena, he calmed down immediately. "Ten percent's a lot. But with my salary, that won't hurt us too badly. My salary is solid, particularly when I get overtime."

"Which I don't like you to work unless it's an emergency. I'd rather have you here at home with me." She sat down on the end of the bed. A dear aunt had given them a wedding-ring quilt when they were married. It still looked fresh and brought back many happy memories.

"The problem is, I've been tucking away a few dollars every month to save for our trip to Spain. With a cut in pay, I won't be able to save as much." Hardly anything at all, she suspected, with such a draconian reduction in salary.

He sat beside her, looping his arm around her shoulders. "I can earn some extra cash. They're always looking for someone for a night security job. It wouldn't be so bad, *querida mía*."

"Yes, it would. I don't want you out at night working by yourself. Besides, you need your rest. I don't want you falling asleep when you're chasing some bad guy at a hundred miles an hour down the highway."

He chuckled, a deep-throated sound that rumbled in his broad chest. A teasing glint appeared in his dark eyes. "Trust me, in a high-speed chase, adrenaline keeps me wide awake."

Folding her arms across her chest, she gave her husband a hard stare. "I don't care what you say, I don't want you to take on any more hours than you're already working. The trip will just have to wait a little longer than I'd hoped, that's all."

"If you're okay with waiting, it's okay by me. But you're a pretty smart cookie. I'm sure, if you give it some thought, you can come up with a better idea than my working graveyard at a twenty-four-hour fast-food place."

She frowned at him. Maybe she could come up with another way to add to their savings without Cesar working extra hours.

At the moment, however, her brain appeared to be in short supply when it came to moneymaking ideas.

The next morning, James and Anabelle were at the computer at the second floor nurses' station logging in for their shift when Elena arrived.

"I've got a great idea!" she announced, bubbly and excited. Her dark eyes sparkled and her caramel skin glowed with good health and energy.

James glanced at Anabelle, and they both rolled their eyes. As nice and fun as Elena might be, not all of her ideas were practical. In fact, some might have come from outer space, as far as James could tell. Still, if he were ever a patient in ICU, he'd want Elena to be his nurse.

"I'm afraid to ask what you've come up with this time," he said, as he checked the computer for new admissions. No new patients had been logged in overnight. A quiet graveyard shift.

The loudspeaker paged a respiratory therapist to pediatrics. James considered how emotionally challenging working with young children every day had to be. Sick and injured adults were hard enough on his psyche.

Taking her turn at the computer screen, Anabelle shook her head. "I'm not going to ask either. It's too early in the morning. My brain wouldn't be able to cope."

"Guys, you gotta ask. It's perfect, I promise." Elena's teeth were such a bright white that her smile lit up her whole face. "Come on, guys. It's a good idea."

Candace appeared at the doorway. Tiny teddy bears decorated her scrubs, perfect for her job in the Birthing Unit. James wondered if Elena had made the outfit for her. He knew she was handy with a needle and thread.

"What's a good idea?" Candace asked.

"Oh no." James groaned dramatically, slapping his chest with his hand as though he were having a heart attack. Nelson wasn't the only actor in the family. "You had to go and ask, didn't you? Now she's going to tell us, and life will never be the same."

Elena punched him gently on the shoulder, and he laughed.

"Okay, Mr. Wise Guy. Since you're so super rich, I guess the cut in pay doesn't bother you. But some of us are looking for a way to make up the difference, and I've found one that will help all of us."

In truth, James had spent half the night trying to come up with a solution to the approaching financial crunch. The effort had cost him hours of tossing and turning and robbed him of a good night's sleep.

"I'll listen to your idea," Candace said. "If you can help me come up with enough extra cash to pay for the braces I'm afraid Brooke is going to need, then I'm definitely in."

Beaming, Elena said, "I'm glad not everyone is as close-minded as some folks I know." She gave James what was meant to be a scathing look, but the twitch of her lips ruined the effort. She could barely stop smiling.

James raised his hands in surrender. "I give up. What has the Queen of Ideas come up with this time?"

Anabelle took off her reading glasses and shrugged, letting Elena know she was ready to listen as well. "Tell all, Elena."

"See, last night I was thinking about what our whole block did a couple years ago. We had a huge yard sale. We advertised it in the paper, and everybody on the block made money out of their old stuff."

She looked so proud of herself, but James wasn't sure where she was going with her idea. Anabelle and Candace appeared equally confused.

The elevator door opened. Moving quickly, a long, lanky respiratory therapist hurried past the nurses' station heading toward the pediatric unit.

"We can have a yard sale in the hospital parking lot," Elena continued. "All the employees can bring white elephants to sell. We can rent space to local clubs and church groups so they can make money too. You know, like a swap meet."

"I like the idea, but it's December," James said. "You can't really count on the weather this time of year to be nice enough for an outside swap meet."

"I think it's a good idea too, but I just don't see how we'd be able to organize a project like that without months of preparation," Anabelle said. "The ladies auxiliary at church works all year to put on their holiday boutique."

Elena's eager expression faded. "I know all that. But this is an emergency. For some people, anyway."

No one spoke as Elena looked from one colleague to another in search of support. Her expression clouded in the face of the less-than-supportive reaction.

"It's still a good idea," she repeated, setting her jaw at a defensive angle, but she'd lost the confident note in her voice.

"It is, and we're on the right track thinking of big ideas, but I don't know if this is the right one." Candace gave her a sympathetic smile and an encouraging pat on the shoulder. "You're full of wonderful ideas. You were the one who thought of the Wall of Hope that ended up generating so much money for the hospital, and I'm sure you're just getting started finding ways that will keep the wolf away from our respective doors."

James wanted to be supportive too. At least encouraging. "You'll think of something else. Thomas Edison came up with three thousand ideas before he landed on the lightbulb."

"Oh great!" It was Elena's turn to roll her eyes. "Only 2,999 ideas to go."

James laughed. So did the others, including Elena. That was a good way to start the shift. Friends, who often prayed together, laughing together.

Unfortunately, the money issue remained unresolved.

Ted Townsend's dispirited mood hadn't changed either, James discovered a short while later.

"How's the pain this morning?" he asked while checking the teenager's pulse. A little elevated but not dangerously so. His color was better than yesterday, his temperature normal. No apparent infection.

"It hurts. What d'ya expect? And my toes itch but I can't scratch them." In total frustration, he pounded the bed with his fist.

"The toes on your missing foot?"

"Yeah. Somebody ought to go find my leg and scratch 'em for me."

"That's a pretty common occurrence with an amputation. It's called phantom pain. The nerves are still sending signals to your brain," James explained. "The doctor has ordered meds for you, if needed. I'll go round them up."

"Great. Knock me out permanently, okay? I don't want to live this way for the rest of my life."

"Your accident didn't affect your brain, Ted."

"Terrific! Then I'll be the smartest cripple in town." The boy's lips twisted into an ugly sneer.

While James was sympathetic to the boy's problem, depressed patients were often difficult to manage and sometimes unpredictable. He didn't want Ted acting out his anger or his frustration. He could too easily hurt himself.

"I'll be getting you up on your feet this morning," he told the boy. "Later a physical therapist will drop by and start you on an exercise program."

"Get up on my *feet*? Don't you mean *foot*? How am I gonna exercise with one foot?"

"You'll manage. I promise."

Disturbed by the boy's negative attitude, James left the room to order his meds. As he stepped into the hallway, he almost tripped over a large golden retriever on a leash. The dog hopped agilely out of his way.

"Oops, sorry, Ace, I didn't see you," he said to the dog before smiling at his owner.

A trim, athletic woman in her midthirties, Diana Zimmer had founded Hope Haven Hounds to bring the comfort of animals to patients. The volunteers and their therapy dogs, who were well trained and affectionate, were carefully screened. Often the dogs provided the best possible therapy for those in pain or feeling depressed.

Ace, Diana's dog, was particularly good with children, patiently letting them crawl all over him if they were so inclined.

James gestured for Diana to step away from the doorway with him. A professional dog trainer, she wore the identifying green jacket of a hospital volunteer, gray slacks and no-nonsense shoes with crepe soles.

Ace wore his Hope Haven Hounds logo on a green bandanna around his neck.

"I think I have a customer for you." Idly, he stroked Ace's head and scratched around his ears. The dog's thick winter coat had been freshly washed. "A patient who's feeling particularly low this morning."

"Nobody can feel down long around Ace. Any problems I should know about?"

Sitting quietly beside Diana, Ace perked up his ears at the sound of his name.

There were certain rules about patient confidentiality in the hospital but James didn't have to worry about Diana—or Ace— giving any secrets away.

"The kid's seventeen and lost his leg in a motorcycle accident a couple days ago. He pretty much thinks that means his life is over."

She grimaced. "Poor kid. Not an easy thing to handle."

"No, it's not. Maybe you and Ace can help." James certainly hoped so. If Ted's attitude didn't take a turn for the better, he'd be at risk of becoming his own worst enemy: someone who gave up when the going got tough.

Chapter Four

ANABELLE HELPED THE PACEMAKER PATIENT TO sit up on the edge of the bed. The pale blue hospital gown slid off his shoulder and he pulled it back in place.

"Any dizziness?" she asked.

"Nope. I think I'm ready for a round of golf anytime the doc gives the word."

"Let's first see how well that pacemaker works with your taking a lap around the bed."

She knelt to help Mr. Rochester put his slippers on. A man in his late seventies, this was his second pacemaker, replacing one with a dying battery. He'd had the routine procedure early that morning; and, assuming no complications, he'd be going home either later this afternoon or early tomorrow. If the rest of his vital organs held together, the pacemaker ought to keep him enjoying rounds of golf on the local links for a good many more years.

She walked him around the room and out into the hall for a few minutes. When she was satisfied his heart was working properly, she escorted him to his room and told him to get some rest. She returned to the nurses' station.

Diana Zimmer was talking with James, her beautiful, well-trained dog Ace sitting patiently beside her.

Anabelle greeted Diana and gave Ace a welcoming pat, adjusting the green bandanna around his neck. "Making your rounds this morning?" she asked the dog trainer.

"I asked her to visit my adolescent leg amputee," James said.

"I'm afraid I wasn't much help," Diana admitted. "The boy's so far down in the dumps, he didn't even want to look at Ace, much less pet or play with him."

Anabelle's heart gave a painful squeeze. Her youngest daughter Kirstie had lost her right leg in a bicycle accident thirteen years ago. The experience had been horrible for Anabelle, maybe even more so than for her daughter. She'd never felt so helpless in her life. Even after all these years, she still had dreams about the nightmarish moment when she had first seen ten-year-old Kirstie crumpled on the ground.

"It will undoubtedly take a teenager a long time to adjust to losing a leg," Anabelle said. "Adults have difficulty coping with an amputation, so you can imagine how hard it is for a vulnerable teenager." She remembered Kirstie's tears of frustration every time she was fitted for a new prosthesis. And her own tearful prayers asking the Lord to help her to be strong for her daughter.

James hooked his stethoscope around his neck. "I thought maybe Ace could cheer the kid up. I guess he's not ready for that yet. Thanks for trying."

"No problem," Diana said.

James turned to check on something, but Anabelle stopped him.

"Maybe I could get Kirstie to visit the boy," she said. "She'd certainly be sympathetic and at the same time be a good example of how life can go on after a tragedy like this." Besides, it would give Anabelle an excuse to call her daughter. She missed Kirstie terribly since she moved to her own apartment in town close to the elementary school where she taught.

"Hey, that'd be great," James said.

"I'll call her this evening."

A patient in James's unit pressed his call button, and James hurried down the hallway to see what the patient wanted.

For the moment, Anabelle's patients were taken care of, paperwork under control, and doses of sympathy dispensed as needed.

"Diana, do you have another minute?"

"Of course. Do you have a patient you'd like me to visit?"

"No, I wanted to talk to you about something." The other day she'd been driving home from work when she saw some children playing with a puppy in their yard. The sight had stirred something inside her—an ache, a longing—for the unconditional love a dog showed its owners. A faithful companion who needed her. She'd been unable to get the thought out of her head. "I've been thinking about getting a puppy."

Diana's light brown eyebrows rose.

"I've been suffering from empty-nest syndrome since my youngest moved out, and I thought a puppy might fill the void."

She lifted her shoulder in a self-deprecating shrug. "Not that Cameron is enamored of the idea."

"Your husband?"

"He's retired from his landscaping business, so he's home most of the time." Their son Evan had taken over the business and was doing wonderful things with it. "In fact, I think a puppy might fill a void for him too. Although he keeps busy, he doesn't have nearly as much personal contact with people as he used to have when he was working."

"It's really better if everyone in the household is committed to having a pet join the family."

Anabelle sat down in the chair behind the counter. Over the years, she'd learned to rest her feet whenever the rare opportunity occurred.

"I know," she said, "but I'm sure Cam would come around in no time. We certainly have enough yard for a dog. Plus two fair-sized pastures." She held out her hand to Ace, and he nuzzled her palm. "You're such a good boy, Ace. Such a good boy."

"Have you thought about what kind of dog you want? What breed?"

"Not really. I don't know that much about breeds. When the children were young, we had a part collie, part mutt. Skipper was wonderful with all the neighborhood children. The boys loved playing fetch. One of the girls even dressed him up with pink ribbons and pushed him around in a stroller."

Diana laughed a high tinkling sound. "You and your husband might not want a dog who's that active."

"Probably not. I do want one that's affectionate and loving, that much I know."

"Most dogs qualify in that department if they're treated well." Diana turned as a hospital aide pushed a food cart out of the elevator and it rattled past the nurses' station with lunch trays for the patients. The faint scent of freshly brewed coffee trailed behind the cart.

"There are lots of other issues to consider," Diana continued. "The size dog you want, how social and easy to train. Long hair or short hair. If he's going to be an indoor or outdoor dog."

"Goodness, our last puppy belonged to a friend whose dog had had a litter. She was giving them away free to anyone with a good home. So we adopted one."

"That's not at all unusual, but it may not be the best way to select a pet." Reaching across the counter, Diana picked up a pad and pencil. "There's a Web site that will give you an idea of what you ought to consider. It will help you make the decision and maybe get you and your husband talking about what's right for you." She jotted down the address and handed the pad of paper back to Anabelle.

She held up her glasses, which were on a chain around her neck, read the note, and slipped the glasses back into the breast pocket of her lab coat. "Good idea. Then I'd at least have something to talk to Cam about. If I can get him on-board..."

"That would be best."

It would, of course, Anabelle thought. Even though retired, Cam kept busy. He'd done a wonderful job landscaping the hospital's new courtyard and supervising the installation of a waterfall. After a huge storm hit Deerford a few months ago, he'd jumped right in, organizing teams to repair roofs and board up broken windows.

She wasn't at all sure she could convince her husband that man's best friend was what they both needed to fill up their empty nest.

Well after one o'clock, James's unit finally reached a steady state, his patients napping or being entertained by their visitors. He took a break to get some lunch in the cafeteria.

The catering company that operated the cafeteria took great pains to serve healthy food at a reasonable price. The food was so good, in fact, employees from surrounding businesses often came for lunch. The expansive salad bar seemed to particularly attract the women who worked in nearby doctors' offices.

James opted for a bowl of chili con carne made with ground turkey, coffee and a slice of apple pie.

When he looked around for a place to sit, he found the room was pretty crowded despite the late lunch hour. The only person sitting alone was Quintessa Smith, the assistant to the hospital's Chief Financial Officer, Zane McGarry.

An attractive and friendly young black woman, Quintessa seldom ate alone. James had the uncomfortable feeling others were keeping their distance because of the proposed pay cuts. Her boss was taking a fair share of the blame for the situation they were all in.

Laying the blame on Quintessa, too, and ostracizing her, didn't seem fair.

"May I join you?" he asked when he reached her table. She had a fashion magazine open in front of her and a half-eaten salad.

She looked up and smiled. "Please do. I've begun to think I either have the plague or a huge zit on the end of my nose and no one wants to tell me."

Chuckling, he sat down across from her. "I guess everyone's upset about the salary cut."

"Tell me about it." She forked a slice of hard-boiled egg into her mouth. "Since the announcement, Mr. McGarry's phone hasn't stopped ringing. We've got employees who are threatening to quit or go on strike. I've even had spouses trying to talk to Mr. McGarry. He's got me taking messages and then never returning their calls. He doesn't want to talk to them."

"Which leaves you in a pickle, I imagine."

"I'll say." She ate another bite of salad, then narrowed her eyes. "You don't want me to take a message, do you?"

"Not really. Doesn't sound like he'd return my call either." The chili had a pleasant zing to it but wasn't too spicy.

"I have to say, I've looked at the balance sheet, and I don't know what else the hospital can do. We've already cut every bit of fat out of the budget that Zane or Mr. Varner can find. The problem, of course, is that we take in patients who are uninsured and can't pay their bills. Worse, sometimes the insurance companies won't even pay the full amount on procedures we do for their people."

"None of which helps the employees who won't be making as much money as they have been come January first."

"I know. I'm sorry."

"Not your fault."

Nor was it his fault. Or Candace's, who had to support two kids on her own. Or Elena's, who'd been dreaming of a trip to Spain since forever.

The niggling headache that had threatened all day jabbed him right behind the eyes.

Maybe a gigantic yard sale wasn't such a bad idea after all. At the moment, it was the only one they had.

After James finished his lunch, he went through the lobby where a twelve-foot Christmas tree stood and stepped outside to get a breath of fresh air. The winter sun cast pale shadows across the parking lot. Casually, he walked a few paces away from the hospital entrance.

There had to be some other alternative to a parking lot sale.

He pulled out his cell phone and punched in the number for St. Francis Medical Center in Peoria. He asked for Human Resources. A pleasant-sounding woman with a broad Midwestern accent answered.

After giving her his name, he said, "I'm inquiring about part-time nursing positions you have open. I have more than twenty years' experience as an RN, both in general medicine and surgery. I also have a military background—"

"By any chance, are you currently employed by Hope Haven Hospital?"

The question surprised him. "Yes, ma'am, I am."

"I see. You're about the twentieth call from Hope Haven employees I've had in the past two days."

He winced. "I guess a lot of us are looking for options."

"I don't blame you. Really, I don't. But unless you live here in Peoria, the cost of transportation and the time you'd spend on the road, particularly in winter, would likely eat up any gains you made. If you think you'd be interested, Mr. Bell, of course you're welcome to submit your résumé electronically." She provided the e-mail address. "I'll look it over and get back to you as soon as I can."

He thanked her for her time but didn't make a commitment about sending his résumé. That was going to take a lot of thought. Fern was right about his not wanting to be away from her and the boys any more than he had to be.

Discouraged, James returned to the second floor. When he stepped out of the stairwell, he heard Ted Townsend shouting his head off.

James broke into a run down the corridor.

"Get out of here! Get out!" the boy yelled. "Your stupid God's already done enough. Get out!"

James rounded the corner into Ted's room, almost colliding with Thomas Wiltshire, the hospital chaplain. Wearing a dark jacket and clerical collar, he looked unfazed by the boy's outburst.

"Your parents asked me to talk to you. They're worried about you, son." Pastor Tom spoke in a soothing voice, a tone developed during years of counseling those who had been injured or were grieving over the loss of a loved one.

The chaplain noticed James and gave him a brief nod to acknowledge his presence.

"I said I don't want to talk to you. Are you deaf or something?" Ted turned his face toward the opposite wall.

"We don't have to talk about your injury. We could talk about the Chicago Bears. They're having a pretty good season this year."

"Football stinks."

James wondered at the vehemence of the boy's anger. Maybe the kid had problems beyond his amputated leg.

"Ah, now, there's a man after my own heart. A baseball fan, huh?" Pastor Tom grinned as though he was just getting warmed up. "The Cubbies. Now there's a team worth rooting for. Talk about underdogs, those boys do their best but it's never enough. The management hasn't the sense the good Lord gave them."

As the pastor continued his monologue, Ted slowly turned back to the preacher with a half-interested expression. Somehow, with the change of subject and talk about sports, Pastor Tom had gotten past the boy's anger, distracting him enough to stop the yelling.

Smiling to himself, James backed out of the room. Not surprisingly, the hand of the Lord was once again working through Pastor Tom.

Maybe they ought to put the pastor to work solving the hospital's financial crisis.

At the nurses' station, James logged onto the computer again. Meds were due for the pneumonia patient in 210. He placed the order with the pharmacy.

More than thirty minutes after Ted's outburst at Pastor Tom, the chaplain stopped by the nurses' station.

James gave him a thumbs-up. "At least you quieted the boy down."

"The young man is simply frightened."

"Understandable," James said. "Lots of unknowns in the future for him."

"True enough. After we got past the relative merits of football, baseball, and soccer, we had a very interesting discussion. He's not only worried about having one leg. He knows, intellectually, he'll be able to get around with a prosthesis."

"But not play soccer."

"More than that. Several universities have been scouting him with full scholarships in mind. His dream is to be an aeronautical engineer, maybe even an astronaut. The astronaut idea is probably out, though not entirely, I would think. The Americans with Disabilities Act might actually give him a leg up, if you'll excuse the play on words."

A pastor cracking jokes, even bad ones, always tickled James. "In either case he could still be an engineer."

"The problem is money. His parents aren't wealthy. His dad was working as an auto mechanic for the Ford dealership just outside of town and hurt his back. He's on long-term disability now. His mother works as a typist in an insurance office. Ted doesn't see how they'll ever be able to help him through college."

A stab of guilt lanced James's chest. He'd been so worried about his own upcoming financial problems, he hadn't given any thought to what difficulties others might be facing.

"Are his grades good enough to get an academic scholarship?" he asked.

"He's put so much time and energy into soccer, his grades have slipped. Now he's missing school." The pastor's clear blue eyes clouded with sympathy. "He doesn't think he has that option."

James wondered. Maybe a seventeen-year-old boy didn't know about all the available options.

Chapter Five

CANDACE PULLED HER CAR INTO THE ATTACHED garage of her split-level home on Fourth Avenue. A familiar ache filled her chest, the spot where Dean used to park his car was now occupied by her mother's old sedan, a daily reminder that her husband was gone.

Forcefully, she banished the thought. Lila Adams, the counselor she'd been seeing lately, often reminded her about the effects of dwelling on her loss. Candace had to admit she had felt some of her loneliness lessening since starting her sessions.

She got out of the car, but before she could reach the door into the house, Howie pulled it open.

"Mommy! Mommy! I gots a stamp."

Candace scooped her son into her arms. "You got a what?"

"A stamp." He held out his tiny fist to show her the back of his ink-smudged hand. The decoration looked vaguely like a red star. Or maybe a Christmas candle. "Miz McCarthy said I know my letters real good."

"Good for you, sweetie." She gave him a kiss. "My smart boy." Howie had been doing quite well in kindergarten, many thanks to his wonderful teacher, Miss McCarthy. It was a real pity the young teacher was engaged and planned to move to California after her marriage early next year.

Candace carried her son through the mudroom into the family room and eased him down. He raced across the room waving his arms, making a noise like an airplane and doing crooked somersaults. He landed in the middle of his Lego set and tossed the pieces up in the air.

Wincing, Candace marveled at how active little boys could be. Since she'd only had one sister, and no brothers, she hadn't been prepared for Howie's high-octane energy.

In contrast, Brooke, whose school had gotten out early, was sitting cross-legged on the floor watching television, her long blonde hair messy from a day of playing. A plate with the remnants of cheese and crackers sat on the coffee table along with an empty glass. Her afternoon snack, apparently.

"Hi, honey. How was your day?" Candace asked.

"Fine, I guess." Brooke's attention remained focused on the TV screen.

Candace frowned. "Have you done your homework?"

Her daughter responded with a noncommittal grunt.

In two quick strides, Candace reached the television and turned it off.

"Mo–om!" her child wailed. "I was watching that."

"I noticed. Where's Grammy?" Candace's mother had moved in with her after Dean died and had been a lifesaver, caring for the children when Candace couldn't be there.

"Upstairs, I guess. Fixing dinner."

"Fine. Now tell me again, have you done your homework?"

Her beautiful daughter, who had such lovely lips, pulled them into a classic pout.

"How about your piano practice?"

The pout remained in place.

"I thought as much." Leaning over, she kissed Brooke on the top of her head. "Upstairs. Now. Homework. Then the piano."

"Mommy, everybody watches—"

"At our house we do homework before TV. Go." She shooed her daughter off with a wiggle of her hand, knowing Dean would have been even more stern than she ever could be.

With little enthusiasm, Brooke complied. Unfortunately, she left the dirty plate and glass behind. Something else Dean might not have appreciated.

Candace felt a certain dread about the teenage years. She hadn't been a perfect adolescent, and she didn't expect her daughter to be one either.

She simply prayed that when Brooke popped out on the other side of those difficult teenage years, that the two of them could be friends.

Later that night, after the children went to bed, Candace and her mother sat in the family room, Janet tilted back in her favorite recliner. Trim and fit at sixty, only her silver hair and a few laugh lines around her eyes gave away her age.

"Any more news about the cut in pay?" Janet asked.

"Just a lot of grumbling, although Elena did suggest we have a gigantic yard sale in the parking lot."

"It's a thought, I suppose." Using the remote, Janet turned the volume down on the TV. "I've been thinking, I have some savings. If you'd let me pay rent—"

"You earn your keep and more, Mom. Without you around, after-school care for two children would cost me half a month's salary. You keep your money. You earned it the hard way." Divorced years ago, Janet had scrimped and saved to raise Candace and her sister Susan, never indulging in any luxuries herself. And she'd done so with grace and joy, never letting the girls know how much she sacrificed.

Candace wouldn't think of taking any of her savings now.

"At least let me pay for some of the children's Christmas presents you've already bought. You shouldn't have to carry the whole burden."

"You've always been generous with Brooke and Howie. They may not get quite as much from Santa this year, but I hardly think they'll feel deprived."

Janet exhaled a long sigh. "You've always been an independent child."

Eyeing her mother with raised eyebrows, Candace produced a teasing grin. "And just where do you suppose I learned that, Mrs. Fuller?"

"Oh, you . . ." Janet turned the TV volume up again and settled in to watch the rest of *History Detectives*. Something about a Civil War sword.

Sitting on the couch, Candace curled her feet up under herself. She yawned. A long day by any measure. And she still had to get to her nightly Bible study.

From somewhere behind her, she heard a faint sound. Someone upstairs in the living room of the split-level house? A sleepless child escaping his or her bedroom?

She turned and called, "Brooke, is that you?"

No answer. Even so, a column of gooseflesh skidded down her spine. She'd just run upstairs to make sure the children were all right.

Anabelle was sitting in front of the computer in her husband's home office. She'd brought up the Web site Diana had recommended about choosing a puppy.

Cameron had settled in his recliner reading an agricultural supply catalog. Since dinner, he'd already gone through the local paper and a hardware catalog.

"Cam, dear, if we had a dog, which do you like best, a large dog or a small poodle-sized dog or something in between?"

"I don't want any dog."

She'd expected that answer. Unfortunately. "Let's say, theoretically speaking, what kind of dog do you like?"

"One that belongs to somebody else and stays out of my garden."

Anabelle sighed and studied a picture of a full-grown Bull Mastiff on the computer screen. If an animal that big wandered into the office, there wouldn't be any room left for either her or Cam. Certainly the many houseplants she tenderly cared for wouldn't stand much of a chance for survival with a Paul Bunyan–sized dog on the loose.

She didn't want to think about what a dog like that might do to Cam's beautifully landscaped yard.

"I think I like a middle-sized dog," she said. "I don't want a lap dog, but not as big as these giant dogs that look like horses."

Cam slapped the catalog closed. "What on earth are you looking at, Annie?"

She pushed her chair back from the computer to face her scowling husband. At sixty-three, he was still the handsomest man she knew, his gray hair and mustache giving him a dignified appearance. He'd be even more attractive if he were smiling.

"Diana Zimmer gave me the address of a Web site that helps you select the kind of dog that would be best for your family. You have to decide how big a dog you want, short or long hair, child tolerant—"

"We don't have any children, at least not little ones."

"We are going to have a grandchild soon. We'd want a dog that would—"

He snapped the recliner's footrest down and sat forward. "Ainslee's baby isn't born yet and won't be old enough to play with a dog for years. Why now?"

Anabelle wasn't quite sure except that it felt *right*. Especially when she thought of all the dogs that needed good homes.

The prospect of a grandchild thrilled her. Although Ainslee had made it quite clear that she was not to interfere or take over the preparations for the baby's arrival. Like buying a new crib for the baby. Which she'd done and then had to return.

Anabelle fought back a sigh. She wouldn't *think* of meddling in Ainslee's affairs or *taking over* where it came to her grandbaby.

Cam leaned back again. "Since we're not getting a dog, we don't have to worry about Ainslee's baby or a dog being child tolerant, do we?"

A wave of disappointment washed over Anabelle. "A dog would be a nice companion for both of us on these quiet nights.

We could take the dog for walks around the neighborhood or teach him to catch Frisbees."

"Anabelle, luv, you're the only companion I've ever needed. I'd be happy to take you for walks anytime you want to go. And if you'd like to learn how to catch a Frisbee, we can do that too. But I think you'd look silly trying to catch one with your teeth."

"Cameron Scott, don't you make fun of me." Tears pressed at the back of Anabelle's eyes. The sight of those children playing with the puppy had set her off. It couldn't be as simple as hormones. She was well past that stage. But with Kirstie living on her own, Anabelle had this great hole in her life.

Cameron was a wonderful husband and a great companion. But he couldn't fill the sense of emptiness that came from not having her children close at hand to hold in her arms.

Silly to think a dog could replace them. Nothing could do that.

But receiving unconditional love from a dog and being needed in the elemental way an animal needed its owner could plug the empty hole in her psyche.

With a sigh, she clicked off the Web site she'd been studying and exited the Internet. She'd go upstairs and do some quilting until bedtime. Maybe while she worked, she'd come up with a way to persuade her sometimes annoying husband that getting a dog was *his* idea.

"Mommy!"

Brooke's scream instantly woke Candace. She was out of bed and on her feet almost before her eyes were open enough to see the clock. Three thirty in the morning.

Grabbing her robe from the end of the bed, she hurried down the hallway to Brooke's room.

"*Mommy!*"

"I'm here, honey. I'm right here." She sat on the edge of Brooke's bed. The bright sunflower quilt had slipped off to one side. In the glow of the night light, Brooke's curls looked tousled from sleep and her eyes were wide open. "*Shh*, honey. It's all right."

"No, it's not, Mommy." Sobbing, Brooke launched herself into her mother's arms.

Her heart aching for her daughter, Candace smoothed her hand over Brooke's hair. "You've had a bad dream, honey. Just a dream. Everything is fine."

Another sob racked Brooke's slender body.

"Do you remember what the dream was about?" Candace asked in a calm, reassuring voice, one she would use with a frightened woman experiencing her first labor. And just as often with the expectant father.

Brooke sniffed, her terror easing. "It was Daddy. I wanted him to come home."

A stab of grief ripped through Candace's chest, so painful it took her a moment to catch her breath. "You know your daddy is always with us, looking out for us from up in heaven."

"No, he isn't. I wanted him to come *here*. Come help you."

Candace brushed the tear-dampened curls away from Brooke's face. After Dean's death, Brooke had stopped speaking for two months and started having nightmares. Candace had taken her to a counselor, who helped Brooke to deal with her grief. Had those same nightmares returned? Why now?

"You wanted Daddy to help me do what?"

"I don't know. I just knew you needed help."

She needed Dean in a thousand ways and always would. But a brain aneurysm had taken him away. Now he resided only in her heart.

Rocking Brooke in her arms, hot tears edging down her own cheeks, Candace quieted her daughter. "It's okay now. You can go back to sleep. Mommy will take care of everything."

Brooke slumped against her. "I want Daddy back *now*."

"I know, sweetie. I know." She rocked back and forth, humming a tune she had lulled Brooke to sleep with when she was a baby. Howie too.

Slowly the child drifted back to sleep in the safety of her mother's arms. Her breathing became a soft snore, a melody Candace cherished.

She wished she could as easily alleviate her own fears and grief.

Chapter Six

THE FOLLOWING DAY, JAMES ARRANGED AN appointment with Leila Hargrave, the hospital's nursing administrator. She shared an office on the first floor with Human Resources. Except for a wedding photo of her daughter, there were no personal items on her desk and no sign of the approaching holidays on her side of the shared office.

In contrast, her office mate had garlands of holly draped above her desk and a childish drawing of Santa coming down the chimney taped to the wall.

Leila indicated the straight-back chair beside her desk. "What can I do for you, James?" She closed the file folder that had been open on her desk.

Noted for her no-nonsense style, Leila wore her gray hair in a tight bun at her nape and rarely smiled. Still, she was effective in her job. The nursing staff always knew exactly where they stood.

"I'm afraid the upcoming pay cuts are going to be hard on my family's budget," James said.

"Your family's budget and everybody else's in the hospital. It was Varner's decision and the board of directors, not mine."

"I'm aware of that, Ms. Hargrave." He tried not to sound defensive or squirm unnecessarily. The chair he was sitting on was so hard and uncomfortable, it seemed designed to minimize the amount of time anyone would want to sit there. "I'm hoping to be able to pick up some overtime to make up the difference. I've worked in most of the nursing departments at one time or another."

"I'm aware of your résumé, James. You're an excellent, experienced nurse. Hope Haven is lucky to have you." She tapped the top of her ballpoint pen on the closed file folder.

"Then do you think it will be possible—"

"Authorizing overtime is going to require my approval and Mr. Varner's. He has already made it clear, unless there's a major disaster, like another tornado blowing through town, his approval will be very hard to obtain."

Disappointment pressed down on him and formed a weighty lump in his chest. "I understand." Working overtime wasn't his favorite thing to do. He hated being away from Fern. But the extra pay would have eased the financial pinch of the pay cut.

"What about switching to graveyard shift?" he asked. "There's premium pay for that."

She cocked her head and studied him intently. "Is that really what you want to do? I'm thinking now of your wife. I understand she's struggling with MS."

Her comment and the flicker of compassion in her eyes surprised James. He didn't know she was aware of Fern's illness and hadn't imagined she'd care. *You've judged her too harshly, James.*

"Our insurance doesn't cover all the meds," he said. "The out-of-pocket expense of those . . ." He left the thought hanging in the air.

"I understand completely." She pulled a file folder from the desk drawer. "You're about the tenth person who's asked for more hours or a shift change. I'll put your name down but can't make any promises. We're fully staffed at the moment. We may lose one or two nurses to Peoria or even Springfield hospitals; but I find, on the whole, our nurses want to stay right here despite the cut in pay. Their families are rooted in Deerford."

"It's a good place to live," James agreed. It hurt to think of leaving Deerford or even working part-time elsewhere. The town was child-friendly, offering lots of recreational activities through-out the year. The schools were excellent, the parents very in-volved. James and Fern had found a good church home in Church of the Good Shepherd. Both boys had been baptized there.

But when it came to his family, he'd do what had to be done. Maybe he could find a part-time weekend job at the clinic where Fern used to work.

He thanked Ms. Hargrave and went back upstairs.

Anabelle and her daughter Kirstie were talking near the nurses' station. In her early twenties, Kirstie had black, wavy hair, clear blue eyes and a sparkling personality that attracted people to her. Wearing slacks and low-heeled shoes, no one would know she'd had her right leg amputated years ago.

"Hey, Kirstie. How's the teaching world going? And why aren't you there?" A dish of hard Christmas candies had appeared on the counter. James took one and popped it in his mouth.

The young woman produced a sparkling smile. "I took a personal day off to get some shopping done. The little munchkins are so excited about Christmas, they can barely sit still. So I'm teaching, but I'm not at all sure there's much learning going on."

"Kirstie has gotten very good reviews from her principal both this year and last," Anabelle said proudly.

"Only because he doesn't know I bribe the kids to behave when he shows up," she teased. "Third graders can be a handful."

"I bet," James agreed.

"Mom said you have a patient you wanted me to talk to." She carried a clutch bag and tucked it under her arm.

"Right. His name's Ted Townsend. Seventeen. A soccer star at Lincoln High. Lost his leg in a motorcycle accident."

Kirstie winced. "Poor kid."

"Yeah. He pretty much thinks the world as he knows it is gone forever."

"Well, he's pretty much right."

Her comment and attitude jolted James. "You've adapted well to your prosthesis."

"Sure I have. When you lose a leg, you pretty much have to adapt. But my life is much different now than it would have been if I still had two good legs."

"Except you'd still be a teacher," Anabelle pointed out.

"Probably true. I love teaching and my kids. But when I meet someone new, particularly men, I have to wonder if and when I should tell them about my leg. Before I lost my leg, I used to love to go to the lake and swim. I don't even own a swimsuit now."

Anabelle pulled her lip between her teeth. "It's still not easy for you, is it?"

"Oh, Mother, it's okay. It's just different." Kirstie kissed her mother on the cheek, then turned to James. "Lead the way, James."

"Stop by when you're finished, Kirstie, and we'll have a cup of coffee together," Anabelle said.

James took her to Ted's room and introduced Kirstie. A couple of sports magazines that looked unread were on the bed, the kid's iPod next to them. Three big vases filled with cut flowers sat squeezed onto a wall shelf and a potted plant was sitting on a pile of get-well cards on the bedside table. The kid had lots of friends, James decided. He'd need all their support as he adjusted to his new reality.

Wanting Kirstie to take the lead, James stood back away from the bed.

The boy narrowed his gaze on Kirstie, his missing leg obvious by the way the blanket flattened where his right knee should have been. "Who are you? Some kind of social worker or something?"

"No. I'm a third grade teacher. Graduated and got my credential from the University of Illinois a couple of years ago."

"Well, goodie for you."

Ted's tone dripped with sarcasm, and that annoyed James. The kid's attitude was really beginning to grate on him.

"Got good grades too," Kirstie said, unperturbed, "and did it all with only one good leg to stand on."

Ted's forehead folded into a frown. "Why should I care?"

Kirstie picked up the bedpan from the table near the sink and knocked it against her right leg. The thud sounded hollow, different than hitting metal against flesh.

Ted didn't seem to get the point.

Dragging a chair up close to the bed, Kirstie propped her foot on the seat and tugged the pants leg up past the calf of her artificial limb.

"My third graders love to play knock-knock on my leg." She demonstrated with her knuckles. "Of course, sometimes they knock on the wrong leg, which isn't so great. Some of those kids are stronger than they realize."

Gaping first at her leg, Ted slowly raised his gaze to meet Kirstie's. "When you walked in, I couldn't tell."

"That's because I've worked hard on my gait so the prosthesis isn't obvious, and I've been working at it since I was ten years old. At the time, I thought it was the end of the world." She grinned at the young man. "Turns out it wasn't, so I learned to live with it." She knocked her prosthesis one more time, then lowered her foot to the floor.

"Can you run on that thing or just walk?"

"I can run with a different prosthesis, though I'm not likely to win any races. But then I've never been particularly athletic. I do have trouble jumping rope, which makes me a terrible failure in the eyes of my third-grade girls. I'm not that coordinated now, and I wasn't all that good when I was in third grade, either."

The hint of a grin curved Ted's lips. "So do you know any one-legged soccer players?"

That stopped Kirstie for a moment. "I don't think I've ever met a soccer player. I dated a basketball player in college who'd had his entire knee replaced. Is that close enough?"

"Not really." Some of the anger and tension had gone out of the boy's expression. The lines of stress relaxed and he came close to giving Kirstie a real smile.

Confident Kirstie could help Ted take a giant stride forward in his recovery, James slipped out of the room. He had other patients to see and a personal financial crisis to face.

About a half hour later, Kirstie came looking for James and found him in the supply room.

"How'd it go?" he asked.

"Ted's a nice kid." She finger combed her hair back away from her face. "All that attitude he's showing is to cover up the fact that he's scared."

"Yeah, I got that. I was hoping you'd be able to reassure him things would be okay." James returned an unused suture kit to its proper bin.

"I did my best. My guess is he'd rather hear that from a one-legged male jock. Which I don't happen to be."

James grinned. No one would mistake Kirstie, a petite young woman with delicate features, for a jock of any kind.

"Guess he's out of luck," James said. "I'm fresh out of one-legged jocks."

Her eyes twinkling as though she had a secret she wanted to share, Kirstie said, "I know where I can find one. I've got a couple of contacts who are active with the Paralympics organization."

James tried to remember where he had heard about that. "Paralympics?"

"Like the regular Olympics, only all the participants are physically disabled in some way. There are dozens of sports—almost every event in track and field, wheelchair basketball, volleyball and tennis, a sport called goalball played by blind participants."

"Really? I didn't know the program was so extensive." He logged the sutures back into the computer and logged himself out, his shift about to end.

"The Paralympics are always held following the regular Olympics in the same host city." Kirstie gave a wave to Anabelle, who was ready to call it a day. "I'll be right with you, Mother."

"No rush, dear."

"Anyway," Kirstie continued, "I'm going to contact these guys I know. If I can get one or two of them to come talk to Ted, it might give him something more positive to think about than simply dwelling on what he's lost."

James's spirits lifted on Ted's behalf. The boy needed a mental boost. Kirstie could well have found the answer.

"That would be terrific, Kirstie. It'll have to be soon, though. I imagine Ted will be discharged soon and switch to outpatient services and rehab."

"I'll make some calls tonight," she promised.

James's spirits were still high as he headed home. The street-lights in town were all decorated for the holiday with garlands of holly. Store windows were painted in Christmas themes featuring everything from baby Jesus in a manger, the three wise men and angels trumpeting Christ's arrival to contemporary visions of Santa and sugar plum fairies.

Tomorrow, he and his family would go in search of the perfect Christmas tree.

He grimaced at the thought. As much as he loved the holiday season and decorating a tree, buying a tree had become a major expenditure. Every year the price had gone a little higher.

This year they'd have to cut back. A smaller tree would do just as well. Fewer presents too.

As he turned onto his street, a few flakes of snow drifted down to land on the windshield. A white Christmas would make up for not having the biggest tree in town.

Chapter Seven

SATURDAY MORNING JAMES MADE A BIG POT OF oatmeal for the family. He'd been up with Fern twice during the night. She'd had muscle spasms in both her legs, and he'd massaged them until the cramps eased.

He glanced across the kitchen table. Fern toyed idly with her oatmeal but had eaten very little, despite the raisins and brown sugar he'd added. Dark circles of fatigue under her lovely brown eyes testified to her sleepless night.

His eyes probably didn't look much better.

Gideon wolfed down his bowl of oatmeal, then made himself a slice of toast spread with peanut butter.

"So when are we going to get the tree?" he asked around a mouthful of peanut butter.

"Soon as we all finish breakfast and clean up the kitchen," James said.

"Some guys are coming over later to shoot some hoops," Gideon said.

"It snowed last night," James pointed out. "You'll have to shovel the driveway." Both James and Fern had always wanted their house to be a place where the boys' friends would feel at home. The basketball hoop mounted on the garage was part of the plan. That was still true even though Fern could rarely bake batches of cookies for them now or hand out sodas on a hot summer day.

"No sweat." Gideon carried his empty bowl and juice glass to the sink. His long-sleeved high school jersey was stretched out of shape and faded from black to gray, the result of dozens of trips to the washer. "The guys can handle it. Besides, I think it's all gonna melt by noon."

"Don't you want to help decorate the tree?" Fern asked, her words slurring.

"I do." Nelson carried his dishes to the sink. "Wouldst thou want your humble servant to fetch the boxes of ornaments 'n' stuff from the attic?"

Fern gave her thespian son a crooked grin. She was enjoying his interest in Shakespeare and eager to see him perform in the play.

"That'd be fine, young Puck," James said with a smile meant for both Nelson and his wife.

"Great." Nelson loped out of the kitchen and up the stairs, his feet thundering on each step. It sounded like the house had been invaded by a herd of woolly mammoths.

"I figured we'd be done decorating by lunch," Gideon said. "It's kind of same ol', same ol' isn't it? Shouldn't take long."

James wasn't sure how he felt about Gideon's lack of interest in helping with the holiday decorations. The project had always been a family affair. But for teenagers, the lure of their peers had a powerful pull.

"We'll see how it goes," James said. "For now, go help your brother bring down the boxes."

Unlike Nelson, Gideon sauntered out of the kitchen, slightly hunched, his arms dangling loosely at his sides, not an ounce of urgency in him. That would all change once he had his hands on a basketball trying to make a shot.

Or when he put on his ROTC uniform.

With a sigh, Fern put her spoon in her still half-full cereal bowl and pushed it away. "I don't think I can manage the Christmas-tree lot this year. Not even with my walker. I'm sorry."

"Sweetheart, you can't get out of helping us pick out a tree. No way." He shook his head. "We've always picked out the tree as a family. Ever since the boys were little."

Her expression clouded with regret. "I can't walk all over the lot."

"Not a problem. You can wait in the van where it's nice and warm. We'll bring the trees to you."

"I'm such a bother."

Picking up his own bowl and Fern's, he bent to kiss her. "It's tradition, sweetheart. You're the best tree picker-outer in the family. The boys and I won't settle for second best. You need to help us find the best. Okay?" Actually, he was thinking of second or third best. Definitely smaller than usual. Given the high price per foot this year, he didn't see any reason to buy a tree rivaling a giant sequoia.

A little teary-eyed, she nodded. "I love you."

"Likewise, sweetheart." The ache in his chest erupted like his heart was being ripped apart. He'd do anything to improve

Fern's health, and there was nothing he *could* do. Talk about feeling helpless.

"Did you take your new meds this morning?" he asked.

"Yes. They're not helping much."

"If Dr. Chopra says they'll improve your condition, they will. Give it a little time."

A half hour later, James carried Fern out to the van, lifted her into the passenger seat and spread a blanket over her lap. Nelson brought the walker in case she wanted to use it later. Gideon found some twine to tie the tree to the top of the van when they brought it home.

Despite an overcast sky, most of the snow that had fallen overnight had already melted. Patches of snow remained in a few protected spots on lawns and under trees. Here and there someone had tried to make a snowman with limited success.

James's favorite Christmas-tree lot was north of Deerford halfway to Princeton. The Cottone family raised their own trees in Wisconsin, hauling them to Illinois every holiday season. Always the freshest and most expensive trees around, the trees were universally well shaped and the needles bounced back when you ran your hand over a branch.

Making use of Fern's handicapped placard, James parked as close to the entrance to the tree lot as he could. "Okay, guys. Let's go find us a tree."

The boys clambered out of the van, their jackets unzipped. In an instant, they'd vanished into the forest of fir and spruce trees.

James opened the driver's door. "If you need me, honk the horn three times," he told Fern.

"I'll be fine. You go ahead and referee the boys. We don't want them bickering over which tree to get."

He hopped out of the van, blew her a kiss and hurried to catch up with his sons. The three of them set off to explore the entire lot, weaving in and out of the rows of trees.

Dozens of families were doing the same thing. Toddlers rode on their fathers' shoulders. Elementary-aged youngsters dashed among the trees, their efforts resembling a game of tag more that a search for the best Christmas tree.

In contrast, teenagers did their I'm-bored-out-of-my-mind, my-parents-made-me-come shtick, but the act wasn't entirely convincing. Their grins appeared too quickly, their whoop of *I found one!* too eager.

"Here's a good one," James said, dragging a five-foot tree out into the aisle for his sons to examine. "Look how symmetrical it is. Perfect all the way around."

"Dad, that tree is shorter than me," Gideon complained.

"Yeah, we don't want a runt tree," Nelson said. "We want a big one with the angel way up on top." He held his hand way above his head.

"We could buy a shorter, less expensive tree and set it on top of the coffee table," James said. "Then it would be tall enough and faster to decorate. Plus there'd be a lot more room for presents under the tree."

His suggestion fell flat. The three of them continued the search, James silently fretting about the expense.

He found a six-foot tree that looked pretty good to him. Nelson and Gideon challenged his choice with a perfect eight-footer.

James lifted his smaller tree. "Okay, guys, let's take both of these trees to your mom and let her choose."

"You know she's gonna pick the big one," Gideon said.

"Yeah, Dad, she likes to fill up our whole picture window."

He knew that. But maybe this year . . .

Sitting sideways with the door open, she examined each tree in turn, a smile on her face. "They're both gorgeous. No bad spots at all." She gave James a questioning look, and he knew she was thinking about the expense too. He hated that he'd told her about the cut in pay. She didn't need the worry.

"We gotta get the big one, Mom," Nelson pleaded. "We always do."

"I don't know, honey," Fern said, glancing at James. "Maybe this year we ought to try to keep things simple."

Despite her words, disappointment flickered in her eyes. The boys' expression mirrored Fern's. Regret curdled the oatmeal in James's stomach.

"The boys are right," he announced. "We'll get the larger tree. It'll be a perfect fit for our living room."

Gideon pumped his fist in the air.

Nelson cheered. "'Now the hungry lion roars, And the wolf behowls the moon,'" he quoted from Shakespeare.

Fern's forehead furrowed. "Are you sure, James? It's a lot of money."

"I'm sure." It was only money. Saving a few bucks wasn't worth disappointing his wife and children. "Okay, guys, get that tree tied down good on top of the van and I'll go pay for it."

"I don't need a new dress!" Brooke all but stomped her foot in rebellion in the middle of the girls' department of the discount store.

Nearby shoppers eyed Brooke with disapproval and Candace with censure.

Candace reined in her anger both at Brooke and the nosy shoppers. She could almost hear them thinking that she should have raised her daughter better, taught her not to have tantrums in public.

She'd brought both Howie and Brooke to the shopping center just outside of Deerford to buy new outfits for the holidays. Howie was easy—a new pair of slacks, a nice long-sleeved shirt, and a pair of shoes to replace the ones he'd started school with in September and had already outgrown. His selections were already in the shopping cart. He was good to go.

Brooke was impossible.

"I always buy you a new dress for Christmas," Candace patiently explained. "You'll want to look nice when you play the piano on Christmas Eve."

"These styles are all dorky." To emphasize her point, Brooke shoved at the clothes hanging on a round rack, setting them in motion.

Howie went down on all fours and into hiding underneath the clothes.

"We can go to a different store, if you'd like." She'd started with the biggest discount store in the shopping center hoping to find a bargain. No such luck. She hadn't even gotten Brooke to try on a single dress.

"The clothes I have are fine."

"Two days ago you were looking at the ad for this store and thought the dresses were cute."

"I can change my mind, can't I?"

The clothes on the rack began swaying wildly back and forth.

"Howie, stop whatever it is you're doing under there." Candace was losing her patience. Crowds of shoppers filled the store jostling each other, parking had been nearly impossible, Howie was getting bored, Brooke mutinous and Candace was hanging on by a thread. She longed for the days when she could pick out a dress for her daughter, and Brooke would be thrilled. The days when shopping was fun.

Now Brooke was eleven going on sixteen and impossible to please or understand.

"Can we just go home?" Brooke pleaded.

Candace rolled her eyes. Fighting Brooke's volatile moods was an exercise in futility, a fruitless effort leading only to frustration.

"All right, young lady. We'll go home. But don't whine to me next week when you realize you don't have anything new to wear for the Christmas Eve service at church."

Brooke whirled toward the checkout lines but not before Candace caught a glimpse of her daughter's chin quivering with the threat of tears.

What on earth is going on with Brooke? First she started having those nightmares, twice in the past week. Now, right in the middle of the store, she pulled a temper tantrum.

It was as though someone had switched her sweet little girl for an alien child Candace didn't recognize.

Please, Lord, I can't handle this without Your help.

"Come on, Howie." Separating the clothes on the rack, she found Howie grinning up at her, his blond hair mussed from his adventures. Unable to stop herself, she grinned back at him.

Boys were so easy, at least as far as shopping went. "Time to go home, honey."

Howie jumped up like a jack-in-the-box and raced after his sister. Candace followed more slowly.

When she got home, she was going to have a talk with her mother. Maybe she'd know how to handle Brooke's wild mood swings.

At the mall, Elena stood in a long line of mothers and their children waiting to talk to Santa Claus. Christmas carols played over loudspeakers as young girls dressed as elves escorted children up a few steps to see Santa. Another elf snapped a photo when the child sat on Santa's lap.

Elena bent down to confer with Isabel. She wore a cute little smock over a red, long-sleeved jersey. Elena had tied a red bow in her hair. "You know what you're going to ask Santa to bring you for Christmas?"

Izzy nodded her head vigorously. "A new doll with a red dress and a two-wheel bike with training wheels and a cake baking set that makes real cakes and a—"

Elena laughed. "Goodness, that's quite a list."

The child looked up with her big, light gray eyes. "I've been good this year, haven't I?"

"Yes, sweetie. You've been very good. But the most important part about Christmas is remembering why we celebrate it."

"Oh, I know why!" Isabel said with a hop. "We learned about Jesus' birthday in Sunday school. *Buela*, how many candles does Jesus need on his cake?"

Elena laughed; Isabel sounded so sincere. "All Jesus wants for His birthday is for us to love each other and be good."

As the line moved up, Elena wondered if she should take a turn on Santa's lap and ask him if he could do something about the pay cut at the hospital. Or, if he'd rather, a couple of airline tickets to Spain for her and Cesar would do nicely too.

With a muted sigh, she acknowledged she was too old to believe in Santa. Or sit on his lap, for that matter.

What a pity.

Chapter Eight

*J*AMES AND FERN SAT TOGETHER ON THE COUCH while a CD played "Joy to the World" in the background. Strings of lights, boxes of ornaments and tinsel were scattered around the room. The scent of fresh greenery perfumed the whole house.

James had sawed an inch off the bottom of the floor-to-ceiling fir and secured the tree in its base. When Gideon's friends arrived for their hoops game, they happily joined in the spirit of the season to help decorate the tree.

"Hey, Gid, is this you when you were a baby?" Scotty Duran held up a see-through ornament with a photo inside.

Gideon flushed. "Yeah, I guess."

"Nice hair, baldy." All the boys laughed.

Gideon's cheeks turned a deeper red.

Pete Montague picked up another ornament. "What's with this bird in a nest? That go on the tree too?"

"Yeah," Nelson said. "Mom bought that when we stayed in a cabin in Minnesota. Every place we vacationed, she bought a Christmas ornament so we'd remember the trip. Our Christmas tree's almost like a 3-D scrapbook we pull out every year."

James winked at Fern and took her hand. "Good memories too. All of them."

"They are. I just wish we could build more memories like that before the boys are grown and gone."

"We will. Dr. Chopra will tame your MS and you'll be able to travel again." They hadn't taken a family vacation in three years because of Fern's progressive disease. James held out small hope they'd find a cure for MS in Fern's lifetime. But controlling the worst of the symptoms seemed within the reach of modern medicine.

Nelson left the rest of the tree decorating to the older boys and found the box containing the nativity scene. He cleared off an end table and moved it to a prominent spot near the fireplace where it could be seen from both the living room and kitchen.

After setting up the stable, he carefully removed each figure from the box—the three wise men and three shepherds, a donkey, a cow and an angel to watch over baby Jesus, placing them in the scene. Then came Joseph and Mary and the manger.

The song on the CD switched to "Away in a Manger" sung by a lilting soprano.

Nelson reached into the box one more time. "Mom, do you want to do the honors? Put baby Jesus in the manger?"

Tears glistened in her eyes. "That's usually your job, Nelson."

The boy looked at the small ceramic figure in his palm. "I'll help you." His words were a plea, a prayer that his mother could still take part in the family's Christmas traditions. A heartfelt wish that her illness didn't exclude her from the life he'd always known.

James saw Fern hesitate, torn between fulfilling her son's wishes and the knowledge of her own weakness.

"I'll help too," James said.

"I've never felt so unstable and wobbly."

Why haven't the new meds kicked in yet? "I won't let you fall."

Standing, James took her arm. Gideon appeared beside her as well, and the room grew silent except for the soprano voice asking the Lord Jesus to stay by her side.

Together, James and Gideon slowly walked Fern across the room to Nelson and the nativity scene. James willed Fern not to fall, not to stumble. He held his breath until his lungs ached.

Nelson placed baby Jesus in his mother's trembling hand and guided her hand toward the manger. Together they placed the baby in his cradle.

"Good job, M-mom!" His voice cracking with emotion, Nelson beamed at his mother's accomplishment.

James knew his son's joy was tempered by a fight against the same tears that burned unshed in his own eyes.

When they'd all finished eating dinner and were still sitting around the kitchen table, James announced that he wanted to have a family meeting.

Gideon glared at Nelson. "Are you in trouble again?"

"Not me," Nelson protested. His head swiveled toward his mother. "I'm not in trouble, am I?"

"No, honey. You're fine."

"No one's in trouble, and no one has done anything wrong," James said. "Except maybe me. There's something I should have told you."

All eyes turned toward him. He cleared his throat and took a deep breath. "There's a reason why I tried to talk you two into getting a smaller, less expensive tree this year. Starting January first, the hospital is cutting my salary. Not by a huge amount but enough that we'll notice the decrease in income."

Two sets of youthful blue eyes widened in unison.

"Are we broke, Dad?" Nelson looked pale and very worried.

"No, not broke. But we will have to cut back some and be careful how we spend our money."

"Your father's worried because my meds are so expensive."

"Yeah, but you can't do without those," Gideon was quick to say in support of his mother. "I can do without a lot of stuff. I mean, I don't need anything for Christmas."

"Me neither," Nelson added. "I'm too old for Santa anyway."

James smiled at his boys. "I think it's safe to say there will be presents for you to unwrap on Christmas morning. I'm thinking more along the lines of saving money by turning off lights when you're not in the room. Taking shorter showers. That kind of thing."

"I'll skip showers altogether," Nelson volunteered. "That'll save a bundle."

Fern waggled a finger at her son. "Oh, no you won't. I don't want any smelly, sweaty boys in my house."

Barely suppressing a teasing grin, Nelson shrugged. "I'm just trying to help."

Gideon picked up Fern's dirty plate and placed it on top of his. "I could get a job for after school. Maybe as a busboy or a job sweeping up at the grocery store. Lots of kids work part-time."

"You have to be sixteen for jobs like that," James pointed out. "Besides, you have your ROTC activities and your studies should be your priority anyway."

"But if I had a job, you wouldn't have to give me an allowance for stuff like lunch at school and downloads to my iPod."

Nelson sat up a little straighter in his chair. "I know what I can do. I could talk to some neighbors and ask them if I can walk their dogs."

Leaning forward, Gideon tapped the table in front of his brother. "We could both shovel sidewalks this winter and mow grass in the spring. A lot of the neighbors are old. I bet they'd pay us real good."

Excited, Nelson said, "And we'd be partners, right?"

"Right. Gideon and Nelson, Inc. We could make up some business cards on the computer."

Nelson frowned. "How come your name has to come first?"

"Because I'm older."

"That's not fair."

"Okay, so we'll do it alphabetically. It still comes out Gideon and Nelson."

Nelson's scowl deepened.

"Whoa, boys." Fern held up her hand. "Why don't you call yourselves the Bell Brothers? That would cover it."

They both looked at her as if she'd just invented the idea of pairing peanut butter with jelly.

A warm sense of pride filled James's chest. He should have told the boys about the pay cut earlier. They'd taken the news like real men, searching for ways to overcome adversity together.

Thank You, Lord, for the insight into my sons' character and for blessing me with two fine young men who are growing straight and true in Your image.

Candace lay in the queen-sized cherry sleigh bed she'd picked out with Dean, staring into the darkness. Unable to sleep, she remained poised, ready to act, if Brooke had another nightmare. She worried that her child had regressed in her youthful battle with grief over the loss of her father. An issue Candace thought had at least been eased, if not resolved, through counseling. It made her sick at heart to think of Brooke still going through all that emotional pain.

From the bedroom down the hall, she heard her daughter whimper, and she was on her feet in an instant. She hurried to Brooke's room.

The blankets were a tangled mess, half on and half off the bed. Brooke was on her knees, her face smashed into the pillow, her rear end sticking up in the air, the way she used to sleep as a small child.

"*Shh*, honey." Candace straightened the bedclothes. "You're having another bad dream."

Brooke muttered something unintelligible.

"Mommy's here. Everything's all right." She eased Brooke flat on the bed, straightened out her legs and pulled the covers over her again. With the thermostat turned low for the night, the air felt chilled. "Go back to sleep, honey. It's all right."

Brooke's lips moved but no words came out, only a long exhale.

Within moments, the dream released its hold on Brooke. The lines of tension in her face relaxed. Her mouth sagged open. Candace brushed the damp curls back from her daughter's forehead.

"Sleep, baby girl," she whispered. "Sweet sleep."

She continued to sit on the edge of the bed until she was sure Brooke was sound asleep, then she slipped out of the room. She met her mother in the hallway.

"Another bad dream?" Fresh from her own bed, Janet wore a lilac-colored velour robe and her gray hair was mussed.

A sick feeling knotted in Candace's stomach and she was on the verge of tears. "I don't know what I'm going to do, Mom. I don't know what's upsetting her so."

"I think you'd better take that child back to her counselor."

"You're right." She hated to spend the money, but there was something very wrong going on with Brooke. She needed to get to the bottom of her daughter's troubles, whatever the cost. "First thing Monday morning, I'll call Tony Evans, ask if he has time to see Brooke."

Tony had done wonders with Brooke, helping her to deal with her grief after Dean's death. Candace hoped the counselor would be equally successful this time. *If* that was the current problem.

Her own experience in grief counseling and working with Lila, her counselor, had helped her through some bad days that would have previously debilitated her. She still went to group meetings regularly.

Yet she still grieved. Her pain was lodged so deep inside her; it was like a festering wound that continued to poison her life.

She couldn't let that happen to her baby girl.

Chapter Nine

JAMES GROANED AS HE CRAWLED OUT OF BED ON Monday morning, leaving Fern sleeping peacefully—at last—after another bad night.

December mornings were darker than an underground tunnel designed to hide insurgents from US forces.

He made his way down the pitch-black hallway to the bathroom and switched on the light. He squinted. Maybe he wasn't all the way awake yet because the vanity lights over the mirror seemed dim. Usually they were—

He glanced up. Sure enough a bulb had burned out. Sighing, he decided to live with it for now. Later he'd ask one of the boys to change the bulb while he was at work.

He finished shaving, dressed and went downstairs, heading directly for the automatic coffee brewer. He poured himself a cup of—

Water? Plain water. Plain, icy cold water.

He stared at the coffee brewer. No red light. He was sure he'd set it to start brewing at five thirty.

He punched the On button. Still no red light.

Closing his eyes, he took a deep breath and forced himself to remain calm. Not having a cup of coffee at home wasn't a big deal. He could always stop by the drive-through to get a cup of java on the way to work.

What he didn't need was the unexpected expense of a new coffeemaker to replace a broken one.

He was pouring himself a bowl of cereal when Gideon arrived in the kitchen. He'd pulled on an old gray sweatshirt over his pajama tops and was barefoot.

"You're up early," James commented.

"We've got a ROTC drill practice this morning."

"During your winter break?"

"Yeah." Gideon opened the refrigerator and retrieved a gallon of milk.

"Do me a favor, son. After you get back home, change the lightbulb in the upstairs bathroom. One of them has burned out." James spooned some cereal into his mouth. "I've got to stop on the way home from work to get a new coffeemaker. Ours conked out this morning."

Cereal box in hand, Gideon gave his father a curious look. "Dad, the coffeemaker's unplugged."

James's head came up. He frowned at his son. "Who unplugged it?"

"I did. Well, Nelson and I did. Appliances that are plugged in all the time are big drains on the electrical system even when they're just sitting there. Unplugging the coffeemaker will save us money."

Jaw slack, James gaped at the boy. "But I like having my coffee ready when I come downstairs."

Shrugging, Gideon poured his cereal and added a generous serving of milk, then filled a glass with more milk. "Okay by me. But you said you wanted to save money."

That was true. James hadn't thought it would interfere with his morning routine. "What about the upstairs bathroom. Did you take the bulb out?"

Gideon pulled out a chair at the table and sat down. "Not me. I think Nelson did."

James thought back over his morning. The hallway had been particularly dark as he walked to the bathroom. He frowned as something clicked.

"The night light in the hallway. Did you unplug that too?"

"Yeah." His son scooped a heaping spoonful of cereal into his mouth and washed it down with a gulp of milk.

"That was only a three-watt lightbulb. We're not going to save much by unplugging that. Besides, Mom needs it."

"Okay. But it all adds up, Dad. A few watts here, a few watts there. We learned about energy consumption and power grids in science class and how it's good to conserve our natural resources when we can."

Mentally, James searched for an argument that would return the household to its former status quo and allow him, in good conscience, to have his coffee ready when he came downstairs.

James couldn't think of any except that he wanted his coffee.

What he'd done by explaining the family's financial situation to the boys was to create a two-man Power Police Force right in his own home.

"I'm gonna take my shower at school later," Gideon said. "That'll cut down on our natural gas bill by not having to heat the water."

James didn't know whether to laugh or bang his head on the kitchen table.

Most of all, he was proud of his sons for taking his words to heart. Perhaps a little too much to heart, but they were on the right track.

As James rinsed his cereal bowl, Nelson entered the kitchen and the overhead light went off.

"Hey," James complained. "There are people here in the kitchen."

"The light over the sink's good enough." The boy grabbed a bowl and a box of cereal. "Mrs. Murphy asked some of us to come by school and help finish painting the sets for the play today. I thought I'd go over some of my lines while I'm there."

"Fine." James looked up at the lightless ceiling. If the boys kept this up, he'd have to buy everybody night-vision glasses just to walk around the house without bumping into things. "Have you got your stuff ready for the Scout meeting tonight?"

"Not yet. I'll do that this afternoon."

James planned to check everybody's camping gear to make sure it could handle below-freezing temperatures during their overnight trip in January. He didn't want to end up with kids suffering from frostbite. Not while he was in charge.

Anabelle sat at the computer at the nurses' station. Between the holidays and employee vacations, putting together a schedule for the nurses in her Cardiac Care Unit was a complicated jigsaw puzzle. Not all the pieces were going to fit.

No, she corrected herself. It was more like a Sudoku puzzle. Nothing added up.

Peering through her reading glasses at the monitor, she tried to will the schedule to take shape.

It didn't work.

"You're squinting. Be careful or you'll get permanent wrinkles."

Startled from her concentration, Anabelle looked over the top of her glasses at Diana Zimmer, standing on the other side of the counter.

"Trust me, my wrinkles are already permanent, and putting the weekly schedule together is giving me even more gray hairs. Not that I need any extra help in that department. I've already got more salt than pepper."

She called Ace to come behind the counter and gave him a good scratch between his ears, her fingers working their way through his thick winter coat.

"Ace, ol' buddy, you are exactly what I need. A faithful friend who asks nothing of me except a dish full of food and a warm place to sleep."

As though responding to her words of praise, Ace wagged his tail.

"Does that mean you've talked Cameron into getting a puppy?" Diana asked.

A renewed wave of disappointment struck Anabelle. Removing her glasses, she slid them into the breast pocket of her lab coat. "I'm afraid not. I tried to talk to him last week about a dog, but he'd hear none of it." Well, he had taken her for a walk after church yesterday. As pleasant as the experience had been, however much she enjoyed being with Cam, that wasn't what she'd had in mind at all. She wanted them to walk a dog together.

"I'm sorry to hear he's still not interested." Diana plucked a hard candy from the dish on the counter. Ace looked up expectantly, but she gave a little tug on his leash, and he sat back on his haunches. "I volunteered at the County Animal Shelter on Saturday. Someone had brought in the cutest puppy, a mix of German Shepherd and who knows what. The friendliest little guy you'd ever want to meet, and I thought of you."

"Oh dear . . ." A spear of regret lodged in Anabelle's chest and her lips tensed. "If he's as cute as you say, I'm sure someone will adopt him."

"Well, that's the problem. The shelter's full of both dogs and cats. He's been at the shelter a week or more already. By the end of this week—"

Anabelle gasped.

"The county simply doesn't have the funds or space to keep so many animals. Some will have to be put down."

"But that's terrible!" The regret that had been gnawing at Anabelle turned to anger. "They shouldn't be allowed to do that to a poor, helpless animal." Anabelle knew she wasn't saying anything Diana hadn't said hundreds of times.

What on earth could Anabelle do? She couldn't go against Cam's wishes. After all, he'd be home with the dog more than she would. Even though she was totally confident Cam would come to love any animal, it wouldn't be fair to Cam if she simply arrived home with a puppy without his approval.

It wouldn't be fair to the puppy either.

"I'm sorry, Diana, I wish I could—"

"It's okay, Anabelle. I thought it was worth mentioning, at any rate. Not every family can provide for a pet."

But she could, Anabelle thought. Cam could too, if only he were willing.

Her jaw tightened. Maybe if she asked him one more time, if she could be a little more persuasive . . .

Diana and Ace went off to do their patient rounds. Anabelle returned to her scheduling task, although her heart wasn't in it.

Maybe the holiday season was depressing her. Kirstie and Evan would come home for Christmas dinner. She'd encouraged Kirstie to invite her boyfriend. But he planned to visit his parents and would be out of town. Ainslee and Doug wouldn't be there for dinner. They planned to go to his parents' home; it was their turn, as Ainslee explained. Instead they'd drop by for dessert on Christmas Eve before they all went to the eleven o'clock church service.

Christmas simply wouldn't be the same without Ainslee.

Discouraged, she sighed. "Just how do you think a dog is going to fix that?" she asked the blinking cursor on the computer screen.

"I've been talking to myself all morning too." Candace swept past Anabelle en route to the supply room. A few moments later she reappeared with an IV bag. "I think every pregnant woman in the county has decided to have her baby today so everyone can be back home by Christmas."

Anabelle swiveled her chair around. "Is that what you've been talking to yourself about?"

"Not really. It's just that I was going to call Brooke's therapist first thing this morning. But when I finally got enough breathing room to make the call, I discovered he's off for two weeks. Visiting his family, I think."

Concern rippled through Anabelle like an icy cold winter creek. Nothing had been easy for Candace since her husband passed away. "Is Brooke having trouble again?"

"She's back to having almost nightly nightmares, and she's acting . . ." She shook her head, causing her highlighted brown hair to shift at her jaw line. "I don't know how else to describe it except that she's acting like an adolescent."

"Then you certainly have my sympathies." When Kirstie hit her teen years, she'd had the double problem of coping with her disability as well as experiencing wildly fluctuating hormones.

"Brooke is only eleven years old and we're already having difficulties communicating. I can't imagine how it will be when she's actually sixteen. Which is why I wanted her to see her counselor as soon as possible." Candace checked the pager hooked onto her scrubs. "Gotta go. Another new mom in labor."

"Good luck with Brooke. I'll say a prayer for you both," Anabelle called after her.

Grateful she had survived the teenage years with her children, Anabelle turned back to the computer.

Compared to the challenges of parenthood, wanting a dog seemed small and insignificant. Even selfish.

And adding a puppy to the household when she was facing a 10 percent cut in pay wasn't ideal timing. There were always vet bills of one sort or another with any animal.

Get over it, Anabelle. Try thinking about all you've been blessed with instead.

Even as she spoke the words, an image of a puppy with big, brown pleading eyes popped into her mind. She slumped and shook her head.

That poor little puppy.

The number of elective surgeries always dropped off the week before Christmas, which meant James had a lighter patient load than usual. He had two discharges scheduled as well, including Ted Townsend, which would reduce his patient census even further. Ted's parents were already in his room getting him ready to go home.

If Varner noticed the light patient load, he'd probably order unpaid furloughs for staff members as a way to reduce expenses.

The elevator doors swished open. Two men in wheelchairs exited the elevator followed by a third man who walked with an uneven gait. Other than their obvious disabilities, all three men looked fit and were under thirty.

"Excuse me, sir." One of the men in a wheelchair rolled up to James. Wearing a blue T-shirt with the Paralympics logo, his arms looked as thick as a Civil War cannon. "We're looking for a kid named Ted Townsend. You know where we can find him?"

"Sure do." James set aside the discharge papers. "You must be Kirstie Scott's friends. She said to expect someone from the Paralympics Committee."

"Yep, I talked with her late last week. Marvin Bloom from Chicago." The man who walked with a limp extended his hand. "I work with the National Paralympics Committee. Talked my buddies into driving up with me."

James shook hands all around. All three had buzz cuts. "Are you all involved with the Paralympics?"

"Jeff and I play wheelchair basketball." He indicated the second man in a wheelchair and introduced himself as Rockie.

"And I'm lead member of the bicycling team," Marvin said. "We have big medal hopes for the next summer games."

James was duly impressed and he gave them all a thumbs-up. "Ted's been one of my patients since last week. He was a standout high school soccer player until he lost his right leg above his knee. That's really thrown him into the dumps. I hope meeting you three, he'll see all he can still do and stop focusing on what he can't do."

"We'll do what we can," Marvin promised.

"I'm glad you got here today," James said. "He's being discharged this morning."

Jeff held up a DVD. "We brought this along for him to take a look at. It's all about the Paralympics, what events are popular in the US, and what the organization can do to help members. He can take it home and look at it later."

"That's great, guys," James said. "Let me take you to his room and introduce you."

He introduced the men to Ted's mother and father and then to Ted. The young man was dressed in jeans and a T-shirt, sitting on the side of the bed, looking as moody as ever. Someone had folded and pinned the empty right leg of his jeans up over his thigh.

"What's this about?" the boy asked. "You brought every gimp you could find to gawk at me? I don't need an audience. I just want to get out of here."

"Be polite, Teddy," his mother warned.

"Why should I?"

Marvin stepped up to Ted, right into his personal space like a Marine drill sergeant. "Feeling sorry for yourself, huh? Think you got a really raw deal, huh? Well think again."

Ted retreated farther back on the bed.

Looking as though she wanted to intervene, Cynthia reached toward her son. Her husband held her back.

James understood Marvin's trying the tough approach. In boot camp it usually worked. He hoped it would with Ted as well.

"See, I could've been dead because I was driving too fast," Marvin continued. "I'm lucky to be alive even though I lost both my legs. I can still drive a car and I can ride a bike. And I mean ride competitively. No wimpy riding around the block for me."

Ted frowned as if he wasn't getting it. "How do you ride a bike without . . . ?" He glanced down at Marvin's legs.

"It's a reclining bike. Fastest man-powered vehicle on two wheels. I use my arms."

Though still unconvinced, Ted nodded.

Jeff rolled closer to Ted. "My buddy died in the same accident that nearly wiped me out." He spoke in a near whisper as though the memories were still raw and painful for him. "He had a shot at a pro-basketball career but he never had the chance to try out. Every basket I make, I make it for him. Whatever the final score is, everybody on my team is a winner."

"You have a choice, Ted." Rockie spoke from behind Jeff. "You can go home, curl up and let your heart and your soul die. Or you can live every day as though it could be your last. That's what we're doing. The Paralympics organization will help you do that."

Jeff handed the DVD to Ted, who looked perplexed. "Look at this when you get home. When you're ready, give Marvin a call." He stepped aside so Marvin could hand Ted a business card. "He'll fix you up with a group you can work with."

Phyllis Getty, an eightysomething hospital volunteer, who was an institution herself, arrived with a wheelchair to take Ted downstairs. She scanned the room, straightened her kelly green volunteer jacket and shook her head.

"My taxi's only got room for one," she said, her voice almost as authoritative as Marvin's despite her diminutive stature. "You other folks are gonna have to get downstairs on your own power."

Jeff did a wheelie and grinned. "How 'bout we make it a race? I'll take the stairs."

Phyllis placed her hands on her hips. "You'd break your neck going down those stairs."

"Okay, then, I'll take the elevator and you take the stairs."

Laughter broke the tension in the room. James helped Ted into the wheelchair and the entire entourage headed toward the elevators, Phyllis in the lead pushing Ted.

James said a silent prayer asking the Lord to watch over Ted and help him face the obstacles he would meet in his new life.

Anabelle lived only a couple of miles from Hope Haven Hospital, which made her daily commute easy even in bad weather.

But as she drove home that afternoon, something made her turn on Bureau Street and drive north out of town. Soon residential areas gave way to farmland where sugar beets, corn and truck farms—some of them raising organic fruits and vegetables—greened the countryside in the summer. This time of year, the ground had been plowed leaving clods of rich, dark earth waiting for the spring thaw to loosen winter's hold on them.

Trees that were planted to form windbreaks around scattered farmhouses were bare of leaves, their branches no barrier to winter storms.

The County Animal Shelter was only a mile or so out of town. There'd be no harm in dropping by, Anabelle told herself. But she wouldn't go against her husband's wishes and bring the little puppy home.

Maybe she wouldn't even bond with the puppy Diana had mentioned.

She turned her Ford Fusion hybrid into the shelter's gravel parking lot, splashed through a puddle and parked near the entrance. Only one other car was in the lot. Not nearly as busy here as the shopping center.

The office was empty, so she pressed the buzzer on the counter. Posters on the wall touted spaying and neutering for all animals. Feral cats had taken up residence in Cam's barn years ago, and they made good mousers. But Anabelle had taken care not to let them overpopulate the place by catching and neutering any new cats that showed up.

After a couple of minutes, the door to the kennels opened, admitting the sound of barking dogs and a young man wearing a tan uniform and matching jacket with a county shelter shoulder patch. His name tag read Josh Johnston.

"Sorry to keep you waiting." He stepped behind the counter and smiled pleasantly. His shaggy blond hair needed a good groomer. "What can I do for you?"

"A friend of mine—Diana Zimmer—mentioned she'd seen a puppy here. I thought I might—"

"Oh yeah, Diana's great." He brightened considerably at the mention of Diana's name, his smile wide enough to show sparkling white teeth. "She helps out at least once a week. She really cares about the animals and is always looking out for folks who can adopt them."

"I'm not actually planning to adopt—"

"She said she knew the perfect couple for a mixed breed pup we got in a week or so ago," he went on without pausing. "Come on, I'll show you."

"But—"

He went out the door to the kennel, obviously expecting Anabelle to follow. She couldn't very well just stand there.

The cacophony of barking dogs rose to a startling pitch in the barnlike structure. Yips and yaps from poodles and dachshunds, deep-throated barks from mixed-breed boxers and huskies. Dogs, two or three to a cage, leaped against the wire enclosures and wagged their tails, all of them pleading, "Take me! Take me!"

It made Anabelle heartsick to think many of these innocent creatures would have to be put down. She wanted to take them *all* home.

And knew she couldn't take *any*.

She wanted to weep.

"Here you go." Josh opened the gate to a pen holding a single puppy. "All the rest of our puppies have been adopted for Christmas. We've only got this little guy left."

Gingerly, Anabelle stepped into the cage. Splay-legged, the brown and white puppy galloped over to greet her. His ratlike tail beat like a metronome counting double time, and his rear end wobbled with the same enthusiasm. One ear stood at attention, the other bent at half mast as though debating if the puppy should grow into a proud German Shepherd or an adorable mutt.

Unable to help herself, Anabelle sat down on the concrete. The puppy launched himself into her lap and began licking her face.

She laughed and turned her head away. "Oh, puppy, I'm so sorry." She played with his ears, trying to straighten the crooked one, and petted his wiggly body. A sturdy little guy who needed a home.

"He's great, isn't he?" Josh said. "If you brought a travel carrier, I can get the paperwork started for you to take the pup home."

Her head snapped up. "No, you don't understand . . . I can't adopt him." The sting of tears burned her eyes and she nuzzled the dog to her neck. He smelled of puppy chow and happiness.

"But I thought . . . Diana said—"

"It's my husband. He doesn't want—" Her chest ached with regret. "I just wanted to see him. Somebody will adopt him. I know they will."

"It's pretty close to Christmas already. After Christmas—" The young man hung his head in defeat. "He won't have much of a chance."

Guilt burrowed into her good sense. She knew she should get up, go home to the man she'd known and loved since high school. Leave the puppy behind.

Leave the puppy to be put down. *If* he wasn't adopted by Christmas.

She eased the dog out of her lap and stood. "Josh, I wonder if I could—" She straightened her spine and pulled back her shoulders. "I can't take him home with me now but I will adopt him if no one else does."

"Well, okay." A puzzled frown pressed his blond eyebrows lower. "When did you want to come and get him?"

"Christmas Eve. But only if no one has taken him by then. I'll leave you my name and phone number."

If it came to that, she'd have to find some way to convince Cam adopting the puppy was the right thing to do. And she only had four days to do it.

Chapter Ten

THE SCOUT TROOP MET IN THE SOCIAL ROOM AT Church of the Good Shepherd. The boys started to straggle in a little before six o'clock, hauling in their bedrolls and duffel bags for James to check for the trip. At the last meeting he'd given them each a list of what they'd need.

"Okay, guys. Settle down. No more roughhousing." Some of the boys were playing King of the Mountain on one of the long folding tables used by the church. While not acceptable behavior, James understood their excitement about the up-coming camping trip. He was pretty jazzed too, despite his worry about leaving Fern overnight. "Spread out around the room, dump out the contents of your duffels and get out your checklists."

The boys, all seventh and eighth graders, erupted into action, each vying for a spot to display the contents of his bag.

"Hey, Pete. You've got enough stuff there to go camping for a week," one of the boys teased.

"Mom said I had to bring two of everything in case I get my socks and pants soaked."

A neighboring boy nudged his buddy. "I'm sure not gonna carry Pete's duffel. It's gotta weigh a ton."

James interrupted the teasing, saying, "Listen up, guys. Stand by your duffel so I know which one belongs to you. And let's keep it down to a low roar, okay?"

He made his way around the room, eyeballing the gear the boys had packed: canteen, mess kit, long johns, extra wool socks, heavy hiking boots. He expected there'd be snow on the ground, and it was sure to be cold. Safety was his number one priority. With a few exceptions, the boys had followed the packing list to a T.

"Nelson, you and a buddy get two tents from our storage closet. We're going to practice putting up the tents outside." The troop was very fortunate that the church allowed them to store some of the troop's gear in the rec room, otherwise it all would have been stuffed into James's garage at home.

Over the years, the church grounds had expanded, the result of the owner of the adjacent property deeding the acreage to Good Shepherd after he passed away. The church had installed volleyball and basketball courts, a softball field and a small playground. The church used the area for various retreats and programs and rented it out to other community groups as well.

James directed the boys to a large grassy area near the picnic pavilion, which was lit by floodlights. For the purpose of erecting the tents, he divided the troop into two groups.

"First thing you do is put down a waterproof ground cover. Trust me, you'll be glad you've got that ground cover if we're camping in the snow. Now spread out the ground cover." He watched as the boys managed that step with minimal effort and only one small complaint about sleeping on the hard ground.

"Now the tent," he continued.

The process looked like a bunch of clumsy circus clowns had taken over the troop. Tents sagged. Poles collapsed. Kids got stuck inside and had to fight their way out.

By the time James had the tents straightened out and the boys had taken them down again to stow them away, James was exhausted and his sides ached from holding in his laughter.

On the way home in the van, Nelson said, "That was great, Dad. I can hardly wait for the camping trip."

"Me too." He mentally groaned, though, praying the Scouts would retain at least some small part of what they'd learned at the meeting that night.

On Wednesday, Mr. Varner called a meeting of employee representatives to discuss the impending pay cuts.

James had previously been chosen to serve on an employee grievance committee and so had Elena. They were joined in the conference room by Eddie Blaine, a hospital custodian and handyman, and Lori Neff, an admissions clerk. Pastor Tom was among the group as well.

With her usual efficiency, Penny Risser, Varner's executive assistant, had arranged copies of the hospital budget, a yellow pad of paper and a pencil at each place at the long conference table. A huge white poinsettia had been placed on the counter behind the CEO.

James pulled the budget closer and flipped through the pages. It looked a lot more complicated than his household budget, involved millions of dollars and showed a huge deficit. Turning off a few lights to save electricity wasn't going to fix the hospital's financial woes.

In his household, James didn't think the effort would solve all of their problems, given the way the cost of Fern's meds continued to skyrocket, but it was a start.

Albert Varner, impeccably dressed in a dark suit and tie, sat at the head of the table. He cleared his throat.

"I believe we're all here," he said. "We'll begin with—"

Penny, who was sitting next to him, leaned over and whispered something in his ear.

"Well, yes," he muttered. "We're all here except Mr. McGarry, our financial officer. I'm sure he'll be along shortly. But we can begin with the reason for this meeting."

Eddie raised his hand. "Mr. Varner, with all due respect, if you're going to announce an even bigger cut in our pay, you can kiss Hope Haven good-bye. The employees aren't going to stand for that. I'm telling you, we'll stage a walkout. Every last one of us."

A red flush stained Varner's cheeks. "No, no. That's not why you're here at all. In fact, preventing a walkout is exactly what I'm trying to do."

James had heard a few rumblings about a walkout, but he didn't think it was a serious threat. Maybe he'd been wrong.

"A lot of the office staff are really worried," Lori said. In her forties, she'd always had a quick smile and friendly disposition. She wasn't smiling now. "We've got several single mothers who are trying to support their families on what little they already make. Taking this big a cut is going to hurt them."

"I'm aware of that." His face still red, Varner shuffled through the papers in front of him. "That's why I wanted to explain— have Mr. McGarry explain—why the cut is imperative if Hope Haven is to stay in business at all."

Penny found the paper he was looking for and put it on top of his stack.

In a nervous gesture, he smoothed his dark hair away from his forehead. "You'll see very clearly on page four that the projected income without the ten percent cuts in salary will not sustain the hospital."

Papers rattled as everyone at the table searched for the page he was talking about.

"I need you, as employee representatives, to be able to explain why the cuts are so necessary. I want the employees to know—"

"It'd be better if you explained to the grocery store why the hospital employees can't pay for their groceries next month," Lori said.

"I understand," Varner said, his voice conveying sincerity. "If it helps any, our entire executive staff—myself included—is taking the same ten percent cut in pay."

"Bravo for you," Eddie muttered under his breath.

Not wanting the discussion to get too far off track, James interrupted. "I think we ought to let Mr. Varner explain why the hospital is short of funds for the coming year. If we know why, then maybe we can help solve the problem instead of putting all the weight on his shoulders."

"Yes, yes." Fumbling with his handkerchief, Varner wiped his forehead. "Let me start from the beginning."

Penny quickly rearranged her boss's papers.

He cleared his throat again. "As you'll see on page one, there are several factors that have created what you might call a perfect storm."

He went on to delineate the funding sources, both public and private, that had reduced or eliminated their contributions to the hospital.

James tried to take notes, but the government jargon, the several insurance carriers involved and the names of various foundations became a confusing blur. The effect of the absent dollars was clear, however. Hope Haven had to cut expenses. The easiest expense to cut was employee salaries, which could be done by closing an entire medical unit, laying off employees or reducing everyone's salary.

McGarry finally arrived and verified everything Varner had said as being the truth.

Varner concluded, "If we close medical units and lay off employees, the entire community will suffer. All of the services we offer are needed right here in Deerford. In lieu of that drastic measure, I made the painful decision to cut salaries by a relatively small amount in order to keep Hope Haven a full-service hospital. The board agreed.

"Meanwhile, I'm working as hard as I know how with our funding sources to get them to restore their grants or reimbursements to previous levels. And I'm working with new sources to replace those that can't or won't continue to support us."

After more than an hour of discussion, Varner ended the meeting and Pastor Tom led the group in prayer. "Dear Lord, once again we bring the problems of Hope Haven Hospital to You to seek Your help and guidance. We humbly ask that You give Albert Varner the wisdom and strength to protect the work we all do in Your name at Hope Haven and give us the understanding to face an uncertain future with courage and determination. We ask this in Your name. Amen."

The weight of hopelessness settled like a stone in James's chest. He'd simply have to find a way to live with a smaller salary. He could see no other choice.

As he and Elena walked upstairs to go back to work, she nudged him. "You're looking all gloom and doom."

"I guess you didn't notice, things aren't looking all bright and cheerful at the moment." He pushed open the door to the second floor and held it for her.

She stepped through the door and stopped in front of him. "Come on now, James. What's happened to your *sanguineness*?"

Frowning, he shook his head. This was no time for spelling games. "What's bloodred have to do with the hospital's budget problems? Except that's the color of the balance sheet."

"Ha! Gotcha!" she said with a grin. "*Sanguineness* means bloodred, but it also means optimistic. I looked it up. And you're the most optimistic guy I know."

A reluctant smile curled his lips. "You're right, you got me."

"Then I say let's be optimistic. Let's get everybody thinking and praying about ways we can help the hospital. It can't hurt. And who knows? Together we might come up with a solution that would turn Varner's balance sheet back to black."

James appreciated Elena's pep talk, but it didn't buoy his spirits a great deal. He was far too aware of Fern's deteriorating health and his inability to help her, plus his upcoming overnight camping trip with the Scouts.

The thought of leaving her and being two hours from home if she needed him knotted his stomach and made his palms slick with sweat.

The scent of stew simmering in the slow cooker greeted Anabelle when she arrived home that afternoon. She shrugged out of her coat and hung it up.

Her search for Cameron took her outside. The horse they were boarding for their neighbor girl came to the corral fence, lifting her head in greeting.

For the moment, she ignored the horse. Instead, she walked to the barn where she found Cam kneeling on the ground surrounded by long planks of plywood, bags of potting mix, plastic water pipe and a rolled-up sheet of heavy plastic. He had on his old work pants and a jacket that had seen better days.

"My goodness! What are you up to, Cam?" The unheated barn was chilly and she rubbed her arms against the cool air.

"I'm building a greenhouse." He stood and massaged the small of his back. "I'm going to start some perennials: black-eyed susans, delphiniums, cone flowers and a couple of lavender plants. Come spring, Evan will be able to put them right in the ground and won't have to buy them from a wholesaler."

"What a good idea. Evan will be pleased, I'm sure."

"We talked about doing this last year, and I never got around to it. Thought I'd better get busy this year. I'm going to set it up to use the barn as a windbreak and lay out the whole contraption so it faces south and gets the most sun possible."

It pleased her that Cam had found a project to keep him busy. He was always happier when he had something constructive to do.

"I'm going to go change clothes. The stew smelled delicious when I came through the house. Thank you for getting dinner started." Since he'd retired, Cam had been good about helping around the house, for which she was very grateful.

"Before you go, lass, there's something I'd like to ask you."

The slight edginess in the tone of his voice gave her a niggling feeling of unease. "What's that, dear?"

"I found a picture on the kitchen table this morning of the kids when they were young playing with Skipper."

"Yes?" She produced her most innocent expression. "The children always had such fun with Skipper."

He grunted a noncommittal sound. "Then, when I sat down at the computer to check my e-mail, I found someone had printed out an article about how the *elderly* benefit from having pets to take care of."

"Really? What else did the article say?" She didn't actually think either she or Cam qualified as elderly yet, but that time wasn't too far off.

"You're still thinking about getting a dog, aren't you?"

Her shoulders slumped and she gave up her pretense. "Cam, I went by the animal shelter Monday after work. I wasn't going to bring the puppy home. Honestly, I wasn't. I was only going to take a peek and come on home. But—" Her throat tightened on her fear for the puppy. "He's absolutely adorable and so friendly. But if no one adopts him by Christmas . . ."

Taking off his old gardening hat, Cam ran his fingers through his gray hair, then resettled his hat on his head. "They'll put him down, right?"

"It's so unfair. He's such a darling boy."

"I'm still not thrilled by the idea of having a dog."

"I know. Maybe if you went to see him . . ." She knew Cameron rarely denied her anything she really wanted. But this seemed like a battle she might lose. That left her feeling empty inside, as though someone had torn a baby from her womb.

He looked off toward the far end of the barn and sighed. "I'm not going to tell you that you can't have a dog, Annie. You know how I feel about it, and we'll leave it at that."

Anabelle wasn't sure how to react now. She could adopt the puppy, but it would still be against Cam's wishes.

"I simply can't bear to think what will happen to the poor little guy if no one adopts him. I told the young man at the shelter that if no one else adopted the puppy by Christmas, I would. I'd pick him up Christmas Eve—tomorrow."

"So be it." With a nod, Cameron turned back to his greenhouse project.

Chapter Eleven

AFTER DINNER, ELENA WENT INTO HER BEDROOM and sat down at her sewing machine. She'd tried to keep her spirits up since the meeting with Varner. It hadn't been easy. She understood the hospital needed to reduce expenses. But the trip to Spain that she'd longed for seemed to be slipping from her grasp like a distant mirage, vanishing just as she was ready to reach for it.

She gritted her teeth. There must be something she could do—

"Buela! Buela!" Izzy came running into the room, using her nickname for her grandmother. Dressed in her pajamas, she clutched her scruffy stuffed pig in her arms. Her dark curls bounced like puppets on a string.

"What is it, sweetie?"

"Is my dress done yet? Can I see it?" Her light gray eyes sparkled with excitement.

Elena held up the red velvet dress, which she'd pieced together over the past few evenings. "I still have to put the white lace on it and hem the skirt."

Taking the skirt in her little hand, Izzy rubbed it over her cheek. "It's soft."

"Yes, it is. And you're going to look so pretty in it." She gave Izzy a squeeze that made her giggle and made Elena's heart fill with so much love, she thought it might burst.

Cesar came into the room. "Hey, what are my two favorite girls up to, making all that racket?"

Izzy squirmed away from Elena and latched her arms around Cesar's legs. "I didn't make a racket, Tito. She tickled me."

"Ah, is that what happened?" Chuckling, he scooped her up in his arms. "How about Tito reads you a book before bedtime?"

"I want *Green Eggs and Ham*," she squealed.

"Again? We read that last night."

Elena smiled as Cesar carried the five-year-old out the door, still discussing the evening's choice of suitable reading material.

Turning her attention back to her sewing, Elena pinned the lace around the collar, gathering it slightly, and slipped the fabric under the needle. From years of stitching together smocks and hospital scrubs and baby clothes, she instinctively set the needle bobbing up and down at the right pace, turning the garment as she went.

This was a skill her mother had taught her and she'd honed over the years. In the way some women relaxed by knitting, she found sewing a way to unwind after a hectic, stress-filled day at the hospital. It was how she coped with bad news. The purr of the machine, the instinctive matching of seams, bringing them together to make a whole and the texture and slip of fabric beneath her fingertips soothed her.

Lost in thought, Cesar's voice startled her.

"You about done for tonight?"

She brought the needle to a halt and looked up. "You put Izzy to bed?"

"She was asleep before I finished the book."

Elena smiled, amazed all over again that her husband, a tough cop, could be so gentle with a child.

"While I was sewing, I had a thought."

"Oh no. Nothing good ever comes from thinking," he teased, stripping off his shirt and tossing it into the dirty clothes hamper.

She snorted. "I'll have you know some of us have excellent ideas."

"Okay, I'll bite. What's your excellent idea tonight?"

She snipped the thread and folded the dress, setting it aside.

"I've been trying to figure out how to make up for the cut in pay I'll be getting so I can still put away a little every month for our trip to Spain." She wanted Cesar to go with her, Rafael and Izzy too, if she could swing the expense.

Sitting on the edge of the bed to remove his shoes, he nodded.

"The nurses at Hope Haven all like the scrubs I've sewn for them. A lot of them have young girls who love frilly clothes. I could take orders for custom-made baby clothes and scrubs and whatever else I can think of and make a little extra money that way."

"Hon, it's one thing for you to make a Christmas outfit for Izzy. It's something else again to work every night just for a few dollars for the trip."

"I don't want to give up my dream."

"You don't have to. We'll find a way to pay for the trip. It might take a little longer than we'd hoped, but you'll get there."

"I can give it a try. See how it goes." She didn't want the sound of castanets and the music of the flamenco to fade from her dreams.

James sat on the couch with only the lights on the Christmas tree illuminating the living room—one of the boys' electricity-saving efforts that brought the family together in a surprisingly pleasant and intimate family evening.

He and Fern had had twenty Christmases together. When they were first married and bought the house, they'd struggled to make ends meet. Their holiday celebrations had been simple. They'd exchanged small gifts. A book of poetry for her, a battery-powered drill for him to make chores around the house easier.

They'd never been happier. And they'd never felt the lack of possessions.

Together, they had all they'd ever need.

Until the boys came along. Gideon and Nelson had filled their lives and their hearts more than James could have ever imagined. They still did.

James had carried Fern upstairs to bed an hour ago. The boys had called it a night soon afterward.

Sapphire, who had curled up in his lap, was his only company now, and he idly ran his fingers through her thick fur.

Over the past several months, Fern had done her Christmas shopping online and somehow managed to wrap the packages for the boys. The colorful boxes were arrayed under the tree, a seductive allure that had the boys itching to unwrap their presents early.

James smiled at the memories of Christmas mornings past, the boys clattering down the stairs before dawn to open their presents, he and Fern almost as excited as they were to see the boys' delight.

He glanced up at the angel perched on top of the tree, and in his heart he heard the words from the book of Luke:

An angel of the Lord appeared to them, and the glory of the Lord shone around them, and they were terrified. But the angel said to them, "Do not be afraid. I bring you good news of great joy that will be for all the people. Today in the town of David a Savior has been born to you; he is Christ the Lord."

The words James remembered from the Bible and the story of Christ's birth assuaged the terror he'd been feeling for Fern's health and for his family, and comforted him. For the first time in days, he felt calm. The Lord had not deserted him; God was at his side ready to carry his burdens. James only needed to let go.

Let the Lord carry the burden.

He need not be afraid.

Closing his eyes, James whispered, "Thank You, Lord."

On Christmas Eve, right before lunchtime, Anabelle slipped into her coat and stepped outside the hospital's main entrance to call the animal shelter on her cell phone. A heavy cloud cover created a monochrome landscape, and the temperature suggested snow was on the way.

When the shelter attendant answered the phone, she gave him her name. "I came by the other day about the puppy, the only one you had left. You remember—"

"Yes, ma'am. I have your name right here. I was hoping you'd call."

"Has anyone adopted him yet?"

"No, ma'am. Are you going to come pick him up?"

Yes! Yes! Yes! Her stomach did a somersault, exhilaration mixing with sheer panic. She wasn't prepared. She had no food for the puppy. No carrier. No leash. She didn't even know where he would sleep.

"I'll . . . I'll come by in an hour or so," she stammered. "If that's all right."

"Sure. I'm going to close early tonight, Christmas Eve and all. Around four. Can you get here before then?"

"Yes, that will be fine. I'll see you in a bit."

She flipped her cell phone closed and stared off into the distance, her brain racing to come up with a to-do list. She barely knew where to start.

"Are you all right, Anabelle?"

She blinked, shook herself out of the self-inflicted trance and smiled at Candace. "I'm fine. I'm adopting a puppy."

Surprise widened Candace's eyes. "Really? I didn't know you were thinking about a puppy."

"Cam didn't want to, but there's this adorable puppy at the shelter and if I don't—" She stopped herself from saying it. "Look, I have to get to the pet store. There's so much I need to buy. Would you stop by Leila Hargrave's office? Tell her I've had a . . . family matter come up. The floor's covered, so I don't expect any problems." The Nursing Administrator wasn't overly fond of staff members taking time off for family issues. In this case, she'd simply have to live with it.

"Sure, I'll tell her," Candace said, still looking nonplused. "Is there anything I can do to help?"

"No, just tell Leila and the gals on the floor. That'll help a lot."

"Of course."

"Wish me luck." Anabelle left her friend and hurried to her car. Her hand shaking, she fumbled with the key. She almost backed into a passing car and had to slam on the brakes. The other driver hit his horn. Her heart rate bumped up to a good 130 bpm, her breathing shallow. If she wasn't careful, she'd go into shock.

"Take a deep breath, Anabelle."

More cautiously, she took her foot off the brake again and eased out of her parking space.

Deerford Feed and Pet Shop was just outside the downtown area on Main Street. A refurbished barn, it was painted traditional country red with white trim around windows that showcased puppies and kittens for sale. The day before Christmas, two puppies and three little kittens were still waiting for a new home.

Anabelle didn't dare take a close look. Cam, still opposed to adopting a shelter puppy, would have a fit if she came home with more than one canine addition to their family.

Inside, a half dozen people were lined up at the cash registers, most of them with last-minute gifts for their pets. Others strolled through the store, checking out the lovebirds and noisy parrots in their cages. Two children were fascinated as they watched a hamster race himself on a wheel. Aerated bubbles rose to the top of several aquariums filled with colorful fish.

Ralph Gustafson, the owner of the store, was in his late fifties. A birth defect had left his right arm underdeveloped and without a hand. Neither the animals nor his customers seemed to notice.

Anabelle cut past the line at the cash register. "Ralph, I know you're terribly busy. But when you have a minute, I desperately need your help." She heard the plea in her voice and hoped he did too.

He ran a customer's credit card through the machine, handed him the ticket to sign, then turned to Anabelle.

Glancing at the waiting line of customers, he said, "Give me a minute or two, and I'll be right with you, Anabelle."

"Thank you. I'll be over in the puppy department."

There seemed to be a dozen different kinds of dog collars, harnesses and leashes; the shelves were stocked with even more brands of dog food.

How could she possibly choose? It had been years and years since she'd owned a dog.

True to his word, Ralph appeared at her side within minutes.

"Now then, Anabelle, it sounded like you have an emergency. What can I do for you?"

"You're right, it is an emergency. I'm picking up a puppy at the animal shelter in less than an hour, and I don't have a thing for the poor little guy. I'm starting from scratch."

He chuckled, the corners of his blue gray eyes crinkling with amusement. "Well, you've come to the right place." He glanced around the store. "Let me get a cart and we'll start filling it up."

He walked off and returned quickly pushing a cart. "How old is the dog?"

"Ten weeks."

He took a bag of puppy food from the shelf and dropped it into the cart. "Okay, you'll need a food bowl and a water bowl. The metal ones that don't slide around are the best." He plucked two shiny bowls from another shelf.

"The shelter attendant said I need a travel carrier for him. And I know I want a leash."

"Right. That means you need a harness to start with and a collar too. Something soft for such a young dog. How about a bed?"

She hadn't thought about that. "If you think I should."

By the time they'd placed everything Ralph thought was necessary in the cart, and added a few chew toys, Anabelle could barely contain her excitement.

Impulsively, she grabbed a bag of doggie treats and a red and green Christmas bow to put around the puppy's neck, dropping them in the already overflowing cart. She might have purchased even more goodies but the time was growing short. She didn't want Josh to close the shelter before she got there.

Her car laden with her new purchases, Anabelle headed for the shelter. Last-minute shoppers crowded the streets of downtown Deerford; traffic was bumper-to-bumper. She tapped an impatient rhythm on her steering wheel as she waited for pedestrians to cross the street. A few flakes of snow had begun to fall, but they weren't sticking yet.

Finally at the shelter, she grabbed the carrier from the backseat and hurried inside.

Josh welcomed her with a grin. "Hey, Ms. Scott, glad you got here in time."

"I wouldn't have missed this for the world."

She followed him into the kennel. Josh opened the puppy's gate, and she stepped inside.

With boundless enthusiasm, the puppy wagged his entire body from tail to nose, jumping and yipping as though he recognized her and knew what was going to happen.

She knelt and took him into her arms. "It's okay, sweetie. You're coming home with me now. You won't have to be here all alone anymore." Tears of happiness edged down her cheeks as she kissed the top of his head and he licked her face in return.

She slipped him into his new carrier, closing the gate behind him.

At the hospital, James finished his rounds, handing over the patients to LaDonna Fields, an older nurse who had volunteered to cover the swing shift on Christmas Eve.

"Hope you have a nice, quiet night," James said.

"As long as Emergency doesn't send too many patients my direction, it should be fine. You have a good evening with your family."

"I will. Thanks." He returned to the nurses' station to log himself off the clock. Candace was doing the same.

"I still can't believe Anabelle is getting a puppy," she said, having told James the news when she returned from her break.

"Sounds like a good idea to me. She and Cameron will enjoy having a dog."

"That's the part that surprises me. She said Cam didn't want a dog but she's getting one anyway."

That was a surprise, but James shrugged it off. Anabelle usually knew what she was doing.

Elena appeared from around the corner. "Who doesn't want a dog?"

Candace laughed and told Elena the news about Anabelle's dog.

"Does seem funny she'd get a dog when her husband doesn't want one," Elena commented. "Cesar can be pretty stubborn when he makes his mind up about something. I assume Cam's that way too."

"Maybe Anabelle thinks he'll come around once they have the dog. Puppies are pretty hard to resist." James had made sure the boys had a dog growing up. But now, given Fern's health, caring for a dog would just add to her burdens.

"At the very least," Candace said, "the puppy will make for a merry, if exhausting, Christmas. Brooke and Howie would go nuts if I brought a puppy home tonight."

"Are you both going to church tonight?" Elena asked.

"Fern and I are taking the boys to the eleven o'clock service at Church of the Good Shepherd. The choir usually outdoes itself at Christmastime and the whole congregation gets to sing along." James hoped the service wouldn't wear Fern out too much. But she'd insisted they all go. "We're going to Fern's parents' house for dinner tomorrow. Her sister Beth and her family are driving up from Springfield."

"Our church has a five o'clock service," Candace said. "This year Brooke's playing 'The First Noel' to accompany the children's choir. She's pretty nervous about playing for the entire congregation; but she's been practicing that one piece so much, I've been hearing it in my sleep. Dean used to play that song. It was his favorite carol. I'm hoping that it will be cathartic for her, bring her closer to her father somehow."

"That would be a good thing," James said.

She glanced away, and James knew Christmas had to be hard for her and her children, the memories of her late husband especially bittersweet during the holidays.

"She'll do fine," Elena said. "It will be a wonderful way for her to honor her father's memory."

"I hope so," Candace said.

"I'm taking Izzy to our five o'clock service too. Cesar won't go with me, though." A hint of sadness touched Elena's dark eyes. "Maybe someday." Blinking, she glanced away too. "Anyway, tomorrow my mother and Granny are coming to dinner. My mother always makes those sweet tamales for Christmas supper. Little Izzy loves them."

"It's my sister Susan's turn to cook dinner," Candace said, appearing to have shaken the sad thoughts. "I'll make pies in the morning after we open presents at home."

They all wished each other a happy holiday, went down the stairs together and headed for their respective cars in the half-empty parking lot.

Chapter Twelve

S ANABELLE PULLED INTO HER DRIVEWAY, nerves fluttered in her stomach. Surely Cam would fall in love with the puppy just as she had.

"Please, Lord, don't let him be too angry with me."

She lifted the carrier out of the backseat and went into the house via the back door. Cam had left his heavy-duty rubber work boots in the mudroom, which meant he'd spent his day gardening. She hoped he was in a good mood.

"Cam, dear, are you home?" she called.

"In the office," he responded.

Taking her courage in hand—and swallowing her anxiety—she went down the hall to Cam's office. He was sitting at the computer.

She set the carrier on the floor. "I'd like you to meet the latest member of our family." She opened the carrier door.

The puppy leapt out of his confinement, yipping and yapping, his tail wagging, and made a beeline for Cam. He sniffed around

Cam's slippers, then rose up on his hind legs and pawed at Cam's knee, his tail still going like a windmill in a tornado.

Eyebrows raised, Cam glanced at Anabelle before turning his attention to the dog.

"Well, hello there, young fella." He petted the puppy, his hand so large the puppy's head nearly vanished in his palm. "You've certainly made a hit with my wife."

"You aren't too mad at me, are you?"

"When was the last time I got mad at you?"

She didn't want to remind him of the time she'd backed the car over a sapling he'd just planted in the front yard. How was she supposed to know a tree had shown up in her yard when she wasn't looking?

"Annie, did you notice how big his feet are?"

She frowned. "They look all right to me."

"Looks to me like this little guy isn't going to stay little for long."

With some concern, she eyed the puppy's feet again. She hadn't been thinking about how big he might grow. Only that he was adorable and so loving.

"I'm sure he'll grow into just the right size," she said with less confidence than she felt. "I had to stop at the pet store to buy a few things for him. If you can watch the puppy for a minute, I'll just go bring them in from the car."

Hearing no objection, she hurried out to the car. When she returned, her arms full, she saw that Cam had spread his morning newspaper on the floor.

"Uh-oh. An accident already?" she asked.

"That's what puppies do." The puppy was now chewing on the toe of Cam's slipper. Cam pushed the dog's head away, but he went right back to the slipper as though it were a yummy doggie lollipop.

"Here, let me take him." Anabelle scooped him up in her arms. "I think we can keep him in the kitchen for now. It'll be easier to clean up any messes he might make."

"The mudroom might be better."

"Maybe at night. I don't want to put him off by himself already. He has to get used to us and his new home."

Cam might not be mad at her, but his frown suggested he wasn't exactly pleased either.

"Ainslee and Doug are still coming over for dessert, aren't they? Are we all going to church together?"

"Oh yes, they're coming. I know Ainslee will be thrilled with our little scamp." She cuddled him close to her chest and took him into the kitchen. She really should have gotten a doggie gate to put across the kitchen door to prevent him from having a free run of the house until he was housebroken. She'd do that right after Christmas . . .

The Church of the Good Shepherd was one of the oldest churches in town. Built of brick, it had a sharply slanted roof with an aluminum cross above the front entrance. At night two spotlights illuminated the cross. On Christmas Eve, snowflakes danced in the two light beams promising the town of Deerford a white Christmas.

James parked in a handicapped spot as close to the church as he could. Still, it was too far for Fern to walk. She'd have to use the wheelchair he'd placed in the back of the minivan.

"Gideon, you want to get the wheelchair out of the back?" he asked.

"Sure, Dad."

Gideon slid the door open and hopped out. Nelson followed him.

James rested his hand on Fern's gloved hand. He'd made sure she was warmly dressed in a heavy coat and knit cap. "Are you sure you're up to this?" James asked her.

"You know this is my favorite time of year. Just look at the snow coming down. It's beautiful."

In James's eyes, Fern was the most beautiful thing he could imagine. Her strength and love of life shone brightly, her face radiant.

"Okay, let's get you into your chair. We don't want to miss any of the sing-alongs."

He climbed out of the van and went around to the passenger side. Gideon had the wheelchair waiting.

"Your chariot awaits, Mrs. Bell." While Gideon held the chair steady, James helped Fern out of the van and settled her comfortably.

Gideon took charge of the wheelchair, pushing his mother along the sidewalk toward the double doors of the church, James and Nelson following behind. Like James, both of his boys were dressed in nice slacks, warm sweaters and winter jackets.

Several members of the congregation stopped to say hello and give Fern's hand a welcoming squeeze.

Their progress was slowed again when Anabelle and Cameron stopped to greet Fern.

"I'm so glad to see you," Anabelle gushed, brushing a kiss to Fern's cheek. "And your boys. Aren't they handsome young men? We don't get to see enough of you and your family."

"My social calendar's been really slow these past few months," Fern said. "But I'm sure to improve soon."

"I do hope so. I've been praying for you." Anabelle gestured toward her daughter. "Here's Ainslee. She's five months along but you'd never know it from her figure. Still as slender as ever."

"Mother, please," Ainslee complained. "We don't have to broadcast to the whole world that I'm pregnant."

In a reassuring gesture, Doug slipped his arm around Ainslee's waist.

Anabelle waved off her daughter's complaint. "A first-time grandmother has the right to be excited, doesn't she?"

Fern laughed. "I'm sure I'll be excited too."

Gideon visibly paled at the thought. "That's not gonna happen anytime soon," he mumbled.

Standing near James, Cameron waited patiently for the ladies to stop their chatting.

James said, "How'd your puppy like his new home?"

Twisting his lips into a wry smile, Cameron said, "The puppy seems fine. He's taken an inordinate amount of interest in my slippers, however. So far he seems to think they're a doggy teething toy."

James winced. That didn't bode well as a first impression.

Fern's parents hurried up the walkway and stopped to say hello.

Frank Driscoll, a tall, muscular man with a quick smile, shook hands with James. "Merry Christmas, son."

"And to you," James said.

Recently, at the age of seventy, Frank had sold his plumbing business to two longtime employees. Driscoll Plumbing trucks were still a frequent sight on the streets throughout the county and beyond.

Marilee Driscoll bent to kiss Fern's cheek. A few years younger than Frank, she wore a knee-length winter coat and a hat trimmed in fake fur. "How are you, dear?"

"I've been better," Fern admitted.

"You're still coming tomorrow?" Marilee asked.

"Of course. The boys wouldn't miss your wonderful sweet potato casserole."

Marilee patted Fern's shoulder, then turned to greet her grandsons, giving them each a hug, to their red-faced chagrin.

James was next in line for a hug, which he welcomed. "Merry Christmas, Grandma."

"Fern doesn't look well," she whispered. "Is there anything—"

"Her new meds haven't kicked in yet. I'll see if I can get Fern to go to the doctor early next week."

"Thank you." Concern shone in Marilee's eyes even as she gave James an encouraging pat on his arm. "I'm so glad she has you."

As James and his family joined the Driscolls and the rest of the congregation filing inside, the scent of fresh evergreens and the sound of the organ playing "O Come, All Ye Faithful" filled the church. Fir boughs tied with red ribbon decorated the end of each wooden pew. Handmade ornaments created by children adorned a Christmas tree near the pulpit, and dozens of red poinsettias were arranged in front of the choir.

James sat in the pew next to Fern and took her hand. "Merry Christmas, sweetheart."

Her loving smile nearly took his breath away, yet he could see tears glistening in her eyes, and they broke his heart.

"Merry Christmas to you, my love," she whispered.

Back home after the church service, Anabelle took off her gloves and shrugged out of her coat. As much as she had enjoyed the singing and the minister's uplifting message of God's love, she was anxious to see how her little scamp of a puppy had fared in her absence.

She opened the door to the mudroom and out he shot. He raced around the kitchen, sniffing every inch of the room.

Crouching, she held out a treat for him. "Come here, scamp. Look what I've got for you."

He galloped to her, all four feet flying and one floppy ear flapping. His behind wiggled with sheer jubilation as he took the treat and ran off again.

She laughed. What an adorable boy he was.

"Anabelle, I think you should come see this."

At Cam's stern tone, her laughter came to an abrupt halt. He stood in the mudroom doorway, his expression dark and brooding.

A sense of impending doom arrowed into her chest and she drew a painful breath. "What's wrong?"

He tipped his head toward the room behind him. "Come take a look."

She stood, hesitant at first and then with dread as she stepped past him.

Before they'd left for church, she'd covered the floor with newspapers, which were now all wadded up at one end of the narrow room. Coats had been dragged off their hooks, rain boots strewn around the room. The doggie bed she'd bought for the puppy was now upside down on top of a pile of newspapers and old magazines set out to be recycled. Bits and pieces of the Christmas ribbon she'd tied around the puppy's neck dotted the room like confetti.

Cam picked up one of his rubber work boots. "That dog of yours has been busy."

Dismayed, she said, "We were only gone two hours. How could he—"

Cam showed her the boot, its toe chewed all the way through.

"Oh, Cam, I'm so sorry."

He didn't say a word. He simply tossed the boot aside and walked into the house.

Anabelle's stomach clenched and threatened rebellion. What on earth was she going to do with that puppy?

The thundering footsteps of Gideon and Nelson racing down the stairs woke James early on Christmas morning.

He groaned and rolled over to find Fern smiling at him in the dim light of dawn.

"They've done that every Christmas morning that I can remember," she said, her voice thick with sleep, her words slurring.

"And I've done this." He kissed her soundly, then rolled out of bed. "You'd think the boys wouldn't get so excited about Christmas at their age."

Fern managed to sit up on the side of the bed. "Oh, I don't know. You had a twinkle in your eye when you found out there was a box under the tree for you."

"Well, that's different. When I get excited, I don't stomp down the stairs shaking the whole house and waking everybody for miles around." He pulled on his terry cloth bathrobe and slipped into his wool-lined slippers. "I always *sneak* downstairs *very* quietly."

She laughed, and James helped her into her pink velour robe and carried her downstairs.

The boys already had the tree lights on and the packages sorted for the respective recipients. James turned on the radio to listen to Christmas music while they unwrapped their presents.

Gideon's favorite present was a new iPod that came with a gift certificate to download songs. Nelson seemed pleased with his new video game and a graphing calculator to use in math class.

When he opened his last present, he uttered an astonished, "Wow! A whole book of Shakespeare's comedies."

Fern beamed at his reaction to her gift. "You seemed to be enjoying your school play so much, I thought you might be interested in other works he wrote."

He flipped through some pages. "Listen to this. *Much Ado About Nothing*. Don John says, 'I am trusted with a muzzle and enfranchised with a clog; therefore I have decreed not to sing in my cage.'" Nelson raised his voice with a question mark before continuing. "'If I had my mouth, I would bite; if I had my liberty, I would do my liking: in the meantime let me be that I am, and seek not to alter me.' Boy, that barely makes sense."

"There are footnotes to explain some of that," Fern said. "That will help you understand the meaning."

Nelson glanced at the book again. "Looks like I'll need it."

"Can we get off of Shakespeare and get on with the rest of the presents?" Impatient, Gideon handed his brother the next wrapped box.

Nelson closed his book and set it aside. "Okay, Dad. Your turn. This is from Mom." Nelson handed James a large box with a big, premade red bow on it.

He shook the box. Nothing rattled. "Guess it's not a new marble set." James still had his father's collection of marbles he'd acquired as a kid, including a couple of unusual agates. The marbles had value as collectibles, but for James it was the sentimental value he cared about.

He pried open the box. Not sure at first what he was looking at, he lifted a navy blue velour robe out of the box.

"Ah, a robe!" he said.

"About time," Gideon said.

"What do you mean, about time?" James fingered his terry cloth robe. "This has lots of wear left in it."

"James, dear, you've worn that old thing bare at the elbows. You've needed a new robe for years."

He checked his elbows. The terry cloth was worn so smooth, only a few threads were holding it together. "*Hmm*, maybe you're right."

Standing, he shed his old robe and tried on the new one.

"Very elegant and handsome." Fern smiled up at him.

"Uh-oh," Nelson warned. "They're gonna start kissing again." He rolled his eyes in mock horror.

Laughing, James did exactly what Nelson had predicted. He kissed Fern and thanked her.

He got another kiss when she opened his present, a warm cardigan sweater woven with bright, variegated yarn.

Finally, Fern opened her present from the boys. The slender box contained a CD. She looked to the boys for an explanation.

Gideon said, "We scanned a lot of the pictures in the family scrapbook and turned them into a screen saver for your computer."

Nelson handed Fern's laptop to Gideon.

"It'll take just a minute to upload this." Gideon tapped a few keys, slid the CD into a slot and tapped some more keys.

He handed the laptop to Fern. "It's like a slide show."

James leaned close to Fern. A photo of one-day-old Gideon in Fern's arms appeared. That was followed by Fern holding Gideon's hand as he toddled across the living room. A few pictures later, Nelson appeared, first as a newborn, then toddler and then kindergartner. Vacation shots of Lake Michigan materialized on the screen and another trip to the Chicago zoo.

In every photo, Fern looked happy and energetic. She glowed with good health.

A lump formed in James's throat. MS had taken so much from her.

He glanced at his wife and saw tears running down her cheeks. She, more than anyone else, knew how much MS had cost her and her family.

Pulling a tissue from the pocket of her robe, Fern wiped away her tears. "Thank you, boys. This is the best present you could have given me. It makes this Christmas Day very special."

"I told you she'd cry," Nelson whispered to Gideon.

Fern's parents lived just outside of town, no more than ten minutes from the Bell household, unless the roads had not been plowed.

The modest, three-bedroom house was set back from the road on a half acre of land that included an oversized garage that had housed Frank's plumbing trucks and the heavy-duty tools of his trade before his retirement.

The only remaining vehicles were Frank's extended cab pickup and Marilee's aging Buick.

Arriving at one o'clock for Christmas dinner, James parked his van in the driveway. Anticipating Fern would be using her wheelchair, the concrete walkway to the front door had been cleared of snow.

The boys hopped out of the van just as Marilee and Frank stepped out onto the front porch, quickly followed by Beth, her husband Joe Ungar and their two children, Andrew and Kim.

Marilee waved. "Merry Christmas to you all!"

Fern raised her hand in response.

The boys knew the routine. Gideon unloaded the wheelchair and both boys helped her get into it. Gideon pushed it to the steps.

Beth hurried down the steps to greet her big sister. Younger by three years, Beth had the same wavy brown hair as Fern but was slightly taller with a more athletic build.

"Hey, sis." She hugged Fern tightly. "High time you showed up. Dinner's practically ready. I had to peel all the potatoes myself."

Fern laughed. "Exactly what I had in mind." She started to get out of her chair. "If you'll give me a hand—"

"Stay put, Fern." Frank came down the steps, moving as agilely as if he were fifty instead of a bit past seventy. "If one of these strapping young men will give me a hand, we'll hoist you up and set you down as gently as a newborn babe."

"Dad, you don't have to—"

Gideon beat James to the task. Frank and his eldest grandson carried Fern, chair and all, to the top of the steps, where her mother welcomed her with a hug.

Frank turned to Nelson and gave him an attaboy pat on the back. "How are you, W9DOY?" he asked, using Nelson's amateur radio call sign, a hobby he had mentored his grandson in while helping Nelson get his ham license.

"I'm good, Grandpa. Haven't had much time for radio lately though."

Frank chuckled. "Wait 'til you're an ol' duffer like me. You'll have lots of time then."

James had always been struck by what a gentle giant Frank Driscoll was. He doubted that Frank had ever raised a hand or his voice to his two children; he was forever patient with his grandchildren.

Beth lingered back beside James. Her brown eyes met James's. "She's worse, isn't she?" Beth whispered.

It hurt to have others recognize what James knew all too well. "She's on a new med. It hasn't helped yet."

The sheen of tears appeared in Beth's eyes, and she pressed her lips together. "I hate MS."

"So do I."

Together they walked up the steps to the porch. Frank extended his hand to James. Almost as big as a baseball glove, Frank's palm was still rough with calluses from his years as a plumber, his grip as strong as ever.

Joe, an auditor with the state government, shook James's hand. About James's height, he had the slender build of a distance runner. "How's it going?"

"We're hanging in there."

James got a hug from Kim, a cute ten-year-old who was into gymnastics. Her brother Andrew, the same age as Nelson and on a fast academic track, chose to shake hands.

The smell of turkey roasting in the oven and the scent of freshly baked rolls filled the house.

They all went into the living room, which was filled with overstuffed chairs and a couch. A curio cabinet in the corner of the room displayed Marilee's collection of porcelain teacups and saucers. In the opposite corner, a small Christmas tree circled by a miniature electric train sat on a low table. The train's route took it past a snowy Midwestern town in miniature.

"How long 'til dinner, Grandma?" Gideon asked. "I'm starved."

"About an hour," Marilee said. "I put out some nuts and crackers and cheese to nibble on, but I don't want you to spoil your appetite."

James chuckled. "Gideon can eat anytime, anywhere, Marilee. I think he's secretly feeding an entire platoon of his ROTC buddies."

"Andrew's the same way," Beth said. "I've tried to get Joe to buy a dairy farm so Andrew could have all the milk he wants."

Everyone laughed sympathetically.

The three boys went out with Frank to mess around in his garage, which always provided a treasure trove of interesting tools and mechanical devices. In contrast to James's father, who'd worked for a cement company and wore a hard hat, Frank seemed endlessly patient and rarely critical of anything his children or James's boys did.

James suspected part of his father's problem had been because his parents were both over forty when he was born. His dad wasn't used to kids and demanded too much. Or maybe it was because he was simply more comfortable working with men who earned their living by hard physical work.

Either way, James had disappointed his father when he joined the army. His father had served in World War II. Like so many other veterans, he'd suffered from post-traumatic stress disorder and wanted nothing to do with the military.

But James had joined the army to be a medic and earn enough money to pursue a nursing career. His dad had had a hard time understanding James's decision, that nursing was his calling.

The women, including Kim, vanished into the kitchen to make final dinner preparations while James and Joe chatted about the state of government.

When they all sat down at the dining table loaded with enough food for an entire army, they clasped hands while Frank said grace.

"Dear Lord, we thank You for the bounty this day has brought us and ask Your blessing on our family both here and elsewhere.

Continue to give us strength to face the challenges in our lives and the faith to know You are beside us each day. Teach us to love as You have loved us. We ask this in Jesus' name. Amen."

They all echoed his amen, and James squeezed Fern's and Marilee's hands. The warmth of Fern's family filled him with love. Once again he counted his blessings that he had found Fern, who had given him two terrific sons and a pair of exceptional in-laws.

Chapter Thirteen

THE MONDAY AFTER CHRISTMAS, JAMES HAD TO WALK through six inches of snow in the hospital parking lot to get to the entrance. The city plows had cleared the major streets in town, but the private contractors hadn't been able to keep up with the snow the current storm had dumped on the area.

The wintry weather had worked in Gideon and Nelson's favor. They shoveled several of the neighbors' sidewalks over the weekend and hoped to stir up more business this morning. Their wallets were growing thicker by the day. Pride in his boys made him smile. Good kids, both of them.

James had stayed home to be with his family for the holiday weekend. Now it was back to work, and the Scouts' camping trip was less than two weeks away.

One thing for sure, if this weather continued they'd have plenty of snow. The kids would earn their badges.

He was also confident he'd spend a lot of the trip worrying about Fern. The Christmas festivities had left her more exhausted than ever, and that troubled James. But she wouldn't hear of him not going.

"Mother and Dad only live ten minutes away if I need something," she had reminded him. "And Gideon will be home. He's becoming a very responsible young man."

All true, James agreed. But that didn't minimize the unease he felt at being two hours away from her.

He changed into his scrubs in the locker room and headed for the second floor. Just as he arrived at the nurses' station, Elena burst out of the elevator.

"Oh good! You're all here." Breathless, she paused at the counter.

Seated at the computer, Anabelle looked over the top of her glasses. "Whatever it is, I can't do it. I've got an out-of-control puppy to deal with."

James suspected the new dog had shredded more of Cameron's slippers by now. If not worse.

"What's on your mind, Elena?" Candace asked.

"When I was at church Christmas Eve, I was praying like crazy about the pay cuts and what we could do about them. And I got this really great idea."

James grimaced and Candace groaned. Anabelle's attention remained riveted to the computer screen.

"Come on, guys. Give me a chance to explain my idea." Elena looked hopefully from James to Candace in search of an ally. "Let's meet for lunch at the Corner. I'll tell you about my plan while we eat. I'll even treat, if you'll just listen to me."

The Diner at the Corner was a popular place for hospital employees when they needed a break from the hospital. James wouldn't mind eating lunch there, but he was skeptical about Elena's newest brainstorm.

"I'll let you buy my lunch," Candace said. "The cafeteria's daily special is tuna and noodles, not one of my favorites."

"Great. Let's say eleven thirty." She checked with James.

He shrugged. "I'll come, but you don't have to treat me to lunch."

"Perfect." Elena scooted around to Anabelle's side of the counter. "You've got to come too, Anabelle. You're so smart and levelheaded, we need you to work out the details of my plan."

Once again, Anabelle eyed her over the top of her glasses. "You're trying to butter me up."

"Of course I am." She grinned and her eyes sparkled. "But I still need you. *Ple-e-e-e-e-ease*." She dragged out the word like a fishing line pulling a tantalizing lure through a deep pool filled with trout.

"Oh, all right. Now will you let me get my work done?"

"Praise the Lord! I'll see you all at the Corner." All but jumping in the air and clicking her heels together, Elena dashed off to the Intensive Care Unit and her patients.

With an amused grin, Candace went to log in on the station's computer.

James waited a moment, then said to Anabelle, "I gather the puppy business isn't going well."

"An unmitigated disaster."

"Oh, I'm sorry."

She leaned back in her chair and took off her glasses. "First, while we were at Christmas Eve service, the little scamp bit a hole in Cam's rubber boot."

"Ouch."

"Then, that night when we left him in the mudroom, which he'd already half destroyed, he cried so loud we couldn't go to sleep. I had to go sit with him in my lap so he'd be quiet. *Every night*," she emphasized, "since I brought him home. I'm exhausted."

James hooked a hip over the edge of the desk. "Maybe he'll adjust in time."

"There's more," she said grimly. "During Christmas dinner, he somehow got out of the mudroom and into the backyard. Cam built a small greenhouse and put it up near the barn. He'd spent all of Christmas morning planting perennials for the spring."

"And the dog dug them up."

"An unmitigated disaster," she repeated. "As soon as it's a decent hour, I'm calling Diana. She's got to help me. I don't know what to do with him."

James assumed she meant the dog, not Cameron. In either case, all he could do was wish her luck.

James was a little late arriving at the Corner for lunch. He'd had to settle a post-op hip-replacement patient in her room. The elderly woman had been in a lot of pain. Getting her meds authorized by the orthopedic surgeon took time, which annoyed James. In his view, a doctor should make sure his patient was entirely stable before moving on to his next surgery.

A nativity scene had been painted in bold colors on the diner's large front window, nearly hiding the cheery yellow café curtains behind it.

When he pushed open the diner's door, the scent of roasting coffee, pumpkin pie and sizzling hamburgers greeted James. Today's dinner specials posted on a chalkboard were turkey and stuffing or honey-baked ham and sweet potatoes. He'd stuffed himself on all of that and more at his mother-in-law's house.

Elena waved at him from one of the dark green vinyl booths along the front of the diner.

He slid into the seat next to Anabelle, who had exchanged her lab coat for a heavy winter coat. Her hospital ID tag, which she wore on a lanyard around her neck, had become tangled with the chain attached to her reading glasses.

Candace, sitting across from James, wore her scrubs decorated with tiny Christmas wreaths. Three mugs of coffee steamed on the table.

"Sorry I'm late," he said.

"No problem," Elena said. "We just ordered."

He looked around hoping to catch the eye of Lindy Yao, the young waitress who usually served him. She was busy with the customers at a table in the back of the diner.

He turned to Anabelle. "Did you get ahold of Diana?"

"Yes, she's going to make a house call this afternoon after I get home, thank the good Lord. I hope she has the magic touch with that puppy."

"We all do for your sake, as well as for Cam's slippers," James said.

Lindy cruised by their table. An attractive Asian American who was saving money to go to college, she had black hair and dark brown eyes. "Your usual coffee?" she asked him.

"Coffee, black, and a turkey sub with everything except onions, and fruit instead of fries."

"You got it."

Elena took a sip of coffee, then set the mug back on the table. "Okay, here's my idea. When the hospital board threatened to sell Hope Haven to that big hospital corporation, the whole town got up in arms."

"And the board reversed their decision," Candace finished.

It had been Elena's idea to create a Wall of Hope in the courtyard as a fund-raising project. People bought engraved commemorative bricks, and their contributions had been one of the things to help stave off the sale of Hope Haven.

Lindy brought James his cup of coffee, and he thanked her.

"So are you thinking we should build another wall?" James asked.

"I think we need a different approach."

"Like what?" Candace asked.

James noticed Anabelle staring off into the distance and not paying attention to the conversation. She had to be extremely distressed by the puppy fiasco. It wasn't at all like her to opt out of important discussions about Hope Haven.

"I made some notes." Elena placed a yellow notepad on the table. "The hospital's income is divided fairly evenly among three major sources: payments from insurance companies and individuals, contributions from the public and charitable foundations and government sources."

"I doubt if we can squeeze any more out of Medicare," James noted.

"We don't have to." Turning the notepad around for him to read, Elena circled two items. "I've talked to a couple of other hospitals in our general area. Based on our patient hospital days, we're not getting our fair share of money from either the state of Illinois or Bureau County, and we're receiving no funds from the city of Deerford."

Lindy arrived with their lunches. James sat back, mulling over Elena's surprising revelation while the waitress placed their meals on the table.

When Lindy left, James bowed his head to say grace. Then he leaned forward again. "So how do you propose we appeal for more government funding? They're all broke themselves these days and laying off employees. It would be tough for them to justify reducing their own staffs in order to keep our pay intact."

"There are many people just thankful they have a job at all these days," Candace commented.

"True." Elena sat up straighter then flipped to the next page of her notepad. "But people need to know that this pay cut affects everyone—we're in danger of losing our very best staff members, nurses and doctors who will go in search of better pay. I know I've heard murmurings of people looking elsewhere."

"Me too," Candace said.

"I actually started making calls," James said. When he noticed his friends' looks of alarm, he quickly added, "It was only going to be part-time to supplement what I earn at Hope Haven."

"It really wouldn't be good for Deerford to have more people transferred as far away as Chicago to receive the care they currently receive here. Near home," Anabelle said, her attention having returned to the conversation at hand. "I feel very strongly about that, especially after Kirstie's accident."

"What we need are strong allies consistently championing for the hospital and its top-notch staff in public. We could start a letter-writing campaign to elected officials and newspapers to try to get them to take up Hope Haven as a cause."

"You've been doing some serious thinking," James said. "There're no guarantees, of course, but your idea might work."

"It will. I know it will." Elena continued down her list. "A politician, for example, could appear before the city council and meet with county board members and the area's representatives in the state legislature."

"That's going to take a lot of man hours to accomplish all that," James commented.

"Hope Haven has more than a hundred employees," Elena pointed out. "I've written up some talking points so people will know what to say in their letters. I know, with the Lord's help, we can do this if we all work together." She handed each of them a copy of the talking points.

"And you want us to spread the word," James said.

"To every employee, your neighbors, friends at church. We need to build a group of supporters who want to keep our special community intact."

To James, considering the current circumstances, that sounded like a very tall order.

After lunch at the Corner, as the four of them were climbing the stairs to the second floor, Candace noticed Heath Carlson coming down the stairs from radiology. She hung back from the others, waiting for Heath on the landing.

"Hi," she said. "A belated Merry Christmas to you."

His grin dimpled his cheeks. "Right back at you. Did you have a good holiday?"

"A quiet one," she admitted. "The highlight of the day was Howie trying out his new sled."

"Great." He glanced down the stairwell. "I'm headed for the cafeteria for lunch. Have you eaten yet?"

"We all went to the Corner. In fact, we were there discussing ways we could help the hospital secure more income so we won't all have to take a pay cut."

Heath seemed interested, so Candace showed him the paper outlining Elena's talking points.

He read over the list, then handed it back to her. "Those are good points to make. If you can get me a copy of that, I'll make sure everyone in radiology gets one."

Pleased he'd volunteered to spread the word, she said, "Let me check the Birthing Unit to see if we've got any mommies about to pop." So far it had been a quiet day. She suspected the OB/GYNs were still recovering from their busy pre-Christmas baby boom. "When I get a minute, I'll make copies and bring them upstairs to you."

Saying he'd see her later, Heath continued down the stairs and Candace headed to the Birthing Unit. Heath was such a solid, reliable man, she knew he'd be able to persuade his co-workers to get on the bandwagon writing letters.

She frowned as she walked down the corridor as she thought of Brooke. It would be at least another week before Tony returned home and could schedule Brooke for a counseling session.

Seeing Brooke feeling so down was like having a toothache. Candace kept worrying the problem. She couldn't get it out of her mind.

There wouldn't be a solution until she got her little girl some help.

Anabelle hurried home after work to be there when Diana arrived. She found Cam restoring the damage the puppy had done to his greenhouse. The puppy didn't appear to be anywhere around.

"Hi, honey," she said. "How did your day go?"

He looked up from his kneeling position. "Fine. And yours?"

"It was pretty quiet. We had a couple of heart attacks admitted in the past day or two. Too much excitement and too much food."

He returned his attention to the bedding soil.

Anabelle got an uneasy feeling in the pit of her stomach. The puppy was nowhere in sight.

"How'd you get along with the puppy today?" she asked.

"Fine."

Generally speaking, Cameron was a bit more articulate than he was demonstrating at the moment.

"Where is he?"

He sat back on his haunches. "In the mudroom. I think he's sleeping."

"Oh. I guess that figures. He was awake half the night." She'd been as well, but she'd had no opportunity to take a nap. "I'll just go see how he's doing."

She went inside via the back door. The puppy raced over to greet her, jumping and spinning around like a top. The mudroom had been totally cleaned out except for his doggy bed and dishes, plus his toys and plenty of newspapers.

Anabelle squatted down on the floor. He leapt into her arms, giving her a considerably warmer welcome than her husband had.

"Hi, sweetie. Glad to see me?"

All wiggle and waggle, the puppy nuzzled up under her chin and licked her face. She couldn't help but smile at his enthusiasm. She wondered if Cam had paid him any attention at all and feared he hadn't.

The doorbell rang. Still wearing her jacket and carrying her purse, Anabelle went to greet Diana. But the moment she opened the door into the kitchen, the puppy shot past her. He raced toward the living room.

"Come here, you little scamp!" She hurried after him, but he was much too fast for her and scampered away.

Anabelle reached the door and pulled it open. "Diana, you are just in time. I can't do a thing with—"

The puppy reappeared, barking and dancing around Diana, leaping against her legs, pawing at her slacks and her sensible shoes.

Diana calmly knelt beside the puppy, holding him firmly. "Sit," she said in a composed voice.

When he failed to comply, she said sit again and pressed down on his rump. The puppy sat.

"What a good boy!" Diana gave him a little treat.

She stood up. The puppy jumped up as well. "Sit." He did, and she gave him another treat.

"I am so impressed." Anabelle beamed at the puppy as though he'd just been awarded first prize in a doggy competition. "How did you do that?"

Closing the door behind her, Diana walked into the living room. "Puppies instinctively want to please their owners. We have to let them know what that is, and let them know repeatedly until the idea is firmly established in their minds."

"I thought dogs had to be at least six months old before you can train them."

"Oh no. In fact it's important they learn the rules right away; the first week is ideal."

Anabelle blanched at the thought of beginning to train the rambunctious puppy right away.

"Where do you usually keep him?" Diana asked.

"In the mudroom. Cameron cleared everything out today so the puppy couldn't get into any more mischief."

Diana followed Anabelle to the mudroom and immediately began the puppy's training. She went through *sit* and *stay* a dozen or more times, never raising her voice and always rewarding the dog with a treat when he—probably accidentally—did as he was told.

To help alleviate his jumping on Anabelle, Diana had her issue the *sit* and *stay* commands.

Eventually, Cam's curiosity got the better of him. He came into the house to watch the action.

"Consistency is extremely important," Diana said. "Give the command, if he obeys he gets a treat. If not, give the command again."

"What can we do about his crying at night?" Cam asked. "Ever since she brought him home, Annie has barely gotten any sleep at all. She's been down here with the dog, keeping him company. She'll be worn out if that keeps up much longer."

Pleased that Cam was concerned about her health, Anabelle listened to Diana's instructions about leaving the puppy alone for short periods of time to get him used to their longer absences.

An exercise in what to chew—and what not to—came next.

Finally, the puppy appeared exhausted from his training. He simply lay down, his head on his paws and looked at the three humans through heavy eyelids.

Diana laughed. "I think we've worn out the poor little guy."

"I'm still not about to let him out in my garden without a leash on him." Cameron had a bitter edge to his voice, the puppy still unforgiven for his greenhouse episode. "He'd dig up our entire three acres, given half a chance."

"There's actually an easy way to stop a dog from digging where he's not supposed to," Diana said. "Find a spot where he can't hurt anything, loosen the soil a bit and hide some of his chew toys in the dirt. He'll spend days trying to find them even after he's dug them all up."

"Really?" With Skipper, except for getting him housebroken, she had been relatively hands-off as the kids descended on him and made him part of the neighborhood pack.

"Well, maybe when we get a couple of feet of snow, I'll let him run loose in the yard," Cameron conceded. "With my supervision. Come spring, though, I'll give your advice a try."

"Which reminds me, do you have a name for him yet?" Diana asked.

"I've been calling him scamp, but I don't think that's a very good name." She glanced at Cam, who was leaning against the doorjamb.

"He reminds me of a sergeant my dad had in the army in World War II. They stayed in touch for years. The guy had the biggest feet I'd ever seen. Long legs too. Kind of clumsy but likable." Cam lifted one shoulder. "We could call him Sarge."

Anabelle's smile traveled from deep inside, quickly working its way up to her face. "Sarge. I like that. Makes him sound like one of the good guys." She knelt and petted the puppy. "What do you think, Sarge? Will that work for you?"

He wagged his tail once, then closed his eyes and went to sleep just like a toddler worn out from a day of play.

Best of all, since Cameron had chosen the puppy's name, Anabelle suspected that would encourage him to bond with Sarge.

Now if she could convince him to do some of the training while she was at work, things between them would go smoothly.

She hoped.

After Diana left, Anabelle went upstairs to change clothes. When she came back downstairs to see to dinner, Cam was in the kitchen setting the table. Sarge trotted in with one of Cam's slippers in his mouth. He looked up at her, his tail wagging proudly.

"Oh, Sarge, Cam isn't going to like that." She reached for the slipper, but Sarge dashed under the kitchen table. "You're still a little scamp, aren't you?" She got down on her knees. Sarge scurried out the other side.

"I got him." Cam scooped up the puppy, took back his slipper and put the dog down again.

"I'm sorry, Cam. He's certainly fond of your slippers."

He examined the toe of the slipper, which seemed to have survived intact. This time. "So am I."

Before Anabelle knew where Sarge had gone off to, he returned with Cam's matching slipper.

"Oh no . . ."

"Sarge!" Cam made a dive for the dog and his pilfered slipper. He missed as the puppy executed a quick turn heading for the living room, Cam scrambling after him.

Wincing, Anabelle decided Sarge was a prime candidate for remedial behavior lessons. And they would be starting immediately!

Chapter Fourteen

ITHIN TWO DAYS, WORD OF THE LETTER-WRITING campaign spread through the hospital staff like a pandemic flu. Everyone caught the letter-writing bug.

James gathered names and addresses of elected officials and contact information for local and statewide newspapers, widely distributing the data.

It felt good to be doing something constructive about the pay cut instead of simply accepting the reduced income as inevitable. Evidently others felt the same way.

That evening after dinner, James sat down at Nelson's computer to compose his own letters to members of the city council. Getting his thoughts on paper and making the problem clear was no easy task. Particularly since Nelson had insisted he only use the desk lamp to read his notes. The overhead light stayed off to save electricity.

He supposed kids could get into worse habits than saving money.

Nelson strolled into the room, his new book of Shakespeare plays in his hand. "How's it going, Dad?"

James stared at the computer screen. "I think I should have taken classes in business communication. My letter's getting so long, nobody's going to read it all."

"You ought to try using bullets. You know, make your points sharp and short, then say you'd be happy to meet with whoever if they'd like more details."

James's eyebrows climbed up his forehead in surprise, and he grinned. "Hey, you're pretty smart, kid, if I do say so myself."

Nelson shrugged nonchalantly. "What can I say? I'm a gift that keeps on giving."

He punched his son lightly on his shoulder. "Easy, youngster. Egos that get too big are likely to get popped like a balloon if they don't watch out."

Nelson didn't seem concerned. He flopped down on his bed, which hadn't been too neatly made that morning. He'd also left a pair of dirty socks on the floor and a couple of dresser drawers weren't closed all the way, bits of clothing sticking out.

James would make sure the room got cleaned by the time school started again.

"I've been thinking, Dad. I went to the mall with Joey today. His mom drove us over. The place was jammed."

"I imagine. All those after-Christmas sales draw a big crowd." He deleted an entire paragraph and pared the rambling thought down to one line.

"Anyway, I was thinking about all those people and how they'd feel if they knew all the nurses and technicians and stuff at the hospital were having their pay cut through no fault of their own."

"Well, I'd hope they'd feel concern about it even if their pocketbooks have been hit by the recession too. We need the public's support if this is going to work."

"So how are they going to hear about it?"

James turned toward his son. "We're hoping to get a letter to the editor in the newspaper. They could read about it."

"Not everybody reads a newspaper," Nelson said.

"True." He hadn't thought that far ahead. How would the employees garner public support? "What are you thinking?"

Sitting up, Nelson swung his feet over the edge of the bed. "I think you ought to organize a protest against the pay cuts. You know, employees marching up and down with signs, talking to patients and families as they arrive and waving at passing cars."

"If you're thinking about us calling a strike, I don't think many of the staff members would go for that. Our job is to help people get well, not walk out on them."

"No, not a strike. A protest, or maybe call it a demonstration. You could call the TV stations and newspapers, get reporters to cover the story. Protests provide great visuals that catch people's attention. That'd be a lot more effective than just writing letters."

James gave the idea some serious thought. "We wouldn't want to disrupt patient services."

"Do it during lunch hour. Swing-shift workers could come in early, and the graveyard shift could stick around for a few hours."

A trickle of excitement jump-started his adrenaline. "*Hmm*, we could picket from eleven in the morning until two in the afternoon. That would allow all the shift workers to participate."

Nelson nodded his agreement.

"Can't picket on hospital property, though. That would be trespassing, I think." James speared both hands through his hair. He'd never considered, much less organized, a demonstration of any kind. "It'd have to be on the public sidewalk."

"Do you need a city permit?"

"I don't think so. You need those for parades."

Brightening, Nelson said, "Yeah, you could have a parade. Would that be cool, or what? I could lead the parade." He hopped up from his chair and proceeded to march around the room, his arm held high as though he carried a picket sign. He quoted from Shakespeare, "'Up and down, up and down, I will lead them up and down. I am feared in field and town—'"

"That would be an 'or what,' son. Let's not get carried away." Could he and his friends and fellow employees pull off a successful demonstration?

More importantly, could they pull it off without getting themselves fired? Or arrested?

"You know, I like your idea. But instead of a protest or demonstration, why don't we call it a Public Awareness Campaign? We just want folks to know how a pay cut could send our best nurses and doctors to Chicago."

Nelson plopped down on his bed and opened his book. "Sure. That would work."

The following day, James called another lunchtime meeting at the Corner. It seemed better to discuss the issues away from the hospital, not on the premises.

Once they were seated and had placed their orders with Lindy, James explained his idea. Or rather, Nelson's idea with his own modification.

"You want me to carry a picket sign?" Anabelle asked, clearly concerned by the plan. "As a nursing supervisor, I'm part of management."

"Not a picket sign like in a strike," James told them. "We're not going to block the driveways or interfere in any way with patient services. We're just trying to make the public aware of the problems we're having at Hope Haven, what effect the pay cut will have on the community, and what people can do to help support the hospital."

"I don't know . . ." Anabelle shook her head. She looked a little tired, and James wondered if the puppy was still keeping her awake nights.

"As long as we're not doing anything illegal," Candace said, "or interfering with patients and visitors, I like the idea."

Lindy delivered their lunches. James had ordered a corned-beef sandwich with coleslaw. Before his first bite, he spread a generous amount of mustard on the meat.

After a few minutes, Elena asked, "So how soon do you think we can stage this protest?"

"Let's call it a Public Awareness Campaign," he said. "It doesn't sound so confrontational."

Elena and Anabelle nodded in agreement.

"Better wait until after the first of the year," Anabelle suggested. "A lot of people are on vacation this week."

James agreed. Besides, it would take a few days to recruit and schedule employees to man the picket line and to notify the press.

"How about the first Wednesday in January? That's a week from today," Candace suggested. "Schools are back in session starting Monday, so everyone should be back from vacation."

Next Wednesday evening was Nelson's performance of *A Midsummer Night's Dream*. That shouldn't be a conflict.

Assuming James wasn't arrested for inciting a riot and locked up, unable to attend.

A frown still furrowed Anabelle's forehead. "I'm a little concerned how Mr. Varner is going to take this, even if we call it public awareness. I don't want anyone to get in trouble, and I truly believe he's doing what he thinks is best for Hope Haven."

"If we stay on public property, the sidewalk," James said, "we don't need his permission."

"I'm not talking about asking permission. I just don't think we ought to drop a bomb like this on him without at least letting him know what we're doing and why."

Chewing thoughtfully, James nodded and swallowed. "I can talk to him. We get along pretty well. But let's wait to see if the rest of the employees will go along with the idea. No need to get Varner in a sweat if we can't pull this off."

That seemed to relieve some of Anabelle's concerns.

"What about the police?" Candace asked. "If they hear there's a riot going on at Hope Haven, they'll come roaring in with their sirens blaring."

Elena shook her salad fork in Candace's direction. "Good point. I'll talk to Chief O'Hanlon and take Cesar with me."

"You're sure he'll do that, talk to the chief?" Candace asked.

Elena grinned and stabbed a shrimp in her salad. "He will if he doesn't want to be eating frozen dinners for a full month. In the backyard."

Anabelle laughed, and James nearly choked on a fork full of coleslaw. He figured Elena would make good on the threat if she needed to.

When they settled down again, Candace asked, "Are we all supposed to make our own signs?"

"Oh, I've got an idea!" Elena piped up.

James groaned. "I hope this one doesn't require a Heimlich maneuver to get me breathing again like your last smart comment."

She elbowed him in the ribs. "We need to have a sign-painting meeting and invite all the employees. We'll buy a bunch of poster board and marking pens and get some sticks. Those who can come can paint their own signs, and we'll paint some with generic slogans for others who can't make it to the party. You know, something like *Supporting Our Hospital = Good Medicine.*"

"Cameron probably has a source for sticks that would work. He uses them to prop up shrubs or tree branches that start drooping."

"I can ask the pastor at Good Shepherd if we can use the social room the Monday evening before our protest," James said, troubled that the meeting would take him away from Fern one more evening. "I could probably get one of my boys to come help too." He'd ask the other boy to stay home with Fern.

"That would also be a good time to brief everyone that this is supposed to be a *peaceful* protest—awareness campaign," Anabelle said, correcting herself. "You know how sometimes fist-fights break out on a picket line."

That would certainly not be the kind of TV or newspaper visual James had in mind to build public sentiment in their favor.

The ideas came fast and furious until the lunch hour had sped by. They divvied up the check, left the money on the table for Lindy and hurried back across the street to the hospital.

By the end of his shift, it was obvious Hope Haven employees were as enthusiastic as James about staging an awareness campaign. He sought out team leaders from various departments and all three shifts to coordinate their units in a way that wouldn't impact patient services.

Then he made an appointment for the next day with Albert Varner to apprise him of their plans, surprised he was able to get in to see the CEO on New Year's Eve.

At the appointed time on Thursday, Penny Risser, Varner's executive assistant, ushered James into the hospital CEO's office, and he sat in one of the two leather guest chairs in front of Varner's desk. A new potted plant sat on the corner of the desk, no doubt a gift from Penny and her green thumb.

As usual, Varner looked the epitome of an executive in a dark suit and tie. In contrast, James wore his green hospital scrubs, his professional uniform.

Varner didn't look pleased to see James. He rested his elbows on his walnut desk and tented his fingers under his chin. His brows were lowered into a frown, his lips thinned.

"I've been hearing rumors that there's a big walkout scheduled for next week. Are you behind that, James?"

"It's not a walkout, sir. In fact we're being very careful not to do anything that will disrupt hospital services, which is why we wanted to let you know what we're doing and why. Our goal is to gain support for the hospital. We're also concerned that pay cuts will hurt morale and cause some of our most skilled employees to look elsewhere for jobs that pay better. That wouldn't be good for Hope Haven or Deerford." James slid an outline of their proposed campaign across the desk to Varner.

While the CEO read the outline, James glanced around the office. One wall featured photographs of Varner shaking hands with virtually every politician in the state from Deerford's current mayor to the governor. Everybody was smiling.

Nobody had a check in their hand.

Varner slid the outline to the side of his desk. "I don't think the board of directors is going to like the idea of you and your friends making a public issue of this. It's bad PR for the hospital."

"They'll like it fine if we actually achieve our goal."

Leaning back in his chair, Varner rubbed his chin. "You do understand I've approached every funding source I could identify. We're in a very difficult economy. The story I get is that times are hard. Money is in short supply across the board. Maybe next year. But the hospital can't wait that long. We had to take action."

"Maybe when they see 150 loyal hospital employees talking about the impact on hospital services, and the community at large, they'll think differently."

Varner paled. "That many will show up?"

"From what I can tell, the whole staff is going to take a turn on the picket line." He'd also sent e-mails to several newspapers and TV stations in addition to the letters to the editor the employees had sent. So far he hadn't heard back from any of them. If they didn't get TV coverage, the impact of the protest would be far less.

Shaking his head, Varner said, "The board isn't going to like the whole staff taking part."

"I suppose if the board reversed your decision to cut salaries, we might be able to stop the campaign. But I have to tell you, everybody's fired up to do this. There's a lot of energy behind this movement. It would take some pretty strong assurances from the board to get them to back down."

"Very well." Varner stood and so did James. "You've notified me of your plans, and I appreciate the courtesy. We'll just have to wait and see what happens."

James thanked him for his time and they shook hands. He didn't leave Varner's office with a good feeling, though.

His skin crawled and a knot formed in his stomach at the thought the CEO would pass on word about the protest to the board of directors. He'd have to, it was his job. He reported to the board and served at their discretion.

In a way, so did James.

No matter that his intentions, and those of the others involved, were to help Hope Haven and the larger community.

He could be summarily fired.

So could the others.

He slowly climbed the stairs to the second floor. He needed to check on a new patient, a hip replacement. The poor woman had been in a lot of pain earlier.

When he reached the nurses' station, Anabelle called him over.

"You've got a phone call," she said. "A reporter from the *Deerford Dispatch.*"

James licked his lips and swallowed hard. The ball had started rolling. There was no turning back now.

Chapter Fifteen

After work, Elena left the hospital on time to make the four o'clock appointment she'd arranged by phone with Cesar and Chief O'Hanlon.

The entire hospital staff and a good many patients had been buzzing all day about the two letters to the editor that would appear in the *Deerford Dispatch* the next day. James Bell and Eddie Blaine, from the maintenance department, would become overnight heroes.

As she changed into street clothes at home, Elena's adrenaline buzzed through her veins in the same way talk of the campaign had circulated through the hospital—at sonic speed.

She glanced at the folder of travel brochures she'd collected to help her plan the trip to Spain. It was nearly two inches thick now. Two inches of dreams delayed if the pay cut went through.

Biting down on her lip, she tried to put the thought aside. Delaying her trip to Spain wouldn't be the worst disaster she might face in her life. She needed to keep that in mind if the public campaign failed to generate additional support for the hospital.

As soon as she finished dressing, she drove her Jeep Liberty the short distance to the police department, located next to city hall on the south side of the town square. Trails of footprints crisscrossed the snow-covered square, which was marked by snowmen melting in the weak winter sun.

Cesar had promised to meet her at the station. The officer manning the front desk waved her through, saying her husband was in the break room.

Cesar, dressed in his uniform, stood as she entered. "Hey, hon. You all set?"

"You bet." She held up the plan James had devised for the demonstration at the hospital.

He winked at her. "Sure hope the chief doesn't think I'm consorting with some wild-eyed radicals set on disrupting the whole town."

"You've been consorting with me for a long time, Officer Rodriguez, and I haven't heard any complaints lately."

He laughed, slid his arm around her waist and ushered her down the hallway to the chief's office.

Cesar rapped his knuckles on the chief's open door, and Brian O'Hanlon waved them in. A tall, well-built man with reddish blond hair turning gray at his temples, he stood behind his desk.

"Hello, Elena. Good to see you." He shook her hand and nodded toward Cesar. "Hope you're keeping this guy in line these days."

"Doing my best, Chief."

"Sit down and tell me what I can do for you."

She handed him James's notes on the demonstration and explained why the hospital employees had decided to stage the event.

"We wanted you to know what was going to happen in case you get some phone calls," she concluded.

O'Hanlon had listened intently and now he nodded. "You're going to keep to the sidewalk? Not block any entrances or exits?"

"That's the plan," she replied.

"I'd like to avoid having to arrest my wife and lock her up in a cell," Cesar said.

Elena shot him an annoyed look. "You better not arrest me or anyone else."

The chief tapped the notes with his fingertip. "Protests with pickets have been known to get out of hand. Emotions can run high when it comes to money."

"I can't think why this one would. We're not angry with anyone. But we do believe that cutting the salaries of people who are vital to the health and well-being of this community is a bad idea."

"Our own officers end up at the hospital more often than we'd like," Cesar pointed out. "Like when McGruff got tangled up in the middle of a domestic dispute last year and was beaned with a frying pan. It's smart to keep the doctors and nurses happy and not cross them."

"I agree," the chief said, tilting back in his chair. "I'll assign a patrol car to keep track of the protest and make sure it's peaceful and that there's no blocking of public access to the hospital."

The chief's response satisfied Elena. She trusted him—and his officers—to keep the peace.

As long as no counterprotesters showed up—and she couldn't think why they would—there shouldn't be a problem.

The New Year's Eve celebration at the Bell house was a subdued one, which matched James's mood. All of his life he'd set goals for himself and generally achieved them. Now he couldn't see the future clearly. Or perhaps he didn't want to. So much depended on Fern's health and their financial situation. Would he be able to remodel the downstairs to add a more accessible bedroom for her? Or should he be thinking about moving them into a one-story house somewhere? Perhaps even changing his job?

Where would they be next New Year's Eve?

For once the future seemed opaque, and he was blind to what came next.

Gideon had walked to a friend's house down the street to celebrate New Year's Eve, promising to be home by one o'clock.

Fern rested on the recliner in the family room, Sapphire curled up in her lap, James sitting nearby. Nelson lay sprawled on the floor while they all watched *It's a Wonderful Life*. The lights on the Christmas tree in the living room reflected back from the picture window and framed a powdery snowfall outside. Tomorrow James would take down the tree, and they'd put this holiday season behind them and hope for a better one next year.

Fern had lost weight in the past few weeks. Every day her speech was becoming more slurred. Often, her legs wouldn't hold her upright at all. Fear for her deteriorating health gnawed at James's awareness day and night.

He didn't want to lose her.

He wanted her back like she was when they met, a bright star in the firmament that had called to his heart.

But that wasn't one of the choices.

"Sweetheart, I think you need to see Dr. Chopra next week," he whispered. "The new meds aren't working for you. There must be something else she can try."

Fern didn't respond. Her head heavy on her chest, her shallow breathing barely audible, her eyes closed in sleep.

Squeezing his eyes closed didn't prevent a few tears from escaping. *Please, God . . .*

James waited until the movie ended. He gave Sapphire a nudge. At the signal that it was time for bed, she jumped down to the floor.

James carried his sleeping wife upstairs to bed, his heart heavy with worry and grief.

Chapter Sixteen

"YOU CAN'T TAKE SARGE TO CHURCH!"

It was Monday evening, and Anabelle was determined to support her co-workers no matter what Cameron said.

"Of course I can." She latched the wiggly puppy's harness in place and attached his leash. "And we aren't going to church. We're going to the social room at church to create our picket signs for the public demonstration." She'd dressed warmly in a sweater and slacks, belatedly realizing that she hadn't yet purchased a sweater for Sarge. She'd have to wrap him in a blanket.

"What if the little fellow has an accident? He's not exactly housebroken yet."

"Dear, I've cleaned up more bedpans than I care to remember. I think I can manage a little puppy accident." Although Sarge was no longer a "little" puppy, as he had put on noticeable weight since she'd brought him home, consuming huge quantities of puppy chow.

Gripping the leash with one hand, she managed to tug a knit cap over her head. "Besides, Diana was very clear about the importance of Sarge being socialized with people and other dogs." Sarge wound the leash around Anabelle's legs. She tried to untwist him.

Mumbling something under his breath, Cameron went to the coat closet and pulled out his winter jacket.

"You don't have to go with me, Cam. I'm perfectly capable of driving to church on my own."

"The roads are icy. I'll take you." He shrugged into his jacket and stared at Sarge. "You can hold the dog in your lap."

Anabelle had had no idea one little puppy would create so much strain between her and her husband. She'd been certain Cam would take to having a dog as quickly as she had.

Apparently she was wrong.

There were several cars in the parking lot when Cam and Anabelle reached Church of the Good Shepherd.

Sarge tugged Anabelle along the path to the brightly lit social room behind the main sanctuary, zigzagging his way in order to mark the piles of snow that had been shoveled to clear the sidewalk.

Anabelle hoped that would take care of any possible accidents.

Inside, long tables the church used for potluck dinners and wedding receptions had been set up. Several hospital employees were already at work with marking pens creating their own special slogans. She spotted Nelson Bell stapling finished signs to the wood landscaping sticks Cameron used to prop up plants and had donated to the cause.

James came over to greet her and Cameron. "Glad you could both come." He shook hands with Cam. "I see you brought the new addition to the family along."

He knelt to pet Sarge, who tried to jump on James's legs.

"Sit," Cam ordered.

To Anabelle's amazement, Sarge sat, and Cameron offered the puppy a treat, which he'd had in his pants pocket. "Good dog," he said.

She looked at Cam suspiciously. It seemed that Cam had been having more interaction with Sarge than he'd led her to believe.

Candace's daughter Brooke came over to visit Sarge. A sweet child with long, blonde curls and blue eyes, she smiled up at Cameron. "Can I pet your puppy?"

"Sure, go ahead," Cam said. "Don't let him jump on you though. We don't want him to get into bad habits."

She squatted down beside Sarge, his tail whipping the air in excitement. "What a pretty boy you are," she crooned, letting him nuzzle her neck and lick her chin. "I wish we had a dog, but we can't afford one."

Anabelle met James's gaze. While the pay cut would hurt Candace more than most because of her single-parent and bread-winner status, a dog wasn't all that expensive to own. Except when they ran up veterinarian bills, of course.

"Is your little brother here?" Anabelle asked.

"No, Howie's got a cold. He stayed home with Grammy. Mommy let me help letter her sign."

"Good for you. I hope your brother feels better soon." Anabelle glanced around the room, spotting several employees she knew including Candace, who was lettering her sign at a table with Heath Carlson. Now that would make for an interesting match, Anabelle mused.

"Brooke, would you like to walk Sarge around and introduce him to everyone?" she asked.

The child's eyes widened. "Can I?"

"Of course. Just don't let go of his leash, and if he starts sniffing around, try taking him outside so he won't have any accidents in here."

Sarge went trotting off with Brooke, no doubt feeling he had found the best of all worlds: an energetic human to adore him.

Anabelle could hardly wait until Ainslee's baby would be old enough to play with Sarge.

"Come on over to the table, Anabelle," James said. "I'll get you started with your picket sign. Do you want to make a sign too?" he asked Cameron.

"Might as well. I don't want Annie to have all the fun."

Anabelle cocked her head. Cameron had decided to march in the picket line? She didn't know when he'd decided that, but his support of the cause and her friends touched her heart and warmed her spirits.

Supplies were arranged on one long table: a stack of poster boards, a shoebox full of colorful markers and several yardsticks and rulers to help keep the words in a straight line.

As Anabelle started work on her poster, she kept an eye on Brooke and Sarge. The girl had stopped to talk with Nelson, and from their respective expressions, Anabelle concluded the conversation was serious. She wondered what the youngsters were talking about. They weren't the type to get into mischief, but one never knew about teenagers.

Employees drifted into the social hall in ones and twos, each person warmly greeted by their co-workers. Excitement and enthusiasm electrified the air. Their mission was a good one, the potential for success exhilarating. Their mood fervent.

Her fellow employees' passion for the cause fired Anabelle's enthusiasm as well. Protesting for a cause was as American as standing for the national anthem. Or eating apple pie.

Suddenly the lively conversations and friendly joshing back and forth came to a halt. The sudden silence shrouded the room.

Sarge started barking.

Anabelle looked up. Sarge had gotten away from Brooke. His leash dragging behind him, Anabelle's adorable puppy had raced across the room and was barking and dancing around the newest arrival—

Mr. Albert Varner.

Heat raced to Anabelle's cheeks, her heart sank to her midsection and she prayed for a lightning strike to blow out the power and darken the room so she could escape without being noticed.

"You better go get your dog," Cam said under his breath.

James recovered from the shock of seeing Mr. Varner at the sign-making meeting faster than Anabelle. He strode across the room and extended his hand, his presence somehow more imposing than when he exercised his nursing skills. Which were quite impressive in themselves.

"Good evening, Mr. Varner. Can I help you?"

Anabelle hurried after James to snag Sarge's leash. "I'm so sorry, Albert." She pulled Sarge away from the hospital CEO. "Sit, Sarge. Sit." He half obeyed then lost the moment and tried to dart off in a new direction. The leash thwarted his efforts.

"No harm done." Albert waved off Anabelle's apology, then turned to James. "I'd like to make a sign for the demonstration on Wednesday."

Surprise shot through Anabelle. "You're going to march with us?" Instead of his usual suit and tie, Albert wore wool slacks, a warm sweater and a heavy winter jacket.

"Of course," he said. "Without the skill and caring of Hope Haven employees, the hospital can't exist. I'm not sure the board of directors understand that, but I do. Where do I get started?"

Candace left the sign-making party earlier than most. While she'd enjoyed working next to Heath, and Brooke had had a great time with Anabelle's puppy, she needed to be home for Howie. He'd been running a low-grade temperature when she left. Her mother was perfectly capable of taking care of a sick child, but that didn't lessen Candace's instinctive worry about her son.

She wondered if mothers ever stopped worrying about their children.

Based on her own mother's example, probably not.

She drove her car into the garage and parked. "Thanks for coming with me, Brooke. Glad you got to play with Anabelle's puppy."

Brooke popped the passenger door open. "It was fun." She hopped out of the car and went inside.

Candace followed more slowly.

She found her mother sitting on the couch in the family room watching TV. Howie was asleep, his head in her mother's lap. Candace remembered doing the same as a child and feeling comforted by her mother's presence.

"Hi, Mom. Is he still running a fever?" Wanting to know for herself, Candace touched the back of her hand to Howie's forehead.

"It's come down, I think," Janet said.

"Good. I'll carry him up to bed. Hopefully he'll feel better in the morning."

Just as she started to pick Howie up, the overhead light went off. She looked at the bank of fluorescent lights overhead. Had both bulbs burned out at once? The TV was still running, the volume low, so there hadn't been a power failure.

The light over the stairs to the main floor of the split-level house snapped off, leaving the central core of the house pitch black.

"What on earth—" A shiver of unease slid down Candace's spine. "Brooke, is that you? Did you turn off the lights?"

"Only the ones we aren't using," Brooke answered.

Relieved it wasn't an intruder plunging them into darkness, Candace shifted her concern to the fear that a member of her family was likely to break their neck trying to get around in the dark.

Brooke appeared as a shadow at the top of the stairs. "I'm going up to get ready for bed. Good night."

Still hunched over in the process of picking up Howie, Candace tried to process what had just happened. Her daughter was turning off lights all over the house? Ones they weren't using?

"I'll be right back, Mom. I'm going to find out what's going on."

Moving carefully for fear of stepping on a giant Lego or a dump truck, Candace reached the stairs. She flicked the family room light on, walked through the living-dining area and up the next set of stairs.

The only light on up there was the small table lamp next to Brooke's bed.

"Brooke, why are you turning off all the lights?"

She pulled her sweater off over her head and tugged her nightgown on. "I'm saving electricity."

Maybe Brooke's science teacher was doing a unit on ecology? "You left Grammy and me in the dark, sweetie. We could've hurt ourselves or fallen on the stairs."

"Oh. I'm sorry. But we have to save electricity. Water and gas too."

Definitely, an ecology unit that was being taken too much to heart.

Candace sat down on Brooke's bed and patted the spot beside her. "Come tell me why it's so important to save electricity."

Brooke sat down next to her. "Well, see, when we were at the church making posters for the demonstration, Nelson Bell told me electricity costs money; and we need to save money. He and his brother are turning off lights they're not using and unplugging stuff that sucks lots of electricity out of the wall even when it's not turned on. They're going to save megabucks every month. I wanted to do the same."

Ah, a small light of insight showed itself in Candace's brain. "Why are you so troubled about money, sweetie?"

Worry lines pleated Brooke's forehead. "'Cause I heard you and Grammy talking about how the hospital is taking away your money and we're going to go broke. And that's why everybody was making those signs tonight, so the hospital would give them back their money."

Awed by the way her child's mind worked, Candace ventured a little deeper. "When did you hear Grammy and me talking about money?"

Brooke shrugged. "I don't know. Before Christmas, I guess."

"Was that about the time your nightmares started?"

"Maybe." Another lift of her shoulders.

"And that's about the time you didn't want me to buy you a new Christmas outfit?"

"I didn't need one."

Candace's heart sank for the burden of worry her daughter had been carrying. All because of a conversation she'd overheard and hadn't fully understood.

"Oh, sweetie . . ." She pulled Brooke into her arms. "You shouldn't be worrying about money. That's a job for grown-ups, for me and your Grammy."

"But I want to help. Daddy's not here, so somebody has to help you. I could maybe even get a job. Nelson and Gideon are shoveling snow for their neighbors."

"You don't have to get a job." Candace's throat tightened on a flood of tears she didn't want to shed. "It's true that the hospital may cut everyone's salary. We're all hoping they won't, but it may happen anyway."

She stroked her hand over her daughter's hair. "Your daddy did plan ahead in case something awful happened to him. He had an insurance policy that helped us. I'm trying hard to save that money and let it grow so it'll be there when you and Howie go to college. Even with the cut in pay, we won't be destitute."

"But we still ought to save money if we can, right?"

"Save, yes. Turning off lights we don't need is a good idea. Turning off too many lights might cause someone to have an accident."

Brooke seemed to be weighing Candace's words.

"Tell you what, sweetie. Why don't you let me decide what we can afford? We won't have to make huge sacrifices, and we'll still be all right. Like if you need a new dress, that would be fine as long as it's not the most expensive designer dress in town."

Slowly, Brooke nodded. "What about jeans? Ellen Radcliff got a pair of really awesome jeans for Christmas. I like them a lot."

Awesome being a positive attribute, Candace gathered. She chuckled and smiled. "Since you didn't get a new Christmas dress, I think we can include jeans in our budget."

Brooke's smile widened. "I know, when I say my prayers tonight, I'll pray you don't have your pay cut and maybe I can have a pair of jeans *and* a new dress."

Pulling Brooke into her arms again, Candace said a silent prayer. *Thank You, Lord, for giving me such a sweet, sensitive child. Ease the burdens she's been carrying, and help me to be a better mother. Amen.*

She kissed the top of her daughter's head. "Sleep tight, sweetie, and no more bad dreams."

She hoped Brooke's worry about money had been resolved and she wouldn't need more therapy sessions with Tony, her counselor.

At least Candace could hope that was the case.

Chapter Seventeen

WEDNESDAY MORNING ARRIVED COLD AND blustery.

At the hospital, anxiety tightened James's neck muscles and bunched his shoulders together. Gazing out a window that overlooked the front of Hope Haven, he massaged his neck to ease the strain. It didn't help.

He checked his watch again. Almost ten thirty, nearly time to begin the demonstration. The whole morning had crept by like someone had drugged his watch and its hands couldn't move. He flicked his fingernail against the watch face. Maybe the battery was running down.

Nelson had wanted to come march with the employees, since the whole idea had been his. But it was a school day and the last rehearsal of the play was scheduled before tonight's performance.

Would the employees who'd promised to join in the march show up? In this freezing cold weather? He didn't want to be the only one with his neck stuck out a mile.

How about the TV station and the newspapers he'd contacted? A story about a small-town hospital wasn't exactly earth shattering. In this weather, reporters might want to cover an indoor event and stay warm. Without news coverage of the demonstration, it wouldn't have any impact on public officials. The pay cuts would already be effective without any objection except from the employees, and there'd be no way to reverse the decision.

Lorraine Wilder, the day-shift nurse supervisor for General Medicine, joined James at the window. A tall, angular woman with dark hair and a prominent nose, she was in her fifties with nearly thirty years' experience as a nurse.

"You must have checked your watch ten times in the past fifteen minutes," she said.

Guilty heat flooded James's face. "Sorry. I'm a little nervous. Any number of things could go wrong—"

"It's going to be fine, James. You've organized the event beautifully. The employees are excited. We'll make a big splash that the public and board of directors will hear. They'll be on our side."

"I hope you're right." James eyed a red cedar tree across the street, its branches waving wildly in the wind. The protesters would be lucky to hang onto their signs.

Even if the public got behind the employees, that didn't guarantee any additional funds would be forthcoming.

Their pay could still be cut.

"Since you're uncharacteristically useless on the floor this morning," Lorraine said, her tone kind and supportive, "why don't you go on downstairs and make sure everything is ready?"

He snapped his head around. "Really? I don't want to leave you in a bind."

"Go, James. The floor's quiet. I'll handle things for you and take the late shift on the picket line when you get back."

He gave her a big smile. "Thanks, Lorraine. You're a champ."

"Probably more like a champion sucker." She jerked her head toward the stairs. "Get outta here. And don't let anybody get frostbite. We don't want the staff out on disability if we can help it."

"Yes, ma'am." He tendered her a casual salute, then hurried upstairs to get his heavy parka and his cap with earflaps from his locker.

Back downstairs, he walked smartly toward the exit and stepped outside. The cold air struck him in the face with an icy slap.

Wincing, he vowed to schedule the next outdoor event he organized during summer.

He retrieved his picket sign from his van along with several signs with generic messages that said things like Honk If You Support the Hospital. The wind nearly turned the signs into kites. Or lethal missiles.

As he walked toward the sidewalk, several employees joined him, all of them bundled against the cold.

"Hey, man," one young fellow said, "sure hope you've got a bunch of radiant heaters lined up waiting for us. This is some arctic blast we got going on."

"Sorry," James responded. "I forgot to put them on special order."

"Oh well, there's a cute chick in admissions I've been trying to cozy up to. Maybe we can keep each other warm."

Good luck with that, James thought.

As employees arrived, James reminded them to picket between the two entrances to the parking lot and the ambulance entrance. No one was to block traffic. Keep moving around in a loop and stay on the sidewalk. Wave to the passing cars.

Excitement replaced James's anxiety when a TV truck from a local station arrived. The TV crew raised a dish antenna on the truck and set up to take video of the protest.

"Excuse me, Mr. Bell?"

James turned at the sound of a female voice and found a young woman with bright red hair and a notepad in her hand. "Yes?"

"I'm Valera Kincaid, reporter for the *Deerford Dispatch*. I'd like to speak to you for a moment, if I can."

Yes! James nearly pumped his fist in the air. Despite the weather, the *Dispatch* and Ms. Kincaid were going to cover the demonstration as she'd promised earlier. So was the local television station. Maybe the tape would reach a wider audience in Springfield, or even nationally.

"Of course," he said. "I'd be happy to talk with you."

"First, tell me what this is all about."

James began explaining the situation to the reporter. Minutes later a pretty blonde TV reporter, who should have been wearing a lot warmer clothes in this weather, stuck a microphone in his face. James kept talking, answering Valera's questions and those of the TV reporter. But he didn't once look at the camera.

The thought of speaking directly to a television audience, even if it was an unseen audience, made his mouth go dry and the palms of his hands sweat inside his gloves.

Traffic on the street began to slow; drivers honked their horns. The picketers began to sing, thoroughly enjoying themselves. Or maybe they were just trying to stay warm.

A reporter from Springfield showed up and started peppering James with questions. He fielded them as best he could and referred other questions to Albert Varner, who was now walking the picket line with his employees. He'd earned their loyalty today by being on their side.

From the corner of his eye, James spotted two long, ten-passenger vans pull into the hospital parking lot and stop. Each van had the name of a local senior citizen retirement home painted on the side, Peaceful Valley Retirement Community.

Bundled up against the cold, the passengers exited at a snail's pace, some with canes, some with walkers and all of them with picket signs.

What in the world—

The phalanx of seniors shuffled over to the sidewalk and fell in line with the employees, who cheered as the oldsters raised their signs: Save Our Hospital.

The reporters and TV personnel hustled over to interview the new arrivals and get more photos and video shots.

James chuckled. *God works in mystenious ways.* This could be the best PR ever!

He strolled over to one of the van drivers, a middle-aged man wearing a red, white and blue knit cap. "How did those folks hear about our protest?"

"A resident's granddaughter works here at the hospital. The ol' gal got all riled up about the hospital cutting her granddaughter's pay. She stirred everybody else up, and here we are. A couple of letters to the editor got them going too." The man shrugged. "I mean, you really don't want to mess with a bunch of old folks. They got time on their hands and like nothing better than to mix it up with those in authority. You wouldn't believe what they do when they're served something in the dining room that they don't like. We're talkin' a hundred angry little old ladies. You don't want to mess with them, I'm telling you."

Smiling, James glanced around. The next shift of employees was making its way to the picket line so the first batch could go back to work or lunch. Everything seemed to be running smoothly except for the traffic trying to get into the hospital parking lot.

"If you and your buddy can drive your vans to the far end of the lot, there's parking there, and you'll be out of the traffic pattern."

"Will do."

James wandered back over to the picket line. A police patrol car was parked across the street, apparently driven by Cesar Rodriguez. But Elena had dragged her protesting husband into the picket line to march along with her.

Farther back in line, Cameron marched beside Anabelle, who had Sarge on a tight leash. The puppy wore a red knitted sweater and little booties on his feet, which Sarge kept trying to bite off.

A wave of regret caught James by surprise. Fern wasn't here, couldn't be here, to walk beside him. The tight grip of multiple sclerosis was sucking the life out of her. And him.

Please, Lord, don't desert us in our hour of need.

Chapter Eighteen

*J*AMES'S MOOD WAS RESTRAINED WHEN HE arrived home. The protest had been a grand success when measured by participation and the publicity they'd been getting.

But no buckets full of hundred dollar bills had fallen out of the sky to solve Hope Haven's financial problems. Or to keep the ax from falling on the employee 10 percent cut in pay.

He was barely inside the door when the phone rang. He hurried to pick up the kitchen phone before it woke Fern, who was napping on the couch.

"I'm calling from Mayor Donald Armstrong's office for Mr. James Bell," said a female voice. "Is he in?"

His eyebrows shot up. "I'm James Bell."

"Mr. Bell, His Honor would like you to make a presentation at the next city council meeting regarding the proposed pay cut for Hope Haven Hospital employees and the potential impact on employees."

A moment of panic closed James's throat. "I . . . I think Albert Varner, the hospital CEO, would be b—better than me," he stammered.

"Yes, I've already contacted his office."

"I'd rather he spoke." Sweat beaded James's forehead and he wiped it away with the back of his hand.

"If you don't feel comfortable speaking at a city council meeting, perhaps you could present the employees' position in a letter that the mayor could read."

"Uh, yes, I could do that." Writing his words down had always been much easier than saying them aloud.

When the conversation with the secretary ended, James hung up and rubbed the back of his neck. Things were moving fast now. The plan had a chance of succeeding.

If they could keep the ball rolling.

Nelson came in the back door reciting his lines out loud. "'If we shadows have offended, Think but this, and all is mended.'" He made a big sweep with his arm. "'That you have but slumbered here, While these visions did appear.' And this idle theme." He grimaced. "No, that's not right."

"Having trouble with your lines?" James asked.

"Did you know I've got the last lines in the whole play? If I blow them—"

"You won't, son. You'll be fine." Proud of his son for accepting a part in the play, James hooked his arm around Nelson in a mock neck hold. "Relax. Don't let your nerves get to you."

Nelson ducked out from under James's grasp. "Easy for you to say." He made a beeline for the refrigerator and poured himself a tall glass of milk. "Mrs. Murphy wants us at school by six thirty. Can you take me?"

"Of course. We'll have an early dinner and get there in plenty of time."

"Great." He headed upstairs. "'And this *weak* and idle theme . . .'"

A couple of butterflies made their presence known in James's stomach. He might have told Nelson not to be nervous, but that didn't stop James from having his own case of the jitters on Nelson's behalf. He had to admire his son's courage when it came to speaking before an audience. Nelson sure hadn't gotten that gene from him.

James had dinner ready by five o'clock: burgers and a hot potato salad Marilee had brought by and he reheated.

He called upstairs to the boys. "Dinner's on the table!"

In the living room, he knelt beside Fern, who was still on the couch. Circles of fatigue underscored her eyes.

Fear for Fern's health mushroomed in James's chest like an atomic cloud. "Dr. Chopra told you to double your meds. Have you been doing that?"

"Yes." Her voice hoarse, she nodded. "James, I can't go tonight. To Nelson's play. I'm so sorry." Tears of disappointment and pain glistened in her eyes.

Dear God . . . "We can use the wheelchair. I can carry you." For her not to attend Nelson's play, or any event where the boys were involved, was unheard of. Fern *always* went to cheer them on. The play, the whole Shakespeare thing, had created such a special connection between Fern and her younger son.

"My whole body is like a wet noodle. I can barely sit up."

"Did your mother take you to physical therapy today?"

"Yes. Not good day. Tired."

"Okay, maybe dinner will help. Let me get you to the table."

He stood and found that Gideon and Nelson were standing nearby, their expressions drawn and tormented with concern.

James helped Fern to her feet. She wobbled like a toddler just learning to walk.

Taking most of her weight and walking backward, James eased Fern toward the kitchen table. Her legs lacked coordination, her feet flopped as though they were no longer connected to her ankles.

This was by far the worst James had ever seen Fern.

One of the boys pulled out Fern's chair. James guided her down and made sure she was comfortable.

Dinner was an agony of indecision for James. He couldn't leave his wife like this. He hated not being there to see Nelson's performance. But there was no choice—

"Nelson, I'll drive you and Gideon to school but I won't be able to stay for the show. I don't want to leave your mom alone. You can call me when you're ready to come home."

Nelson looked stricken.

"I'll stay home with Mom," Gideon said quickly. "Shakespeare isn't really my thing. I've got homework to do anyway."

"I don't need a babysitter," Fern protested.

"It's no big deal, Mom," Gideon assured her. "I was looking for an excuse not to go anyway."

James knew that wasn't true. Despite their occasional bickering, both boys supported each other as best they could, attending everything from each other's swim meets and track meets to spelling bees.

"You're sure you're okay staying home?" he asked Gideon.

"Yeah. I'm cool." He helped himself to another big spoonful of potatoes making sure he got plenty of the bits of bacon on top.

"Okay. I'll leave my cell on vibrate. If you need me, don't hesitate to call. Or text me. I'll come right home."

Fern tried to protest again but her efforts weren't convincing. Which troubled James all the more.

If only he could transport Fern *Star Trek* style to the school to see the play. That would surely give her a lift. But Captain Kirk and Mr. Spock weren't around, and twenty-first-century engineers hadn't yet invented a device to do the job.

After dinner, James slipped upstairs to call Dr. Chopra. She sounded concerned that Fern wasn't responding better to the new medication but remained optimistic that the increased dosage would improve her condition.

The all-purpose cafetorium was set up with risers for a stage and folding chairs for the audience. A couple of plywood trees that the kids had painted and a wooden bench provided what little scenery the actors needed.

The costumes were more contemporary than medieval. Nelson as Puck wore Levi's, a shirt with red and yellow patches sewn on, and a court jester's triple-pointed hat.

Theseus—a duke, according to the printed program—wore a dark suit a size or two too large for him. Queen Hippolyta had borrowed her sister's prom dress, carefully pinned in back to fit her better.

James joined Marilee and Frank Driscoll in the audience.

Frowning, Marilee asked, "Fern and Gideon aren't coming?"

"No, she was too tired. I didn't want to leave her home alone."

"This afternoon's physical therapy session absolutely exhausted her. I've been so worried."

"I know. So have I." Worried deep down in his gut.

James looked up as Duke Theseus strode onto the stage from one side and Queen Hippolyta with her attendants appeared from the other. The play was under way.

"'Now fair Hippolyta,'" the Duke began in a strong voice, "'our nuptial hour draws on apace. Four happy days and you will be mine.'"

Mrs. Murphy had apparently modernized some of Shakespeare's language to make the performance easier and more understandable for the students—and the audience.

As the play progressed, some of the kids forgot their lines and were prompted by Mrs. Murphy. Others stumbled along, gathering giggles from their classmates as well as from the audience.

At the end of the play, Nelson stood center stage to speak Puck's final lines. "'So good night unto you all. Give me your hands, if we be friends, and Robin shall restore all as it should be.'"

The cast bowed in unison, and the audience applauded enthusiastically. In that moment, James regretted Fern had missed the play even more now than he had earlier.

Cast and audience mingled, giving and accepting congratulations, gathering up students to take them home.

Marilee gave Nelson a hug, and Frank shook the boy's hand. When it was James's turn, he lifted his hand for a high five, then hugged his son.

"You were really great," he told Nelson.

"I messed up a couple of lines," he admitted, "but I think it went okay overall."

"Better than okay! I was very proud of you. And your friends," James added.

Frank said, "We'd better be on our way home. The roads are pretty icy."

"Thanks for coming, Grandpa. You too, Grandma." Nelson watched his grandparents make their way through the dwindling crowd, then turned to James. "I wish Mom could've been here."

"Me too, son." He frowned as one possibility struck him. He didn't have to transport Fern to the school. He could bring the play to Fern. "Hey, do you think your friends would come over to our house and do the show all over again?"

Nelson brightened. "Really? That'd be great."

"Why don't we ask your teacher? See what she thinks."

Mrs. Murphy, who had dark, wildly curly hair, didn't look much older than her students, several of whom were inches taller than her. Her cheeks were flushed with excitement and her hazel eyes sparkled with enthusiasm. No wonder the kids loved her.

James introduced himself. "Congratulations for putting on a great show."

"Oh, the credit goes to the students. They all worked hard and were wonderful. Our young Puck did a great job."

"Does that mean I get an A in English?"

She tilted her head. "Let's see how well you do on next week's punctuation and grammar test."

Nelson groaned and made a face.

"I'm sorry my wife couldn't be here," James said. "She's been looking forward to the play for weeks, but she wasn't feeling up to coming tonight."

"She's got MS," Nelson added.

"Oh, I'm sorry," Mrs. Murphy said. "I didn't know that."

"Nelson and I were wondering, would it be possible for the cast to come to our house and do the play again? My wife would love that."

Taken aback, Mrs. Murphy blinked and glanced around the room. Most of the students and parents had already left. "I'm not sure . . ."

"You could ask them in class tomorrow, Mrs. Murphy," Nelson suggested. "Even if everybody couldn't come, we could have someone else read the lines for them."

"It would be an act of kindness my wife would very much appreciate," James added.

"When did you want to—"

"How about tomorrow night?" Nelson glanced up at James. "If we don't do it right away, Dad, everybody will forget their lines."

James couldn't think of a reason tomorrow wouldn't work. On Saturday morning, he and Nelson were going on their scouting trip, so the weekend was out. And Fern did need an emotional lift.

"Tomorrow night would be fine with me," he said.

"All right, Nelson. Remind me to ask the class tomorrow. We'll see how many can make it for tomorrow night."

The next morning, James woke up to good news.

Still in her nightgown, Fern sat on the edge of the bed. "I almost hate to say anything for fear I'll jinx myself, but I slept much better last night than I have in a long while. I feel almost human."

Relief and hope combined into a heady sensation that made James want to cheer. "Your color's better and so is your speech."

She looked as pleased as James felt. "Looks like doubling up on the new meds was the right thing to do."

He helped her downstairs for breakfast with a lighter heart than he'd had in weeks. He told her about Nelson's class possibly performing in their own living room, and she was thrilled.

He was still feeling ebullient a half hour later when he arrived at the hospital. In the staff lounge, someone had posted the article Valera Kincaid had written in the *Deerford Dispatch* about the demonstration. James had been quoted at length.

He got a lot of attaboys and pats on the back from his fellow employees.

He'd barely settled into the morning routine of checking on his patients, when he had a phone call at the nurses' station. A reporter for the Springfield newspaper wanted to know more about Wednesday's event. He wanted to interview James over the phone. James promised to call him back during his lunch hour.

He didn't dare spend any more time away from his patients or he'd risk losing more than 10 percent of his salary.

He'd risk losing his job too.

Chapter Nineteen

CANDACE LEFT WORK ON TIME AND DROVE TO Deerford Middle School. Although they lived only a couple of blocks from the school, she preferred to pick up Brooke when she could, or asked Janet to. Call her paranoid, but she'd already lost one person she loved. She didn't want to risk losing her child to an accident or worse.

Candace parked her Honda CR–V behind a long line of other parents waiting for their children.

The dismissal bell sounded. Within seconds, children exploded out of the school's main door and flew down the walkway or across the snow-covered lawn as though a mass escape from prison had been orchestrated by the teachers inside.

Candace spotted her daughter at the same time Brooke broke off from a gaggle of her friends and headed for the car. She opened the car door, tossed her backpack inside and jumped into the backseat after it.

"Hi, honey. You have a good day?"

"MaryBeth's mom saw you on TV last night."

Candace turned to face her daughter. "She saw me?"

"Yeah, when you were marching at the hospital. It was on the news. Everyone's talking about it."

There'd been a lot of talk around the hospital about the TV and newspaper coverage. But she hadn't realized she'd been identifiable on TV and hadn't watched television last night. She didn't like making a spectacle of herself.

With any luck, most of the focus had been on James and Mr. Varner, not her.

"So everybody says no way will the hospital cut your pay now." Brooke leaned forward and put her arms on the back of the front seat. "So do you think we could go shopping again? All my clothes are old. I promise I'll still turn off the lights when we don't need them, and make Howie do it too."

Candace laughed out loud. She couldn't help herself.

It appeared her daughter was back to normal.

She could only pray that her salary would remain normal as well.

When Anabelle returned home from work that afternoon, she received an exuberant welcome from Sarge.

She knelt and he jumped up to lick her face.

"Hello, sweetie, did you miss me?"

"Tell him to sit, Annie," Cam said in a resolute voice. "We have to be consistent with our discipline. We don't want him jumping on people when he gets bigger."

She looked up at her husband, who looked very much at home wearing khaki pants and a flannel shirt. "So now you're the expert on training dogs?"

Sarge continued to jump, his tail whisking wildly through the air.

"Sarge, sit," Cam ordered in a normal voice.

Sarge sat and looked up at Cam expectantly.

Cam made the dog hold his position for a couple of seconds before offering him a treat. Sarge gobbled the nibbly down in one swallow. "Good boy," Cam said.

"I can see I have some catching up to do in the doggie training business. I think I'll take Sarge for a walk before it gets dark."

Her announcement sent Sarge into a whirling dervish of jumping and dancing around the kitchen.

"I'd suggest when you want to take Sarge for a w-a-l-k that you spell it," Cam said. "He's one smart dog."

Slightly peeved at Cam's fast mastery of training the dog, she said, "Sarge, sit."

The puppy cocked his head to the side, looked at her with curious brown eyes and did nothing.

"Sit," she repeated.

"Push his rear end down. And here," Cam handed her a treat, "give him this when he complies."

She tried again, doing as Cam had suggested. This time Sarge complied and got his treat.

"I'm going to take Sarge for a l-o-n-g w-a-l-k. We'll be back."

She retrieved the puppy's harness and leash from the mud-room, hooked up Sarge and went out the back door. It wasn't her fault that she hadn't been able to spend much time training the puppy. She worked full-time while Cameron was home to do all the training. She just had to remember Sarge would eventually listen to her like he listened to Cam.

The temperature was above freezing, the sun still shining, so the street was clear of snow. She didn't really plan to go far. Mostly, she wanted a little fresh air and some time spent with Sarge.

Sarge, however, appeared interested in everything *but* her. He dashed back and forth at the end of the leash, sniffing and poking his nose into every crevice he could find. Every time he reached the end of the leash, he yanked her arm, and she half stumbled after him. For a little puppy, he was amazingly strong. And determined.

"Ouch!" she cried when he yanked harder than usual. "Sarge, sit!"

He did no such thing. He continued to sweep back and forth like a radar gun in search of the enemy. Or a friend.

She'd barely gone as far as the neighbor's house when Ethel Dickson waved from her front porch.

"Hello, Anabelle, lovely day isn't it?" A lively eighty-year-old, Ethel came down off the porch, the broom she'd been using in her hand. As usual when she did housework, she wore a frilly apron over her dress. "I see it's your turn to walk that sweet little puppy of Cam's."

Sarge raced to the end of his leash to greet Ethel.

"Actually, I was the one who—"

"Your Cameron is such a dear man. He does love his puppy. Walks him two or three times a day. He's taught him to sit and heel. He's quite devoted, you know."

"Actually, no. I didn't know—"

"You can tell a lot about a man by the way he treats his dog. Yes, indeed. I remember when Sam had that old hound dog of his. Rufus, he called him. They were inseparable, those two. Wherever Sam went, Rufus went along too. Just like your Cameron and that puppy."

Cameron hadn't let on he was spending so much time with Sarge. She'd still thought he wasn't happy about having a dog while all the while he'd been doing exactly what she had hoped for—bonding with Sarge.

That evening, Gideon and Nelson helped James rearrange the furniture in the living room to clear space in front of the window to serve as a stage. In addition to most of the cast members, a few parents were expected to come, those who hadn't been able to attend the performance the prior evening because of work or other commitments.

Fern'd had a reasonably good day, though she looked tired now. But her spirits were high.

Some of the weight of worry James had been carrying in his chest lifted with her improved health. If only the improvement continued . . .

Carloads of kids began to arrive along with a few parents. Sapphire, never comfortable in a crowd, lit out for upstairs to hide under the bed. Her safe place.

Nelson began organizing the cast.

"Okay, guys. Over here by the bookcase is stage left. Lynette, that means you and your attendants enter from there."

"There isn't enough room for everybody," she complained.

"Just squeeze together," Nelson said. "Jason, you enter from stage right." He indicated the general area of the entryway.

"Got it!" The kid in the too large suit lumbered across the room to take his proper place.

James noticed Fern's smile and the amused twinkle in her eyes. When she glanced in his direction, he winked at her and they shared a moment of joy.

Moments like this had been too rare in recent weeks, and James prayed this was the first of many more to come.

"Joy Ellen couldn't come," Nelson said, "so Alice, you read Hermia's lines, okay?"

The petite dark-haired girl wrinkled her nose. "That means I'm supposed to be in love with Lysander. Yuck."

"Hey, I'm not too happy about that either," announced the boy who was playing Lysander.

James swallowed a laugh.

Eventually, Nelson had everyone sorted out and Duke Theseus stepped to the center of the living room. "'Now fair Hippolyta, our nuptial hour draws on apace . . . '"

To say that the performance progressed somewhat differently than it had the prior evening was an understatement.

James lost count of how many lines were forgotten. Alice had trouble remembering she was playing Hermia, complaining that her supposed true love Lysander had cooties.

In turn, the boy playing Demetrius, who apparently really liked Alice, kept defending her and overacting his role as Hermia's suitor.

By the time Nelson spoke his final lines of the play, all of the adults and many of the youngsters were laughing so hard they could barely speak.

James's sides ached from laughing, and there were tears in his eyes. If given a chance, he knew William Shakespeare would deny he had ever written such a slapstick comedy.

In Deerford, this version of *A Midsummer Night's Dream* was a hit show that would be remembered by every performer long into their waning years. James's chest filled with pride for his son and the other students who had given this gift of laughter to him. And to Fern.

As the cast took their final bow, the audience all stood to applaud. James hooked his hand under Fern's elbow to steady her. She looked up at him and whispered, "Thank you. I wouldn't have missed this for the world."

James would have willingly climbed the highest mountain or swum the widest ocean if it meant her eyes would glow with this much happiness and vitality every day for the rest of her life.

Surely the downward spiral of her MS had bottomed out now, and she was on the path to improved health once again.

Thank You, Lord!

Before going home, the cast took time to help put away the folding chairs and put the living room back in order. Then they enjoyed some cookies and apple cider Fern's mother had been kind enough to drop by earlier in the day.

When everyone left, the boys went up to their rooms.

Sitting on the couch, Fern yawned and shook her head. "I think I'm done for the day. I'm ready for bed."

"You've put in a long day," James agreed.

"And enjoyed a fun evening," she added with a satisfied smile.

"Okay, let me help you—"

"For a change, I think I can make it without you carrying me." Using her walker, she pulled herself upright.

"Now, don't overdo," James warned.

"I'm feeling so much better today . . ." She took a few steps toward the stairs. "But you might want to stand by ready to catch me."

"I'm right here, sweetheart." The last thing Fern needed was to fall and injure herself. James intended to stay as close as possible.

At the foot of the stairs, she set aside the walker and grabbed the banister for support. Slowly, she went up one step, two steps . . .

James folded the walker and carried it up behind her. On about the sixth step, she wobbled and locked two hands around the banister.

"Uh-oh, that was close," she said.

"Let's do it the fun way." Setting aside the walker, James scooped her into his arms, carrying her the rest of the way up the stairs.

"Well, I tried," she said with a discouraged sigh.

"Tomorrow you'll be better," he said, though he knew there was no guarantee that came with his promise.

The next morning, James found himself in the staff lounge being lauded once again for organizing the campaign.

"My mom's neighbors saw you on TV," one of the orderlies said. "They're going to write to the governor about our pay. You did great, man."

James smiled and nodded. He really needed to get changed into his scrubs and get to work.

"Good job!" A night-shift nurse high-fived him as she passed by.

He mumbled his thanks.

This was far more attention than he'd intended to generate for himself. He wanted everyone—including possible funding sources—to focus on the hospital staff as a whole and what good work they all did.

He finally disengaged himself from his co-workers, changed clothes and hurried down to the second floor. His unit had had two admissions overnight—a raging case of flu that looked like it might morph into pneumonia, and an emergency appendicitis who'd had surgery earlier that morning.

James made sure he took extra precautions with the flu patient. He gloved up and wore a mask and a covering over his scrubs. One of his greatest fears was that he'd bring home a contagious disease, and Fern, with her lowered resistance, would catch an illness she wasn't equipped to fight.

At about midmorning, he was logging the meds he'd delivered when the elevator door hummed open. A young man in a wheelchair rolled out and headed toward the nurses' station. It took James a moment to recognize Ted Townsend. The boy had been discharged more than two weeks ago.

James stepped out from behind the counter. "Hey, Ted, how's it going?"

The kid gave him a full-blown smile. "Not so bad. I just came from physical therapy across the street."

"Right." The outfit that provided physical therapy was housed in the Deerford Medical Services Building opposite Hope Haven. "They getting you up on your feet?"

"More than that. They're making me work harder than Coach Everett ever did in soccer. I'm doing one-legged jumping jacks and I can bench-press a hundred twenty pounds."

"Wow, that's impressive. You're holding up okay?"

"Oh yeah. A little thing like an amputated leg isn't going to stop me. Besides, I'm getting my prosthesis in a week or two. Then there'll be no stopping me."

James marveled at the change in attitude Ted had undergone. "That's great. I knew you'd be okay."

The laundry cart picking up dirty linens rumbled by.

"Yeah, well . . ." The boy glanced at the passing cart, then back to James. "I wanted to apologize and thank you."

Leaning back on the edge of the counter, James crossed his arms. "I don't need any apology or thanks, Ted. I just did my job. Now you're doing yours."

"No, it's more than that. It's the Paralympics. I've been talking a lot the past couple of weeks to Marvin Bloom, the guy who came up from Chicago with his buddies."

James acknowledged that he recalled the three men Kirstie Scott had contacted.

"Well, anyway," Ted continued, "turns out the Paralympics has a college scholarship fund for athletes who excel in the program. Marvin thinks I'd have a pretty good shot at doing well in track. I mean, I ran track at Lincoln High when it wasn't soccer season, so I could probably be pretty competitive once I get used to the leg they're gonna give me."

"I think you're right. You'll do real well. You were a good athlete and that hasn't changed. And if you're determined—" Sensing the boy's excitement and resolve, James gave him a thumbs-up. "I'm betting there'll be no stopping you."

"Yeah, and if it works out, I'll be able to go to college after all. So that's why I wanted to thank you." Ted extended his hand. "And apologize for having such a bad attitude when I was here."

James took his hand. "Tell you what, Ted. You let me know when your first track meet is, I'll be there. How's that for a deal?"

"Deal!" The kid grinned again. "And tell that good-looking girl, the one who lost her leg, that I owe her for getting Marvin up here. Tell her thanks."

"I will."

Ted did a tight turn in his wheelchair and rolled toward the elevator.

Anabelle came up behind James. "What was that all about?"

"He's a former patient, the one Kirstie hooked up with the Paralympics."

"Oh yes, I remember."

"Tell Kirstie she did well. He says thanks. As soon as he gets his new leg, he's planning on training to run track."

Surprise sparkled in Anabelle's eyes, and she smiled. "That's wonderful, James. Kirstie will be very happy, I'm sure."

Feeling pleased with himself, and proud of Ted's new-found direction, James went back to logging the meds he had administered.

A few minutes later, Lorraine Wilder, his nurse supervisor, told James that Mr. Varner wanted to see him in his office. Stat.

"What does he want?" James asked, puzzled.

"He didn't say. He seemed a bit more agitated than usual though." She tucked a couple of loose strands of her dark hair behind her ear. "You'd better take care of whatever it is in a hurry. I'll cover for you up here."

An uneasy feeling of approaching trouble skidded down James's spine. Varner had been on the employees' side during the protest. Had he changed his mind?

Or was something else going on?

James took the stairs to the first floor.

When he stepped into Varner's executive assistant's office, he asked Penny, "What does Mr. Varner want from me?"

She didn't look up from her well-organized desk, every piece of paper in its proper place. "I'm sure he'll tell you himself. Go on in."

Neither her tone nor her words were reassuring.

He rapped once on Varner's open door, then stepped inside.

"There you are, James." Varner stood and extended his hand across his desk for a handshake. "Sorry to take you away from your patients. I know you're a very busy man." He waved James to one of the two guest chairs. "Sit, sit. Everything is fine. Just fine." Words spilled out of the CEO as though he was in the middle of a hyperactive meltdown and needed to take a tranquilizer.

James sat, but only on the edge of the chair. "What did you want to see me about?"

"It's just a little thing. They're not asking much of you." He shuffled the papers in front of him as though he'd forgotten the subject of their meeting.

Suspicion raised the hackles on the back of James's neck. "Who are *they*?"

"The board of directors, naturally. I work for them, you understand. Which means we all work for them. More or less."

"What do they want from me?"

"Well, you know, the demonstration you organized was all well and good. Free speech and all that. But maybe you got just a little carried away with all the TV coverage and newspaper articles."

James nodded. An ill-defined feeling of distress tightened his neck muscles.

Varner straightened the half dozen pens on his desk, putting them in a neat row. "The board members, some of the members, have been receiving phone calls from their associates. Calls that suggest it's their fault that the hospital is short of funds."

"Approving the hospital budget is their responsibility," James pointed out.

"Yes, well, that's true. And they do have some responsibility in terms of fund-raising."

"So why are they upset if people are calling drawing attention to what their responsibilities are?"

He transferred all the pens to the center drawer of his desk and shoved it closed. "Since the demonstration, the pressure— the heat, if you will—has increased considerably. The members are hoping there's something you can do to, ah, cool down the temperature a bit."

"Surely you're not asking me to announce that the employees are suddenly accepting of what amounts to a rather draconian pay cut for many of us." He knew others in the community were facing similar financial straits, and it complicated the issue a bit.

But all he knew was that he was very protective of his friends, and he was fighting for them right now.

"No, no, I wouldn't expect that. Not at all." Varner took the handkerchief from his coat pocket and mopped his forehead. "They're thinking you might tone down the rhetoric. Not make so many public statements. Let things simmer for a while."

Cautiously, James asked, "And if I did that, stopped talking to reporters and so on, what would the employees get in return?"

"Well, I . . ." Perspiration had formed above his lip, and he wiped that away. "Hope Haven employees have always prided themselves on being loyal to the organization. To the patients, as well."

"We're still loyal," James argued. "That's why we don't want to see the situation deteriorate due to lower morale or our top talent leaving Hope Haven for better jobs elsewhere."

"Yes, of course, I quite understand your position. Still, I'm hoping, as a personal favor to me, that you'll follow the suggestions of the board."

James leaned forward, resting his arms on Varner's desk. "Albert, I have been asked to present our position to the city council next week. I can't suddenly turn down that invitation without being able to tell them the issues in question have been resolved. You understand that, don't you?"

Varner backed his chair away from the desk. "Of course I understand. In this case, I'm simply the board's messenger. I've delivered the message. The next step and whatever happens after that is yours."

The implied threat brought James up short and stole the breath from his lungs. Was Varner suggesting the board would take action against him personally? Even fire him if he didn't comply with their wishes?

The board was trying to impose a gag order on him. They could probably make it stick too, unless he hired an attorney. Which he couldn't afford. They probably knew that.

James stood. "Mr. Varner, you and the board of directors will know my answer to their request next Tuesday night at the city council meeting."

While he might have sounded brave and determined, James knew he was walking a narrow line. Did he dare risk getting fired—and losing Fern's insurance coverage?

Chapter Twenty

AFTER DINNER, JAMES CARRIED HIS GEAR FOR THE camping trip downstairs and stacked it by the front door ready to be packed in the roof rack basket on the van. He had fifteen Scouts going on the trip plus two other dads who drove SUVs. That meant lots of gear to haul. They'd be leaving early in the morning from the church parking lot.

Nelson came down the stairs with his duffel and subfreezing sleeping bag. In his socks, he padded across the entryway.

"You got everything, son?"

"Yeah." He dropped the sleeping bag next to James's.

"Did you use the checklist?"

"We went over all that stuff before Christmas."

Mentally, James rolled his eyes. That answer meant Nelson hadn't checked his list.

James pulled his list out of his pocket. "Two pair of wool socks?" Nelson nodded. "Extra pair of pants? Extra shorts? Gloves? Warm cap? Canteen?"

Nelson yawned and nodded affirmatively to each item.

"In the morning you'll add your toothbrush and toothpaste, right?"

Nelson's brows scrolled closer together. "I already put my toothbrush in the duffel."

"Really? I guess you're going to use Gideon's toothbrush tonight and in the morning?"

"No way!" Gideon shouted from the family room where he was watching TV.

Muttering something under his breath, Nelson dropped to his knees, unzipped his duffel and rooted around inside.

Repressing a grin, James decided Scouting provided all sorts of preparation for adulthood, including packing properly for a trip.

Leaving Nelson to recover his toothbrush, James went into the family room. Gideon was sprawled on the floor watching a reality show and eating popcorn. Like Nelson, he was shoeless and his shirt hung open, revealing a white T-shirt underneath.

James sat on the recliner near him. "You're going to stick close to home and your mother this weekend, right?"

"Sure, Dad."

"She seems to be feeling better, but she could have a relapse."

Gideon mumbled an acknowledgment.

Bending down, James picked the remote up off the floor and muted the sound.

Gideon looked up. "What? I was listening."

"Son, I'm counting on you. You've got Grandma Marilee's number if there's a problem. Your Aunt Beth's too, but it would take her longer to get here."

"I know, Dad. Their numbers are all in my cell."

"I'm taking my cell with me, but I'm not sure whether there'll be reception at the river camp. If you can't reach me by voice, try texting. Sometimes that goes through when nothing else will."

Sitting up straighter, Gideon swiveled around to face his father. "Dad, I was the one who taught you how to text. I think I can handle it, okay?"

James chuckled. "You think I worry too much, huh?"

"Hey, I worry about Mom too. I'll keep a close eye on her. I promise."

Gripping Gideon's shoulder, James gave his son an affectionate squeeze. "Thanks."

Later, as James went upstairs to bed, anticipation about the trip and anxiety about leaving Fern churned together with a dose of adrenaline that was bound to keep him awake for hours.

He undressed in the light from the hallway so he wouldn't wake Fern, who was already in bed.

"Are you and Nelson all set to go in the morning?" Fern's voice was thick with sleep.

"Sorry I woke you," he whispered, crawling into bed beside her. "Assuming Nelson remembers to get his toothbrush back into his duffel in the morning, we're set to go."

"You'll both have a good time."

Knowing how much he'd worry about Fern while he was gone, he wasn't quite as optimistic as she was about having a good time. "Are you sure you're going to be all right on your own? I could drive the boys up there and be back here by noon. Then on Sunday—"

"You'll do no such thing. You haven't gotten away from here in ages for any sort of a vacation. You need a break, James. You'll enjoy being with the boys, and Nelson is tickled that you're his Scout leader." She reached for James's hand and brought it to her lips. "Gideon will be here if anything goes wrong. We'll both be fine."

James prayed she was right.

Even so, the troubling possibility that she might need him kept James awake for a long time. When he finally fell asleep, that same fear invaded his dreams with malignant, terrifying tentacles.

Sitting at her sewing machine, Elena ran the side seam for the nursing scrubs she was making. She snipped the thread, then flipped the garment over to run the second seam.

Cesar, who'd been trying to fall asleep in bed, lifted his head. "Aren't you coming to bed soon?"

"In a minute, honey." She matched the edges of the cotton fabric. "One of the girls in pediatrics bought this Dr. Seuss material and thought it would be cute for scrubs." It would be too. Even young children would be able to identify the colorful characters.

"You're going to be exhausted if you don't get your sleep."

Granted, her eyes were already burning with fatigue but she didn't want to stop yet. "I want to get this done by Monday, and it's hard to sew when Izzy is awake. She's always wanting something. I'll sleep late in the morning."

Cesar remained silent as she ran the second seam.

"Are you sure it's worth it, hon?" he said as the machine quieted.

"It's an extra twenty-five dollars, all profit, in our travel account." If she could add that much to their savings every week, it would certainly get them to Spain all the sooner, no matter what happened with the pay cuts at the hospital.

She heard her husband mumble something. Turning, she discovered he'd pulled the pillow over his head to block out the light and the noise.

A spear of guilt stabbed her. She was keeping Cesar from his sleep too.

Just a few more minutes, she promised herself. Then she'd go to bed.

Finishing the tunic top would take her one small step closer to her dream.

By six the next morning, a light snow had started to fall. The flakes floated past the parking lot lights at the Church of the Good Shepherd, dusting the cars of parents delivering the Scouts for the weekend outing.

James tossed a duffel to Nelson, who stood on the back bumper of their van. He stuffed the duffel into the cartop carrier and turned to catch another one. Like James, all the boys were wearing their Scout shirt over a long-sleeved thermal shirt plus a warm jacket and cap.

The two fathers who'd volunteered to come along on the camping trip were busy helping the boys.

Ron Beckwith, a big man with a voice to match, had loaded his SUV with food for the weekend and enough four-man tents to shelter the Scouts and leaders. Bud Singh was hauling cook-stoves and firewood in his vehicle as well as his share of Scouts.

James left Nelson and his friend to finish stashing the remaining sleeping bags and duffels in the back of the van and strolled over to talk with Ron.

"How's our head count?" James asked. Boys in heavy ski jackets and their parents milled around the three vehicles. At this early hour, there was little talking and no horsing around. That would no doubt come later when they reached the campground reserved for the troop.

"Pete Switzer hasn't shown up yet."

James peered through the falling snow. He'd hate to leave one of the boys behind, but he'd have to if the kid didn't get here soon. Being left behind was a tough lesson for a youngster to learn.

"I checked the weather this morning," Ron said. "Snow flurries throughout the day, clearing by tomorrow. We ought to be okay."

"As long as they keep the highway plowed." Still worried about leaving Fern, James reminded himself that he'd only be gone for about thirty hours. He'd be back home by lunchtime tomorrow.

Nelson jogged over to him. "Dad, the duffels are all stowed."

"Good." Pushing back the sleeve of his jacket, James checked his watch. Six twenty. He'd give Pete ten more minutes and then they'd get on the road. "Let's mount up, boys. It's about time to go."

"Here comes Pete," someone shouted.

A dark sedan pulled into the parking lot, sliding on the wet asphalt. As soon as the car came to a halt, Pete leaped out and made an awkward dash toward James's van with one boot on, the other in his hand. His father followed with the boy's duffel and sleeping bag.

"Sorry. I overslept." Pete tossed his gear in the back of the van, then had to retrieve his boot that he'd thrown in with everything else.

His buddies razzed him. "Poor Petey. Didn't get his beauty sleep."

"Didn't your mommy wake you up on time?"

James swallowed a smile. Nothing like a little peer pressure to shape up a kid. Or a new recruit, he recalled from his army boot camp days.

He checked his cell phone one last time to make sure it was on and dropped it in his shirt pocket. Gideon would call if Fern had a problem.

Amid waves and good-byes from parents, the three-vehicle caravan headed out of the parking lot. On a good day it was about a two-and-a-half-hour drive to the campground northwest of Deerford on a bluff above the Mississippi River. Today it was likely to take longer, the falling snow making visibility poor and the road through flat farm country slick.

James set a moderate pace in the lead car. This was no time to risk sliding off the road or colliding with an oncoming vehicle.

Despite its being the weekend, Candace woke at her usual time. She and Brooke were going shopping this morning, making it a girls' day out and leaving Howie home with Janet.

As she made her bed and straightened the quilt, she glanced at the framed photo of Dean on her bedside table. The familiar ache twisted in her chest. He'd been so handsome. So carefree. So full of life.

Then in a single instant he'd been gone.

Squeezing her eyes shut, she quoted Psalm 31:9 out loud. "Be merciful to me, O Lord, for I am in distress; my eyes grow weak with sorrow, my soul and my body with grief."

With a sigh, she knew she couldn't go back to letting grief consume her. She had her children, her mother and her faith. Somehow they would sustain her.

Downstairs, she put on the coffee and made up a pot of oatmeal, adding raisins, nuts and brown sugar. Big, fluffy flakes of snow drifted by the kitchen window, as pretty as a Christmas card. She wished she could capture the view on the note cards she made by hand using her collection of stamps and watercolors, but she wasn't that talented. Brooke, however, was showing signs that she had a real flair for art. How very special that would be.

Janet came downstairs for breakfast, quickly followed by Howie and Brooke. Janet poured herself a cup of coffee and carried it to the kitchen table.

"I've decided since you two are going shopping," she said, "that Howie and I ought to do something special today too."

Howie's green eyes popped wide open. "What're we gonna do, Grammy?"

Smiling, Candace delivered bowls of oatmeal to the table. Her mother always thought of something special to do with Howie so he wouldn't feel left out when Candace went off alone with Brooke.

"Well, young man," Janet said, "I read in the paper yesterday that the YMCA is having an open house. They're going to have games and cookies and punch and . . ."—she paused for effect— "a snow slide!"

"A snow slide!" Howie grinned from ear to ear.

"That's right. You climb up to the top and ride down on an inner tube and then climb right back up again. The street department's bringing in a whole truckload of snow. Though it looks like Mother Nature is helping too."

"That's boring," Brooke commented, adding an adolescent lift of her nose. "I'd rather go shopping."

"So where do you want to start?" Candace asked. "The mall or the discount store?"

"The mall! Betsy got the cutest outfit for Christmas. It's a skirt with matching leggings so she doesn't even get cold at recess." She scooped up a spoonful of oatmeal and swallowed it down. "I want some jeans too. Maureen got these really cute jeans with patches on the knees and cuffs. They're totally awesome."

With a prepubescent daughter in the household, Candace had to be careful what she wished for. She was more than relieved that Brooke's fears regarding their financial situation had been allayed.

Now she just had to worry about paying for everything that had suddenly appeared on Brooke's wish list.

The big after-Christmas crush had eased at the mall. Nonetheless, there were plenty of shoppers checking out the stores for good buys and discounted prices.

Brooke was able to find the skirt with leggings in a cute navy blue print but the stores didn't have the jeans she wanted in her size. Fortunately, she found another pair that was just as *totally awesome* in Brooke's view.

Deciding to have lunch, they went to the food court. Brooke chose a bean burrito, Candace a taco salad. They both ordered sodas.

When Candace looked around for a place to sit, she decided the entire town of Deerford and half of Peoria had had the same idea about lunch. The food court was jammed with people, all laughing and talking loudly to be heard over the piped-in music.

"You see any tables open?" she asked Brooke.

"Nuh-uh. Everything's full."

As Candace scanned the room, she heard her name called.

"Candace! Over here!"

She turned and spotted Heath Carlson waving them over to his table.

Pleasure at seeing him brought a smile to her face. "This way, honey. A friend from the hospital has room at his table."

Juggling food and the shopping bags, they wove their way around the jumble of tables until they reached Heath.

"This is a madhouse, isn't it?" He held a chair out for Candace.

"I thought there for a minute we'd have to sit on the floor." She gestured for Brooke to take the chair opposite her. "Honey, remember Heath Carlson from the sign-making party? He's a radiologist at Hope Haven."

"Hi." Brooke bit into her burrito.

Heath sat back down in front of his half-eaten slice of pizza and a small salad. "You're the young lady who plays the piano, right?"

Brooke's cheeks colored. "Yeah, a little."

"She played at church Christmas Eve and was wonderful." Watching her daughter play "The First Noel," the same carol that had been Dean's favorite, had brought tears to Candace's eyes and a lump to her throat.

"I bet you were great," Heath said.

Brooke shrugged and took another bite of burrito.

Apparently amused by Brooke's shyness, Heath grinned. "My mother made me take piano lessons for three years. I had to beg her to let me quit, and now I'm sorry I did. It'd be nice to be able to play some kind of an instrument."

"You could still take lessons," Candace pointed out.

"Not me. I'm afraid my brother, Shaun, got all the musical talent in our family. Of course, his wife makes him play his drums out in the garage so he won't wake the baby."

Candace laughed. Something about Heath always lifted her spirits and made her smile. He seemed so genuine and down-to-earth. Even in a crisis, which happened from time to time at Hope Haven, he kept his sense of humor.

Candace appreciated that in a co-worker.

Chapter Twenty-One

JAMES WATCHED AS FOUR BOYS STRUGGLED TO set up their tent in a blowing wind that whipped up the bluff from the river. In summer, this park was filled with picnickers and campers. Winter was a different matter. James's Scout troop had the campground all to themselves.

"Come on, guys," James said to the floundering boys. "We've practiced this. What do you do first?"

"Secure the corners," one boy responded.

"Right. So why are you trying to raise the tent before the corners are secured?"

The four of them looked dutifully sheepish. Starting over, they spread out the tent floor with the opening facing the fire pit. At the edge of the group campsite, birch and maple trees stood with their bare limbs shaking in the breeze.

Reasonably confident they'd get the tent up this time, James walked away. He pulled out his cell to check for coverage.

He stared at the tiny screen. No service. That wasn't good.

Troubled, he strolled back along the road that led into the campground. He wondered how far back the signal had given out and wished he'd been checking as he'd driven here.

Failing to raise even one bar after a half-mile walk, he returned to the campground. Maybe the cloud cover was too thick, preventing a satellite connection. Or maybe his cell phone company didn't provide service this far out in the boondocks.

He went back to the camp to check with Ron.

"I'm not getting anything either," Ron told him. "Hate the thought of being out of touch with the rest of the world if something happens to one of the boys."

Or if something happened to Fern, James thought with a grim twist of his lips.

He got the same answer from Bud. No service on his cell. None of the Scouts who had cells with them could get service, and James berated himself for not checking something so vital before he had set up this trip.

Hoping that a text message might make it through, James sent a brief one to Gideon. No cell service. Text go thru?

He waited impatiently for a response.

All the tents were up now, and the boys were dragging their bedrolls inside. The patrol in charge of lunch had cranked up the propane stove to heat a pot of chili.

His cell played a version of "Home, Sweet Home," identifying the caller as a member of his family. He flipped the cell open. The message from Gideon read Txt ok Mom ok.

James uttered a heartfelt *Thank You, Lord*, and sent Gideon a TK U message.

To eat their lunch, the troop sat on stones and logs that circled the fire ring. A small amount of heat from the blazing logs reached James, warming his face and hands.

After lunch, the Scouts secured the campsite and used their knot-tying skills to raise the food boxes to a height that couldn't be reached by roaming bears. Of course, since there were no bears at all in Illinois, as far as James knew, the technique was something he wanted the boys to know for future camping expeditions.

Then they broke into patrols and went on a hike. The object was to use their compasses to follow trails around the park and identify any animal footprints they might discover en route.

Periodically James checked his cell for service. No luck.

The boys kept busy until almost dinnertime. A snowball fight broke out, but the snow had melted to slush so it turned into mostly a mud-ball fight. James kept his distance and let them have their fun.

Darkness fell and a few stars appeared as the temperature dropped below freezing. Dinner, a few stories around the campfire and it was time to call it a night.

"Be sure you change into dry socks," James admonished everyone. "We don't want anyone getting frostbite."

Sharing a tent with Ron and Bud, James took off his boots by the door and crawled inside.

"I'm beat," Bud said. "Those kids have more energy than a flock of geese on uppers."

James chuckled. "They're probably going to tell ghost stories and not get to sleep for hours."

"We'll get even when we blow reveille before dawn," Ron said.

With a groan, Bud flopped back onto his bedroll. "Count me out on doing anything before dawn."

Smiling, James checked his cell one more time, then slid into the cold sleeping bag, zipping it up tight. Even in dry socks, his feet were like blocks of ice. He pulled his knit cap down over his frigid ears.

The ground beneath him was as hard as concrete. Rocks poked at his back. When he shifted to escape one stone, he found another larger one that jabbed at his shoulder or hip.

He couldn't remember the last time he'd been camping. In the years since they'd been married, he'd rarely slept anywhere except next to Fern in their own warm bed. Or maybe at a motel during a family vacation.

He closed his eyes and tried to block his persistent anxiety about her well-being. *She knows not to overdo it*, James told himself. Gideon was a smart kid. He'd keep a close eye on his mother.

Still, the thought of Fern needing him and his not being there drilled its way into James's head and wouldn't go away. Like dangling from a rope over a bottomless crevasse, he twisted around and around trying to escape the worry and fear that harassed him.

Dear Lord, watch over Fern and keep her safe from harm. Restore her strength and ease her pain. I ask this in the name of Jesus Christ, my Lord and Savior. Amen.

James heard the boys in the neighboring tent laughing and carrying on. Bud had begun to snore, so maybe he had been extra tired. So was James.

As his feet finally warmed, he felt himself drifting off to sleep. Somehow "Home, Sweet Home" wedged its way into his dreams. A peaceful sound that soothed—

"James! Your cell is going off." Ron punched him in the back.

James snapped to a sitting position. Disoriented, he tried to clear his head. The air was colder than the inside of a freezer. Wind ruffled the sides of the tent.

He dug into his pocket, pulled out the cell and flicked it open. In the pitch black of the tent, he read the screen: Mom fell—called ambulance—hsptal w/ gran.

Dear Lord! He sucked in an icy lung full of air. His worst nightmare . . .

He wrestled his way out of the sleeping bag. "Ron, my wife's in the hospital. I've gotta get home."

Ron sat up and turned on his flashlight. His dark hair was mussed from sleep. "What happened?"

"I'm not sure. She fell. I don't know how badly she's hurt." James pulled on his boots. Had she fallen down the stairs? She could have broken something.

Bud switched on his flashlight as well. "Leave everything here. We'll bring your gear home with us tomorrow."

James tried to think but his brain was muddled, a frozen slush, and operating in slow motion. "I'll get Nelson and take him with me. Maybe I can come back tomorrow—"

"No, stay with your wife," Ron insisted. "We'll get the boys home. There's enough room in our two SUVs since we won't be carrying firewood and food on the return trip."

"Okay. Fine. I'll see you . . ." James ducked out of the tent and struggled into his ski jacket. It had started to snow again, an inch or two of newly fallen snow already covering the ground.

Realizing he needed his flashlight, he scrambled back inside the tent to find it. Retrieving the light, he backed out again.

His heart pounded in his chest like artillery rounds going off. His breathing was shallow, and every breath hurt. Sweat covered his palms. And all the time he silently chanted *I'm coming, Fern. Don't leave me, sweetheart. I'm coming, Fern. Don't leave me, sweetheart. I'm coming . . .*

He rousted Nelson out of his tent. As alarmed as James, he staggered to the van carrying his boots and jacket.

"Mom's gonna be all right, isn't she?" he asked in a small, shaky voice when they were both inside the van.

"I hope so, son. Dear Lord, I hope so."

The van's windshield wipers forced their way back and forth, beating a heavy, morbid rhythm.

A combination of snow and fog devoured the headlights only feet in front of the van. The yellow center line lay hidden beneath two inches of snow. Keeping one eye on the side of the road, James could only creep along despite his need to speed to Fern's side.

The snow tires on the van could handle the conditions—if James didn't run them off into a ditch.

His muscles were taut, his nerves raw.

"Do you have your cell?" he asked Nelson, not letting his eyes stray from the road. His breath fogged in front of his face. The heater hadn't kicked in yet.

"Yeah, I got it."

"Check to see if we're getting service. If we are, call Gideon. I need to know what's happening."

"Okay." His jacket zipper scraped and the heavy fabric crackled as the boy dug out his phone.

"Any yet?"

"One bar."

"Text Gideon that we're on our way."

James had a death grip on the wheel. His hands started to ache and he flexed his fingers.

"Okay, I sent the text," Nelson said.

"I probably should have had you bring your ham radio along on this trip."

Nelson kept his eyes on his cell phone. "Not sure it would do any good. I might not be able to bring up a local repeater from here. Besides, I haven't charged the batteries in a while."

"From now on, keep the batteries charged and bring it with you." Next time, James would remember to check for cell reception before he took any more trips away from Fern.

Since the snow started, no vehicles had passed to leave tracks James could follow. On this unfamiliar road with little or no visibility, James was driving blind.

Somewhere up ahead, the road intersected with the north-south highway. He didn't know how far. He'd be lost if he missed the turn.

"Gideon got the mes—sage," Nelson's voice cracked. "He responded: 'Mom in emergency. Gran says drive slow.'"

"I don't have much choice," James murmured, as much to himself as to Nelson.

They drove in silence until a flashing red signal light appeared ahead of them. The highway. James gently pumped his brakes to slow for the turn south.

"I've got service," Nelson announced. Without being told, he hit Gideon's cell number.

"Gideon, it's me. Nelson."

A punch of relief landed in James's chest. "Ask him how your mom is and what happened."

Nelson began to relay Gideon's answers. "Mom got out of bed and she fell. She was real weak and talking funny. Gideon couldn't get her back in bed, so he called Grandma." Nelson paused, listening. "Grandma said he should call an ambulance. Then she and Grandpa came over to get Gideon."

"So what's happening now?"

Nelson repeated the question and waited. "Dr. Weller is taking care of Mom, but he hasn't come out to talk to Gideon and Grandma yet."

Dr. Weller was a terrific Emergency Room physician, but he didn't have a whole lot of experience. James could only hope he was doing the right tests to find out why Fern had fallen. Why she'd been too weak to get back up, even with Gideon's help.

A million possible scenarios flashed through his mind. A stroke or heart attack. Blood clot. Aneurism. A negative reaction to her meds. The onset of some disease unrelated to MS.

The problem with being a nurse was that James knew too much, had seen too many seriously ill patients and there seemed to be no end to the problems that could fell a person at any given moment.

"Gideon says the nurse came out and told them Dr. Weller has called mom's doctor for a consult."

Good. If the problem was related to Fern's MS, Dr. Chopra would discover what had gone wrong. At least, James prayed that would be the case.

The fog had begun to lift above the highway, and the snow wasn't falling so hard now, improving visibility. Still James couldn't speed up too fast. Not on a snow-covered road.

"Tell Gideon we'll be there in an hour, maybe an hour and a half. If he has a chance to see Mom, tell her I'm coming. That I love her."

Well after midnight, the overhead lights illuminated only scattered cars in Hope Haven's parking lot.

James pulled into a spot near the well-lit Emergency entrance. Nelson had drifted off to sleep, his head resting against the side window. James woke him and they hurried inside.

"Hey, James." The Emergency Room reception clerk greeted him. "I've been watching out for you. About a half hour ago, your wife was moved to a room on the second floor. She's doing fine."

James's knees wobbled and his legs almost gave out on him. Steadying himself against the counter, he drew a relieved breath. He asked for Fern's room number.

Upstairs, they found Gideon sound asleep on a couch in the waiting room. Poor kid had had a hard night. Grandpa Frank was snoozing in a chair, his legs stretched out in front of him, his mouth hanging open.

Knowing there'd be plenty of time to catch up later, James let them sleep and went directly to Fern's room. He noticed an autumn-colored leaf posted on the outside of the door, meaning the patient inside was not supposed to get up without assistance. A reasonable decision considering the whole incident started when Fern fell. Until the doctors knew why, they'd take every precaution.

Inside the room, James glanced first at the monitor above Fern's bed. Good systolic rhythm, no sign of bradycardia or tachycardia. Breathing normally with adequate oxygen intake.

Marilee was sitting in a chair next to Fern's bed in the dimly lit room. She stood and produced a weary smile. "You made it." She opened her arms to give him a hug.

"How is she?" he asked.

She gave Nelson a hug and patted his cheek. "She's resting. The doctor ordered a CAT scan. No sign of any trauma. He thinks it must be an underlying MS problem, which is why he called Dr. Chopra."

"Has she been in to see Fern?"

"Not yet."

Since Fern was stable, the doctor would probably wait to show up during early rounds, or so James hoped.

"James?" Fern's eyes fluttered open, her voice thready. "Is that you?"

He sat down in the chair Marilee had just vacated and took Fern's hand. "I'm here, sweetheart."

"I'm sorry."

"Nothing to be sorry for."

"Your one night out."

"*Shh*, we're here now. Nelson too."

"Hey, Mom." Standing on the opposite side of the bed, the boy leaned forward and kissed his mother's forehead.

She lifted her hand, her fingers trembling, to touch Nelson's cheek. "Oh, you shouldn't have left the—"

"Yeah, we should have," Nelson said. "That tent was so cold, it was like we were at the North Pole. I'd rather be here with you where it's warm."

She managed a weak smile.

"Go back to sleep now, sweetheart." James stood and bent over to kiss her, smoothing a few strands of her wavy brown hair away from her face. "I'll be nearby if you need me." He hadn't been there for her tonight though, not when she fell. Not when she'd needed him.

The realization that he'd failed her twisted in his gut.

Fern didn't fight the need for sleep, and she drifted off quickly.

James joined Marilee and the boys in the waiting room. Strange to be on this side of a medical emergency instead of being the one to help resolve the crisis.

Marilee handed James a brown paper sack. "I picked up all of Fern's meds I could find. I thought maybe the doctor would want to check them."

"Good idea. Thanks."

"I put a nightgown for her in one of the drawers and some makeup for when she feels ready for that."

Frank came awake slowly and stretched. "How is she, son?"

"Sleeping. Thanks for stepping in for me," James said.

"Not a problem. She's our little girl, you know."

"Yeah. I know."

Gideon struggled to sit up and knuckled the sleep from his eyes.

"Hey, Dad."

"Hi, son. Thanks for taking care of your mom."

Barely awake, he yawned and nodded.

Marilee said, "We'll take the boys back to our place. They can catch up on their sleep. Tomorrow, or rather later today, you can let us know what Dr. Chopra says."

James agreed that was a good idea. He gave both of his boys a hug and thanked Marilee and Frank again.

When they'd left, he returned to Fern's room. He placed the sack of Fern's meds on the bed table, settled into the chair and simply watched his wife sleep until his own eyes closed with fatigue.

Chapter Twenty-Two

WHILE IT WAS STILL DARK OUTSIDE, THE NIGHT
nurse came in to check Fern's vitals.

James woke up with a start.

"She's doing fine," the nurse said quietly. "Someone just made a fresh pot of coffee in the staff lounge. You should go up and get a cup."

"Thanks." He checked his watch. A little after six. The lines on Fern's monitor moved steadily across the screen. "I think I'll do that."

The nurse left, and James stretched, rotating his head to loosen the taut muscles of his neck. He hadn't started the weekend meaning to camp out in a hospital room half the night. At least his feet were warmer here than they'd been in the tent.

With Fern still sleeping, he slipped upstairs to get a cup of coffee and brought it back with him. The taste was far better than the vending machine dregs that visitors were forced to consume when the cafeteria was closed.

When he returned, he found Dr. Chopra talking with Fern. The monitor had been turned off as no longer necessary.

"Good morning, doctor," James said. "You're here early for rounds."

Wearing a white lab coat, she turned to greet him. A petite woman with dark hair pulled back from her face, she had large, luminous brown eyes and a retiring manner. She was also a leading expert on multiple sclerosis and other diseases affecting the nerves.

"I am having trouble understanding why Fern did not respond better to the latest medication," she said, her slight accent a leftover from her childhood growing up in India. "It has been quite effective with my other MS patients."

"It's probably 'cause I'm ornerier than most," Fern quipped, though her speech was still slurred.

"I suspect the cause is something a little different than that, but we will see."

Noting the doctor was carrying Fern's chart, James said, "Last night Fern's mother brought all of Fern's meds from home. Would you like me to check them against your records? Maybe there's some sort of discrepancy." He picked up the brown paper sack from the bed table and showed the doctor the stash of pill bottles.

Normally James wouldn't suggest a member of the patient's family check medications, nor would it be medically acceptable. But as an RN, he was qualified to handle the task.

Dr. Chopra's forehead furrowed as she considered the idea. Before she reached a decision, her pager interrupted. She checked the caller's number.

"I have to take this," she said and handed James the chart. "I will be right back." She stepped into the hallway.

James bent to kiss his wife. "Good morning, Sleeping Beauty. Feeling any better?" Her color seemed better than last night and she wasn't feverish, which meant no virus had invaded her weakened immune system.

"A little better. Did you stay here all night?"

"Since about two o'clock when I got here from the Scout camp." He sat down in the chair with Fern's chart and the bag of pill bottles. "I didn't see much point in going home. I'd only have to come right back."

"Where are the boys?"

He flipped open the chart. "Your mother took them home. She'll let them sleep late this morning."

"And then spoil them with waffles and all the bacon they can eat."

"Probably." He chuckled and started checking off the medications one at a time as they were listed on the chart, then setting the bottle aside. Some of the meds Fern took once a day, others were "as needed." A couple weren't familiar to James, and he noted one prescription had expired.

He held the bottle up for Fern to see and asked her if she was still taking the expired medication. If the old med had lost its efficacy, that could be the problem.

She squinted at the bottle. "No, Dr. Chopra had me switch to a different formula. It should be there somewhere."

"Okay, I'll throw this one out then."

He finished checking all the pill bottles against the chart. Everything seemed to be in order. Still, Fern's MS had taken an unexpected turn for the worse.

Why? Just as important, when had the plunging downturn started?

He thought back over the past few weeks. The doctor had ordered a new medication. James had picked up the new prescription at HHH Pharmacy across the street just like he always did. But Harold, the owner and regular pharmacist, hadn't been there that day. There'd been a death in the family.

A new pharmacist had filled the prescription. A new, young pharmacist overwhelmed by too many customers waiting in line.

And James had been distracted by the news of the upcoming pay cut. He hadn't checked—

Spurred into action, James quickly found the new prescription bottle among the others. He examined the medication and the dosage and checked that against the chart.

"That's it!" he shouted, his eureka moment propelling him to his feet. Why hadn't he checked this before? Confirmed the dosage with the doctor when Fern started having more problems and not improving? He was a medical professional. He should have known better. In the past, he'd caught errors just like this here in the hospital.

Why hadn't he caught the mistake in Fern's case?

Fern looked at him as if he had lost his mind. "What's it?"

"The pharmacist filled the prescription with the right medication but the wrong dosage. Instead of a hundred milligrams the doctor had ordered, she gave you ten-milligram pills."

Shaking her head, Fern said, "Harold wouldn't make a mistake like that."

"He didn't. He had a young woman filling in for him that day. Maybe she read the prescription wrong. Dr. Chopra's handwriting isn't the best. Or if she called it in, there could have been a misunderstanding." A weak link in the system from James's perspective. It was too easy to misread handwritten notes on a chart or a prescription or misinterpret verbal instructions.

Fern's puzzled expression suggested she wasn't convinced. "Would the milligrams make that much difference? I was in a downward cycle when the doctor gave me the new medicine. Maybe it's the same cycle just getting worse."

"That's possible, but I suspect stopping the old medication and taking only ten milligrams of the new was like no medication at all." He glanced toward the hallway. "I'm going to find the doctor. We'll see what she thinks."

He found Dr. Chopra standing near the nurses' station, still on the phone.

James waited impatiently to speak to her.

As the morning had progressed, activity on the floor had steadily picked up. The meal service cart arrived, rattling down the hallway. The wheels on a laundry cart squeaked as it rolled by, a high-pitched sound that put James's teeth on edge. Somebody ought to oil those wheels instead of letting them inflict pain and suffering on people who were already sick.

Finally the doctor ended her phone conversation.

"I think I've found the problem," he told her, guilt burrowing into his conscience for not checking Fern's meds at the very beginning. "Here's the latest medicine you prescribed." He pointed to the chart and handed her the pill bottle. "That's what she's been taking. In the past day or two, you told her to double up on the meds." Which might have accounted for her slight, and all too temporary, improvement.

Dr. Chopra scanned the chart and checked the label on the bottle. "Oh no, that is not correct. Ten milligrams is not enough to offset Fern's MS symptoms. This is very bad." She completed a prescription form and looked up at James. "Would you please order the correct medication from the hospital pharmacy immediately. We will start Fern on the proper regimen this morning and see if she will improve."

"I'm not on duty this morning. If I'm not logged in, the computer won't allow me to order meds."

"Oh yes, of course." She turned to the day-shift nurse on duty. "Order this stat, please. Administer a dose as soon as it arrives."

"Yes, doctor." The nurse gave James an encouraging smile. "I'll make sure they get on this right away."

"Thanks." James exhaled in relief. His inattention to Fern's meds had cost her dearly. He wouldn't let that happen again. Ever.

The doctor tucked her pen back in the pocket of her lab coat. "I would like to keep Fern overnight to see how she responds to the medication in the proper dosage. If she does well, you may take her home tomorrow."

After the morning service at Holy Trinity Church, Elena went to retrieve Isabel from her Sunday school classroom.

"I didn't spill any juice on my dress, *Buela*." The five-year-old made the announcement while twirling around in the red velvet Christmas dress she'd insisted on wearing again this morning. Elena had plaited her dark hair, and it whipped around the child as she spun.

"What a good girl not to spill." Elena helped the child into her coat and then took her small hand and they walked toward the parking lot. "What did you learn today?"

"About a big, big whale that ate up nobody and then spit him out."

Elena suppressed a smile. "Do you mean Jonah?"

"I dunno." Using both feet, she hopped over a crack in the sidewalk. "Can I wear my new dress to my school tomorrow?"

"Oh no, sweetie. That dress is too nice to wear to school. You'd get it all dirty." Not to mention the damage she might do to the dress while crawling around in the sand box or painting at an easel.

"But I want my friends to see my new dress."

"They'll see it some other time."

Isabel pulled her hand free of Elena's, dug in her heels and planted her fists on her narrow hips. "But I want to wear it tomorrow, *Buela*."

Elena wondered where Izzy had gotten her stubborn streak. From Elena's own son, Rafael? Or from the child's mother?

"Izzy, sweetie, we'll find you something else to wear tomorrow."

"No!" She stomped her foot. "I want to wear this one."

A passing couple eyed both Elena and Isabel with disapproval.

"We'll talk about it later, Izzy." Hoping her granddaughter wouldn't make an even bigger scene, Elena kept on walking. "We have to get home now to feed your Tito and your daddy their Sunday dinner."

"My daddy will let me wear my dress to school."

Unlikely, but Elena wasn't in the mood for an argument. "Do you know where we parked?" she asked as a diversion. "I don't see my car."

"I do! I do!" She pointed, then ran across the parking lot in the direction of Elena's small, green SUV.

"Izzy!" Fearing a car might strike the child, Elena raced after her. "Wait for me!"

Isabel beat her to the car. "I found it! I found *Buela's* car."

Breathing hard—and saying a quick prayer of thanks that Izzy was safe—Elena knelt in front of the child and took her firmly by the shoulders. "You know better than to run off from me when there are cars around. You could've been hurt."

The child's gray eyes widened. "I didn't do anything wrong."

Elena eased her grip. "Yes, you did, sweetie. You ran off without watching for cars and you nearly scared your *Buela* to death."

Suddenly, Isabel threw herself into Elena's arms.

"I don't want you to die, *Buela*. Please don't die."

Please, Lord, give me the patience I sorely lack. "I'm not going to die for a long, long time, little one. But you must learn to be more careful."

If only Cesar or Rafael had been here, they could have been holding Isabel's hand more tightly than she. Isabel wouldn't have run off on her own.

But the two men in Elena's life, whom she loved more than any others, generally refused to attend church, with the rare exception of the times Isabel performed with her Sunday school class. And then only Rafael would attend with her.

That thought created a lump of regret in her throat that was hard to swallow.

James arranged to take Monday off as a personal day to bring Fern home. He didn't want her to be alone. Not yet. Not when she was fresh out of the hospital.

Sunday afternoon he'd gotten a call from Ron Beckwith that the Scouts were home safely with no traumas to report. James had been relieved his sudden departure hadn't created any problems.

After Ron's call, he'd picked up his rested and well-fed boys from the Driscolls. This morning he'd gotten them off to school, then headed to Hope Haven anxious to learn if the meds in the proper dosage had improved Fern's condition. Although asking for a huge improvement overnight was like praying for a miracle.

He took the stairs two at a time to the second floor. Instead of scrubs, he was dressed in jeans, flannel shirt and his warm jacket. He'd brought a comfortable velour lounging outfit and a jacket for Fern to wear on the way home.

Taking off her reading glasses, Anabelle greeted James at the nurses' station. "Why didn't you let us know Fern was in the hospital? We would have come to visit her yesterday."

"I spent most of the day with her." In truth, he hadn't thought to call his colleagues. He'd been solely focused on his wife and her needs. "By afternoon she was pretty worn out. More than anything, she needed rest. And you know how hard that is to get in a hospital."

Anabelle nodded her agreement. "Too true, I'm afraid."

Candace popped her head out from the storeroom. "I was shocked to see Fern's name on the admissions list. I haven't had a chance to drop in to see her yet."

"We hope she's feeling better today," Anabelle said. "Is she being discharged this morning?"

"That's the plan if she's responded well to her new meds. Has Dr. Chopra been in yet?"

"Not that I've seen." Candace shook her head.

Anabelle asked, "Are you still planning to speak at city council tomorrow night?"

He winced. Between the scouting trip and Fern's crisis, he'd all but forgotten he had agreed to provide a public statement about the hospital's plan to reduce expenses on the backs of the employees.

"Yeah, I'll give them a written statement, but I haven't a clue yet what it's going to say."

"You'll think of something," Candace assured him.

"Some of the employees are planning to come to the council meeting to support you," Anabelle said.

"Great. Then I especially hope I don't make a fool of myself."

Lorraine Wilder, James's day-shift supervisor, approached the nurses' station and smiled. "I just checked on your wife. She's alert and ate a good breakfast. I imagine she'll be going home this morning."

"That's good to hear. Thanks."

He left his co-workers and went down the hall to Fern's room. She was sitting up in bed watching a talk show on television. She'd combed her hair, put on a trace of makeup and changed into her own nightgown.

"Hey, there, Sleeping Beauty. You're looking good this morning." He crossed the room to give her a kiss.

"So are you, handsome. No work today?" She punched the button to turn off the TV.

"Nope. I hope I'm going to spend the day with you at home."

A tiny frown pinched her brows together. "You don't have to do that. Mother could come over if I need her."

"I think she spent most of yesterday cooking for the boys and then sent home a casserole with me. She could use a rest too."

"I'm certainly a bother, aren't I?"

"We all love you, Fern. There's nothing the boys and I, and your parents, wouldn't do for you."

By ten o'clock, Dr. Chopra had checked Fern out, asked her to call in daily and released her.

As James helped Fern dress in her street clothes, he could already tell her strength and stability had improved. Thank the good Lord. He prayed the improvements would continue, although he knew Fern would never entirely regain her health. That wasn't how MS worked. Not until they found a true cure.

"Knock, knock." Wearing her kelly green volunteer jacket, Phyllis Getty pushed a wheelchair into the room.

"I've come to help you make your escape," she announced in a surprisingly deep voice for such a small woman who was years past her eightieth birthday. "I've got the warden tied up in his office and the guards are all asleep. Let's get this show rolling before they wake up."

Fern laughed and so did James.

"We're ready." James took control of the wheelchair and helped Fern ease herself into it.

"Now don't you start thinking you're going to wheel your wife out of here because you're a nurse, James Bell. No, sir, this is my job and that's why I get paid the big bucks."

"Maybe you ought to trade jobs with her, James," Fern teased.

"I just might do that."

"Maybe not." Phyllis shouldered him away from the chair. "But I admit, we volunteers can have a lot of fun and speak our minds without getting fired."

Hoping Phyllis didn't have any inside information about his employment status, James picked up Fern's sack of meds and personal items.

Pushing Fern, Phyllis started down the hallway but they didn't get far.

Anabelle stopped their progress to give Fern a hug. "You take care of yourself, you hear? We love having you drop in to visit, but don't feel you have to get sick just so you can make a social call."

Next in line, Candace gave Fern another hug and much the same message.

"Where'd this traffic jam come from?" Phyllis complained. "I can't get my work done if folks are always jumping in the way." She pushed ahead, nearly running over Candace.

Bringing up the rear, James shrugged and grinned. Phyllis was a hospital institution he had no intention of crossing.

The elevator responded to Phyllis's call and the doors swept open.

"Wait!" Elena came running down the hallway. "Fern can't leave until I give her a hug."

Phyllis rolled her eyes and *huffed* in mock protest while Elena wished Fern good health.

Finally in the elevator, Fern glanced up at James. "You have some very nice friends here."

"I know. Hope Haven is a great place to work because of the people."

"I do hope I'm counted among your friends and fellow co-workers," Phyllis said.

"Absolutely," James said.

Fern reached behind her to pat Phyllis's hand holding the wheelchair. "Hope Haven wouldn't be the same without you."

Chapter Twenty-Three

USING GIDEON'S COMPUTER, JAMES SPENT THE better part of Monday writing his statement for city council, taking frequent breaks to be sure Fern was okay.

She seemed stronger than she had in a long while. She even had enough energy to get on her laptop to check in with her MS friends in the online support group. James suspected she was warning them to always double-check their meds.

James wished someone had reminded him more frequently.

After several false starts, he finished the draft statement, printed it out in large type and took it downstairs to Fern.

"Take a look at this, will you? Tell me if it's totally the wrong approach, and I'll do it over."

She took the two sheets of paper from him. "You're going to read this at the council meeting?"

"No, I'm just giving copies to the council and the mayor will read my statement."

She gave him a curious look before turning her attention to what he'd written.

On bad days, her MS caused Fern to experience blurred vision. Today she seemed to be reading better than usual, which was another positive sign that the corrected dosage of her medicine was working.

After a few minutes, she looked up. Tears shone in her eyes.

A discouraged knot formed in his stomach. "It's that bad, huh?"

"It's beautiful, honey. You have a wonderful way with words and this is . . ." She hesitated. "Touching. And very personal."

He relaxed a little. "You don't think it's too much? I mean I didn't put any facts in there about how the pay cut will affect individual employees."

"No, but you've told them how the cut will affect the community. For the city council, that should be even more important than individual stories."

James hoped she was right. Besides, he was still counting on Varner to make a presentation, which presumably would be filled with all the statistics anyone could possibly want.

On Tuesday night, James wore his dark blue suit to make his presentation to the city council. Fern had made him buy the suit years ago when her sister Beth asked them to be Kim and Andrew's godparents.

The suit was probably out of style now, assuming suits changed style, and it had smelled a little musty when he'd dragged it out of the closet. In the past few years, he'd only worn the suit a handful of times, mostly to funerals. He didn't suppose the deceased cared about the style.

As he entered city hall with the copies of his statement in hand, he ran his finger around inside his collar and straightened his tie. He would have felt a lot more comfortable in a nice pair of slacks and a sweater, but Fern had vetoed that idea.

"You're going to be speaking to important people in the community, who will all be wearing suits," she said. "You need to look like you're just as important as they are if you're going to persuade them a pay cut is a false economy for the hospital and will impact everyone, not just the employees."

He countered with, "Maybe if I wore my old jeans with holes in them, the council would take pity on us poor underpaid hospital employees."

She lifted one eyebrow in censure, a trick she could do only when her medications were doing a good job of controlling her MS symptoms. James had celebrated the moment.

"Mr. Bell! Mr. Bell!" A wiry little woman with snow white hair, and standing no taller than five feet, came charging toward him. "I'm Jacqui Jackson, Government Relations Coordinator for Peaceful Valley Retirement Community. I wanted you to know we're here to support you and all the employees at Hope Haven." She stuck out her hand.

Taken by surprise, James accepted her handshake, discovering she had an amazingly strong grip. "That's very nice of you, Ms. Jackson."

"We came in two vans. Could've been more of us except Maddie and Elsworth Token have the croup. Terrible coughs, don't you know."

"Yes, ma'am." He looked around for an avenue of escape.

She leaned forward and lowered her voice. "It's possible that Elsworth wanted to stay home to watch basketball on television and fibbed about how sick he was."

James nodded as if he understood the situation. Which he supposed he did.

"We were all at your demonstration last week, even Elsworth, probably because there aren't any basketball games on in the morning," she announced. "Jolly good fun that was."

Ah, the van loads of seniors who showed up unexpectedly. "The employees really appreciated your support," he said.

"Yes, I know. My granddaughter works in the lab. She thought it was great fun too." She glanced around at the people streaming into the assembly room, some of whom James recognized from the hospital. "Best get yourself a seat. We'll be rooting for you."

Amazed by the elderly woman's high energy level, James entered the assembly room.

Across the front of the room, seats for the seven members of the city council were arranged behind long tables on a raised dais. Members of the audience were seated on interlocking folding chairs with a center aisle down the middle of the room.

He spotted Elena standing in one of the front rows, and she waved him down the aisle to the seat she and Anabelle had saved for him. As he walked to the front, hospital employees greeted him with encouraging words.

"Tell 'em how it is, James."

"We'll be cheering for you."

By the time he reached his seat, James's stomach had turned into a bundle of nerves. All he had to do was present his statement and sit down. Anybody could do that. No need to break into a sweat. Other than handing someone copies of the written statement, he didn't have to actually speak.

Mayor Donald Armstrong, a former government teacher at Lincoln High School, walked out onto the dais followed by his fellow council members. The crowd quieted down, and a cute little Girl Scout in her green uniform led the flag salute. That was followed by the invocation.

Once everyone was seated again, the mayor called the meeting to order.

"Good evening, everyone. Nice to see such a big crowd here tonight." Smiling, he scanned the room, which was almost full. Although the mayor used a microphone, he had the kind of teacher's voice that could carry to the farthest corner of any room. "I know many of you are here regarding a Hope Haven issue, so with the permission of my colleagues, we're going to take that item out of order on the agenda and start with that."

There seemed to be general agreement both among the council members and the audience to proceed.

"I regret," the mayor continued, "that Mr. Albert Varner, the CEO of Hope Haven Hospital, has a conflict this evening and will not be able to speak to us."

James's heart sank somewhere down around his ankles. He'd been counting on Varner to interpret the situation objectively and support the employees' position, as he had during the protest. Clearly, the board of directors had ordered him not to participate.

"Fortunately, we have with us tonight James Bell, a nurse at the hospital and an individual who was in a leadership position organizing the recent public awareness campaign."

"I didn't do it all by myself," James said under his breath to Anabelle, who was sitting next to him.

"I believe Mr. Bell has a presentation for us, and then we'll open the microphone for comments from others who may wish to speak to the issue. Mr. Bell?"

James sat paralyzed in his seat. The speaker's podium at the front of the room where he was supposed to stand loomed like Mt. Everest. A shiver shook James's body.

Anabelle nudged James with her elbow. "You're up, James. Everybody's waiting."

Her admonition prodded James to his feet. Feeling as unsteady as Fern so often was, he made his way to the podium. He opened the manila folder that held copies of his statement.

"H-honorable Mayor and m-members of city council." His tongue expanded to fill his mouth. His throat contracted, barely allowing sound to escape, and his lips had developed a mind of their own. "I'm pleased to present my statement to you."

He leaned forward to pass the statement to the city clerk, who sat in front of the dais along with the secretary recording the meeting. The clerk handed a copy to each member of the council.

"Go ahead and read your statement, Mr. Bell," the mayor said. "The audience is anxious to hear what you've got to say."

James swallowed painfully and sweat crept down the side of his neck. It'd been a long time since he'd felt this nervous . . . so nervous he felt sick . . .

"Is there something wrong, Mr. Bell?" The mayor's tone was one of concern, not censure.

"I, ah . . ." James looked down at the remaining copy of his statement. His vision blurred.

Behind him, the audience stirred impatiently.

Panic threatening to overwhelm him, James glanced over his shoulder at Anabelle. "I can't—" His voice sounded more like a croak than human speech.

Anabelle sensed the problem. She slipped out of her seat and came to the podium. "Are you all right?"

He shook his head and pointed to his throat.

"Laryngitis?"

He nodded and handed her the statement. "Could you?"

Looking unsettled, she addressed the mayor and council, first by introducing herself and her position at the hospital. "I'm afraid Mr. Bell has a bad case of laryngitis, Your Honor. He spent part of the weekend at a Boy Scout camp out in the snow. I'm afraid he may be coming down with something."

James blessed Anabelle for coming up with an excuse so quickly to explain away his behavior.

"With your forbearance, Your Honor, he's asked me to read his statement."

"Yes, by all means. Please proceed, Mrs. Scott."

Lifting an apologetic hand to the mayor, James bolted back to his place in the audience and scooted down in his chair, wishing the floor would open up and swallow him. He berated himself for the episode. He never should have agreed to present even a written statement. He should have let someone else make the case for the employees. There were plenty of qualified people who could handle that.

Why had he stuck his neck out?

Slipping on her glasses, Anabelle began to read. "Honorable Mayor and members of city council. Over the weekend, my wife—who suffers from multiple sclerosis—had a medical emergency while I was out of town. She was taken to Hope Haven Hospital by ambulance where she received the finest treatment available anywhere in the country."

Anabelle glanced back at James and smiled. The audience murmured sympathetically.

"The Emergency Room staff and doctor saw to her care with all of the professionalism of a big-city hospital. Tests were ordered, from simple blood tests to a CAT scan. Her personal physician was notified of her condition.

"The staff did all of this, not because she is my wife. Or because I am a fellow hospital employee. They are that thorough, that conscientious, with every patient who enters the hospital. Even those who are unable to pay for their care."

Anabelle paused, and a ripple of approval circulated through the room.

Holding his breath, James kept wondering if they understood what it meant, how critical it was, to have skilled, caring staff taking care of someone you love.

Anabelle continued. "It is the people of Hope Haven, the staff, from the lowest paid employee to the staff doctors, who are the heart of the hospital. The heart of *our* hospital. To cut their pay, as has been proposed, is like slicing a part of the hospital's heart—its staff and the staff's morale—away. It may not look serious on the surface, but even the smallest cut can fester and spread poison through an entire system."

Again, Anabelle paused. Her hand trembled as she lifted the statement to better read the words.

"That's what I don't want to happen—to let a small cut fester and infect something as good as Hope Haven Hospital. And neither do any of the employees. We love our work, the lives we save, each of us making our own contribution to the health of the community. The last thing any of us want is to see a top-notch doctor leave in search of what he or she used to have right here in Deerford."

James closed his eyes as Anabelle continued to read in a strong, persuasive voice filled with passion, experience and empathy for others.

"Your Honor, I hope that you and your fellow members of the city council will do whatever you can to locate the funds necessary so that the hospital can rescind the proposed pay cuts. Not because of me or my family. But for your sake and for the sake of this entire community. This community we love calling home."

Anabelle removed her glasses and looked up at those sitting on the dais.

The room remained silent. Not a sound. James was sure he'd blown it. His statement hadn't moved anyone. Hadn't convinced a soul that the hospital was too important to risk losing the heart of the institution to a cost-cutting frenzy and the infection of lowered morale that would spread.

Just when James knew he'd failed, from the back of the room, someone began to clap. At first only one person. Then others joined in, the applause growing to a thunderclap of approval and validation. Finally, the entire audience stood and the council members stood as well, all of them applauding, and it turned into a standing ovation.

Anabelle turned around to face the crowd and beamed a smile at James.

"Beautiful! Congratulations," James heard her say, and his heart soared once again with hope.

As the commotion died down, Mayor Armstrong called the room back to order.

"Mr. Bell. Mrs. Scott. You and your fellow employees can be justifiably proud of the work you do. Hope Haven Hospital has the highest reputation. As a community we owe you all a great debt of thanks."

Several people in the audience applauded.

James got an uneasy feeling that raised the short hairs on his nape. From the mayor's tone he heard a "but" coming.

"As you are well aware, unemployment in our community—our country—has risen. During that same period, the city has seen tax revenues drop; and we've had to respond by tightening our belts, just like our neighbors across the country have."

The mayor glanced at his fellow council members, and James realized the city wouldn't be able to provide more funding. A sense of hopelessness pressed his head down and he studied the tips of his dress shoes. Shoes that Fern had polished to a high sheen so he'd make a good impression.

"We have responded to this crisis," the mayor continued, "by asking a sacrifice from many of our employees. Noncritical employees will be required to take two days of unpaid leave a month."

A murmur of dismay hummed around the room.

"While we can sympathize with the difficulties Hope Haven is facing, it would be irresponsible of us as members of the city council to divert any of our limited resources when all of our employees are already facing reduced hours, and the community is affected by reduced services.

"I have spoken with several representatives at both the county and state level, all of which are facing similar financial challenges. The financial outlook for our city, in the near term anyway, is dim."

All of the effort, the energy, the *hope* James's fellow employees had placed in him and his plan had come to nothing. He'd led them on a futile path, and they'd blindly followed him into a barren desert.

He scrubbed his hand over his face. Dear God, he was so sorry.

Chapter Twenty-Four

THE DAY FOLLOWING JAMES'S SUDDEN ONSET OF laryngitis in front of the city council, Valera Kincaid reported the meeting in the *Deerford Dispatch*. She included quotes from the mayor and several council members, all of whom expressed concern about the future of Hope Haven Hospital as well as the city of Deerford.

The Springfield newspaper also picked up the story.

So far there'd been no reaction from Albert Varner or the board of directors. In fact, there was no sign of the hospital CEO at all.

As far as James was concerned, the Public Awareness Campaign, the demonstration in front of the hospital, all of the press releases, and the TV coverage had been a waste of time.

As James and his colleagues discussed the situation, Anabelle said, "I dropped by Penny Risser's office trying to poke around and find out what's going on. She hasn't seen Albert since yesterday afternoon and claims not to know where he is."

"Do you think she knows and just isn't talking?" Candace asked. Her new scrubs featured cuddly teddy bears and angels with halos on a light blue background. Elena had made them for her.

"Hard to tell," Anabelle conceded.

"Not that it matters." Discouraged, the weight of failure hung heavy over James and the efforts they'd all made. "Varner's been known to go into hiding when faced with a difficult problem." Worse, the payday that would bring a 10 percent cut in pay to the entire staff was fast approaching. Unless some miracle happened, everyone would have to learn to live with a lot less income.

"The only news I've heard," Candace said, "is that the board has called a special meeting. Penny placed a request to set up the boardroom for them and provide a light supper."

James hooked his hand around his neck and tried to rub the tightness from his muscles. "Bon appétite."

Seeing how discouraged he was, Anabelle patted his shoulder. "Don't give up hope, James. Sometimes it takes the Lord longer to answer our prayers than we'd like."

And sometimes the answer is no.

That evening after dinner Harold Hopkins, the pharmacist, came by James's house. He had a huge bouquet of flowers in his arms. A short, stocky man, the bouquet was so large he was nearly hidden behind the gladiolas.

James opened the door wide to admit the pharmacist and a wintry blast of cold air. "Wow, Harold. Are you on your way to a funeral?"

"Thank the good Lord, no. These are by way of apology to your wife."

James's eyebrows rose in response to Harold's surprise admission. He ushered Harold into the living room where Fern was sitting curled up on the couch, Sapphire in her lap. While not fully back to where she'd been health-wise two months ago, this had been a good day for her.

"You have a gentleman caller," James announced.

Fern looked up and her eyes widened. "Mercy, what are all those flowers for?"

Without taking off his heavy plaid jacket, Harold knelt in front of Fern. Startled by the stranger, Sapphire leaped off Fern's lap and scooted up the stairs to hide under the bed.

"Mrs. Bell, I cannot tell you how very sorry I am about the incorrect medication you received. Rest assured, that young lady who filled your prescription has been reprimanded."

"Oh, Harold, I don't want anyone getting in trouble because of me." Fern caressed a rose petal and bent the stem in order to better smell the floral perfume. "These are lovely, but you really shouldn't have."

"It's the very least I could do." With some difficulty, he raised himself up from his kneeling position. He eased himself into the armchair next to the couch. "She's only been out of school a few months and, from all accounts, she was a brilliant student. I'm reluctant to disrupt her career when she's barely gotten started. But I will report her to the licensing board if you feel the damage she did to your health by filling the prescription incorrectly warrants such action."

Quickly, Fern shook her head. "Oh, please don't. I'm much better now that I'm on the correct dosage."

As always, James's heart filled with love for the woman who was so forgiving. "Harold, the pharmacy was extremely busy when I picked up Fern's meds. I had the sense Ms. Yang was doing her best, but she wasn't used to that big a crush of customers."

Harold glanced up at James, who had remained standing, and nodded. "And that, I'm afraid, is my fault. I should have found a more experienced pharmacist to fill in for me."

"You couldn't have known what would happen," Fern said.

"Perhaps not, but I should have considered the possibility. I have suggested to Ms. Yang that she find a position where she could work under an experienced pharmacist for a time. Give her a chance to get used to the pressure of retail pharmacy operations."

"Good idea," James said. "And the fact is, I accept some of the blame myself. I didn't confirm the dosage with Dr. Chopra. Rest assured, that won't happen again." His vow contained equal parts of grim determination mixed with a large dose of guilt.

"Well, then . . ." Harold stood. "I won't keep you longer, but I did want you to know how deeply apologetic I am to have caused you unnecessary discomfort."

"The flowers are beautiful, Harold. You're very kind to think of me. I'll enjoy them for days." Fern extended her hand.

Gallantly, Harold brushed a kiss to the back of her hand. "Mrs. Bell, you are a kind and generous woman. I cannot express my gratitude enough that I have been able to be your pharmacist for so many years."

James showed him out, then returned to the living room and sat down next to Fern on the couch.

"Well, what do you think?" he asked.

"I think we don't have a vase nearly large enough to hold all these flowers."

"True." He admired them for a moment before saying, "How about I put them in the scrub bucket?"

Fern giggled. "And put them in the middle of the kitchen table? I could hide behind them and the boys would never know I'm there."

Sliding his arm around Fern's shoulders, he gave her a hug. "Fortunately, I'll always know just where to find you." Kissing her, James sent up a silent prayer of thanksgiving for Fern's improved health and asked the Lord to sustain them both in the future as they faced new challenges.

A dark cloud settled over Hope Haven Hospital as the clock ticked inexorably toward payday. Except for necessary exchanges, few words were spoken. Squeaky food carts rolled through the hallways like robots in a prison going from cell to cell.

Sympathetic doctors made their rounds, their expressions funeral somber.

Maintenance and housekeeping did their jobs with little enthusiasm.

No one laughed.

James hated the demoralizing malaise of helplessness that spread through the staff like a new strain of deadly flu.

He'd heard of two nurses who had already quit for better paying jobs, and a clerk in admissions had decided to return to college full-time.

For his part, James tried hard to remain positive and upbeat when he was with patients. And with his family. He wasn't always successful.

The day that had come to be thought of as Black Friday arrived. Checks were delivered, or in most cases, a pay stub with a record of direct deposit to the employee's bank account.

Standing by the nurses' station, James hesitated to open the envelope. As if putting the inevitable off would change anything, he mused.

Anabelle offered an encouraging pat on the back. "We did our best, James. No reason to beat yourself up over the pay cut."

"At least one good thing has come out of this." He fingered the envelope, easing one corner open. "My boys have made a bundle of money shoveling snow off the neighbors' driveways. For now, they don't need any allowance from me."

Candace joined them, her check unopened as well. "Make that two good things. Brooke turns off the lights the minute she leaves the room and she's making Howie do the same. No wasted energy at our house."

"It all adds up," Anabelle said.

James smiled. His boys had been pretty good about turning the lights off too, though he had convinced them to leave the nightlight on for safety's sake. And his coffee-pot plugged in.

The stairway door flew open, admitting Elena to the second floor. She skipped . . . *skipped?* . . . toward the nurses' station. For a fortysomething woman, she was light on her feet as she twirled and snapped her fingers over her head.

"What's gotten into her?" James asked, feeling no urge to follow Elena's lead.

Candace shook her head. "Too much caffeine?"

Prancing back and forth, Elena continued to snap her fingers.

"What in the world are you up to?" Anabelle asked.

Breathing hard, Elena stopped snapping and dancing. "My dearest friends, I have just come from the staff lounge. I was there when our own Mr. Varner posted a memo on the announcement board and put copies in all of our mailboxes."

"He's back?" James asked.

"About time," Candace commented.

Elena did another twirl accompanied by a series of snaps. "You ask what I am doing. I'm doing the flamenco! My trip to Andalusia is back on the table!"

James's jaw dropped. Candace and Anabelle reacted with the same stunned expression.

"How?"

"You won the lottery?"

"Cesar's been promoted to chief of police?"

Her robust laugh careened around the nurses' station. "No, sillies. Varner's memo. The board has rescinded the pay cuts. They've instituted a hiring freeze for all nonmedical personnel. They're going to negotiate prices and contracts with our suppliers. Of course, the board has done away with any cost of living or merit increases this year, but I can live with that."

James tried to keep his excitement in check. Maybe he'd misunderstood. "Varner has *permanently* rescinded the pay cuts?"

"Well, there is one small glitch. The board's going to review the situation in six months and make any necessary adjustments then."

"So our current salaries are good for six months," James tried to confirm.

She twirled and snapped her fingers. "That's what I'm saying, boyo! And the ten percent cut in today's paychecks will be added to next pay period's check."

Feeling light-headed, James leaned back against the counter. A six-month reprieve was more than he'd been hoping for this morning.

With a sigh, Candace sat down heavily in a chair. "Thank You, Lord!"

Grinning, Elena said, "I gotta get back to ICU."

"Wait." Anabelle stopped her. "I think we ought to take a minute for a prayer circle and give thanks to the Lord. A lot of people are going to feel grateful for this news."

"Can't right now," Elena said. "How about I meet you all in the chapel when our shift is over?" She hurried off with all the energy of a ten-year-old ready to enter a jump-roping contest.

Meeting in the chapel sounded like a good idea to James, particularly since two patients in his unit chose that moment to hit their call buttons.

Still feeling both stunned and relieved, he rushed down the hallway to find out what they wanted.

A little after three o'clock, James and Candace took the stairs to the first floor.

"I called my mother to tell her I'd be a bit late getting home and asked her to pick up Brooke," Candace said, her voice echoing in the stairwell.

"She was okay with that?"

"Oh yes. Having her live with us has made it so much easier for me and the children. I don't know how I would manage without her."

James imagined what her experience must be like. Being a single parent meant juggling huge responsibilities while praying nothing fell to the floor to crash and burn.

As he opened the stairwell door to the first floor, he heard hurrying footsteps above him. Looking up, he spotted Elena and Anabelle coming down and waited for them.

As they crossed the lobby area, Mr. Varner appeared from his office carrying his overcoat.

"Albert!" Anabelle greeted him with an enthusiastic wave of her hand. "We're all so grateful the pay cuts have been rescinded."

"As am I," he conceded, flushing slightly. "It required a great deal of persuasion on my part, but the board finally realized they had to be supportive of our employees and couldn't let you down."

"We appreciate that," Candace said.

"To convince them, I had to first approach every other possible source of funding. The foundations that contribute to the hospital, government grantors, even Medicare management. To no avail, I'm afraid. If there was to be a solution, the board had to come up with it."

James had misjudged Varner, thinking he'd been warned off by the board of directors and had betrayed the employees. Apparently the opposite had been the case. He'd worked as hard as a man could to keep employee salaries intact.

"Rest assured, the board endured some very heated discussions but did finally find their way through the maelstrom." Varner checked his watch. "Now, I really must go. Yet another meeting, I'm afraid."

He hurried off, leaving the four friends standing in the middle of the lobby.

"Wow." Elena broke the silence. "I didn't think Mr. Varner could pull off something like that. He really stuck up for us."

"I suspect the Lord had a hand in Albert's success," Anabelle said.

Thoughtful, they walked into the chapel to find it was already packed with employees. Giving them a broad smile, Pastor Tom waved them inside.

"Come in, come in." Wearing his usual navy clerical shirt and white clerical collar, Tom stood to the side of the room at a small altar. A large wooden cross hung on the back wall above a water feature, the sound of flowing water soothing to those in distress. "We're here to celebrate and give thanks to the Lord for delivering us a gift we've all been praying for. So many hands have had a part in this gift that together we can all take some credit. But it is the kind and loving hand of the Lord working through us that has blessed our lives in both large and small ways that we thank today. Let us pray."

Along with everyone in the chapel, James bowed his head in gratitude. Together, the hospital and everyone on the staff as well as the board had faced adversity.

Together, from the clerks to the doctors, they had grown stronger as a unit.

Together, they had walked with the Lord. Although they may have stumbled and felt weak and hopeless from time to time, they had endured.

Now was the time to open their hearts and give thanks unto the Lord.

About the Author

Charlotte Carter has been telling stories since a very early age when she and a friend acted out *Bambi* stories. Her friend got to play the role of Bambi; Charlotte was Thumper. Now the author of fifty published novels, Charlotte's books have appeared on Waldenbooks best seller lists and been translated into a half dozen different languages. Her honors include a Career Achievement Award from *Romantic Times* and winner of both the National Readers' Choice Award and the Orange Rose contest.

A native Californian, Charlotte and her husband of forty-eight years have one spoiled cat, two married daughters and five grandchildren, who they are occasionally allowed to babysit. In her spare time, Charlotte pursues her lifelong goal of performing stand-up comedy.

Charlotte Carter can be reached through her blog at www.CharlotteCarter.com.

Read on for a sneak peek of the next exciting and heartfelt book in *Stories from Hope Haven.*

It's available through Guideposts' direct mail program by calling Customer Service at (800) 932–2145.

A *Simple Act* OF *Kindness*
by
Pam Hanson & Barbara Andrews

I T WAS PAST TIME FOR HER BREAK WHEN CANDACE finally had a chance to go to lunch. Usually she ate in the hospital cafeteria; but on a whim she'd brought a sack lunch: a salad and one of the blueberry muffins her mother had baked for the kids' breakfast. After her hectic morning, it would feel good to sit in the staff lounge and relax.

She was about to enter the lounge when Penny Risser barged out of the room wearing her habitual scowl. Penny was only a couple of years older than Candace, but her brusque, disapproving personality made her seem middle-aged at thirty-nine. Some of the younger staff members had nicknamed her "The Dragon," since she fiercely guarded access to the hospital's CEO, Albert Varner. As his executive assistant, she usually kept herself aloof from other staff members, so Candace was surprised to see her leaving the lounge.

"Hi, Penny," Candace said in the most pleasant voice she could muster. "How are you today?"

"Too busy for chitchat," the woman said in her usual abrupt manner.

Candace watched her walk away, wishing someone would tell her that olive green was not a flattering color for her to wear. But then, Penny didn't seem to have close friends on staff, and no one would risk her wrath to give fashion advice.

Going into the lounge, Candace reflected about the way some people used and abused important positions. She was thankful that harmony usually prevailed among the members of the nursing staff.

As soon as she opened the door, she was assailed by two familiar voices having a heated discussion. They stopped when they saw her, but she couldn't conceal her surprise. Of all the nurses in the hospital, Elena Rodriguez and James Bell were the least likely to have a disagreement. In fact, they often kept the staff entertained with their good-humored teasing.

"Candace, you got here just in time to referee," James said with a halfhearted grin.

"Oh dear, that doesn't sound good."

James was the only male nurse on the second floor and, having recently turned fifty-three, one of the older ones. Tall and solidly built with graying hair and warm blue eyes, he set a good example for younger nurses, always patient, sympathetic, and helpful.

"James is exaggerating," Elena said. "I just can't understand why Penny Risser thinks she can lord it over us."

Although Elena was approaching her late forties, she had the energy and spark of a teenager, always full of ideas and willing to do anything for her friends.

"She has to keep Varner's confidences," James said in a reasonable voice. "After all, he is her boss."

"That doesn't make her *my* boss," Elena said heatedly. "It was just plain ridiculous of her to tell us that there's going to be a big announcement soon, then refuse to say what it involves. Maybe the hospital board is going to try to cut our salaries again, or even worse, lay people off."

"You don't know that," James said in a calm voice, even though his expression gave away his agitation.

"When is this big announcement coming?" Candace asked, sitting on the couch, momentarily forgetting about her lunch.

"Who can say?" Elena said. "Risser told us just enough to make me worry."

"Don't worry until there's something to worry about," James said philosophically.

"Maybe it won't affect us at all," Candace said hopefully, although she couldn't imagine why Penny would deliberately hint at something big if she wasn't supposed to talk about it.

"You sound like my husband," Elena said, flashing one of her brilliant smiles. "Don't worry today about tomorrow."

Candace had thought more than once that Elena could have been a fashion model with her long, slender body, lovely caramel skin, dark eyes and lustrous dark brown hair. Fortunately, she loved her work in Intensive Care, and patients greatly appreciated her kind, efficient ways. It still warmed Candace's heart to know that Elena had recently renewed her relationship with God and was working hard to understand what the Bible had to teach. She often wished that her own faith was fresh and vibrant again, unaffected by her husband's death.

Just then, Anabelle Scott, a nurse supervisor in Cardiac Care, entered the lounge. At sixty-three, she was also one of the older nurses, and Candace valued her friendship as much as she did James's and Elena's. Anabelle was a kind, compassionate nurse, but she was also the voice of reason in the small group of friends.

"Ah, Anabelle, you're just the person we need," Elena immediately said, going on to explain Penny Risser's veiled warning.

"It may have nothing to do with the nursing staff," James pointed out.

"Maybe Penny was only making herself sound important," Anabelle said. "Unfortunately, she does that sometimes."

"That sounds like playground nonsense," James said. "Like, 'I know something that you don't.'"

"Possibly," Elena said, sounding unconvinced.

"Anyway, we'll find out when Mr. Varner wants us to," Anabelle said. "We just had one pay-cut crisis. Let's pray it's not anything like that."

Elena nodded, but her expression remained grim. After a beat of silence, she said, "Back to work for me."

"Me too," James said. "Bye, you two." They headed down the hall together, Elena animatedly waving her hands as she reiterated her point to James.

Anabelle shook her head and then turned to Candace and peered over the top of her reading glasses that she kept on a chain around her neck.

"I didn't want to add fuel to the fire, but I've been hearing some rumors myself," the older nurse said. "What do you suppose our superiors have in store next?"

Candace sighed. "Who knows?" She didn't want to add Penny's vague warning to her list of worries.

The next evening Candace debated whether or not to go to her grief counseling session headed by Lila Adams. She had initially started going at the urging of her mother several months ago and had made great strides since. But she still felt she should be ready to face the future without support from Lila and the others. Candace had become more a listener than participant, not wanting to deprive the recently bereaved of their chance to express their sorrow.

Still, her counselor seemed very happy to have her continue. Lila had opened her heart and her home to those in need of help. Not only was she a wise counselor, letting her patients work out their own solutions, but she brought together people who had a great deal in common. Candace counted many members of the group as friends, and she'd formed an especially close bond with Megan Gallagher, a widow herself who was struggling to come to terms with her loss. Sometimes, when the session didn't run too late, they went out for ice cream afterward. It helped to know someone who'd experienced the same kind of loss.

The stately old homes on Lila's block were frosted with glistening crystals, and the counselor's Queen Anne Victorian home reminded Candace of a birthday cake with its snow-covered roof and multiple chimneys sticking up like candles. She parked her black, compact SUV on the street several houses down from Lila's. Some of the group members were quite elderly, and she liked to save the closer parking spots for them on nights when the pavement was so slippery.

Lila loved old things; but unlike many collectors, she used her antiques to create a warm and nurturing atmosphere. Candace let herself in, hung her coat, and went to the closed door where the group sessions were held. The décor was a feast for the eyes; and every time she arrived, she still found something new to admire. She especially admired a coffee table Lila had made from a stained glass window found at salvage yards. It reminded her of the way the counselor salvaged shattered lives and made them whole again.

Megan wasn't here tonight. In fact, it was a rather small gathering with a half dozen people, no doubt due in part to the wintery weather. She knew Olive and Verla quite well, having heard their deepest sorrows and taken them into her heart. Lila soon came into the room with her usual plate of cookies. If she was disappointed by the small turnout, she certainly didn't show it.

Candace nibbled on a cookie as she listened to others' stories and challenges they'd encountered over the past week. Olive cleared her throat to chime in.

"I've found a wonderful new way to console myself and commemorate my husband," the older woman said. "I've been making a memory book of all the places we visited and things we did when we were traveling the country and selling my pottery."

"How lovely," Lila said, dressed tonight in sleek brown wool trousers that matched her hair, and a beige cashmere sweater.

While Olive described her scrapbook, Candace thought of all the photos and memories she had randomly stored in boxes. Most were high up on closet shelves where her children never went. The idea of mounting all of Dean's pictures and souvenirs in one book that her children could enjoy was a good one. Maybe Brooke and Howie would benefit from a big project like that. When Dean first died, memories of him were too painful to relive; but now she felt she might be able to take on this kind of project.

"How did you feel as you were making the memory book?" Lila asked.

"I thought it would make me sad," Olive said, "but instead I remembered all the good times we had. It didn't make me miss my husband less, but I felt more and more thankful for all the wonderful experiences we shared."

Candace sat up a little straighter in her chair as she mulled over the idea of a memory book.

As the session came to an end, the women chatted about the slick road conditions. Candace hadn't spoken much, but she took away the idea of doing something with all the photos that were haphazardly stored in different boxes and drawers around the house. Images of her husband and all that he'd accomplished in his too-short life deserved better treatment. With a resolved nod, Candace determined Brooke and Howie needed to see what a vibrant and caring person their father had been.

A Note from the Editors

Guideposts, a nonprofit organization, touches millions of lives every day through products and services that inspire, encourage and uplift. Our magazines, books, prayer network and outreach programs help people connect their faith-filled values to their daily lives.

Your purchase of *Stories from Hope Haven* does make a difference! To comfort hospitalized children, Guideposts Outreach has created Comfort Kits for free distribution. A hospital can be a very scary place for sick children. With all the hustle and bustle going on around them, the strange surroundings, and the pain they're experiencing, is it any wonder kids need a little relief?

Inside each easy-to-carry Comfort Kit is a prayer card, a journal, a pack of crayons, an "I'm Special" wristband to wear alongside the hospital-issued one and a plush golden star pillow to cuddle. It's a welcome gift and has a powerful effect in helping to soothe a child's fears.

To learn more about our many nonprofit outreach programs, please visit www.guidepostsfoundation.org.